BEN SEES I

With his usual knack of getting into trouble, Ben the tramp finds himself hunted by the law and the lawless in this breathless adventure of murder and blackmail.

Son of novelist Benjamin Farjeon, and brother to children's author Eleanor, playwright Herbert and composer Harry, Joseph Jefferson Farjeon (1883–1955) began work as an actor and freelance journalist before inevitably turning his own hand to writing fiction. Described by the *Sunday Times* as 'a master of the art of blending horrors with humour', Farjeon was a prolific author of mystery novels, with more than 60 books published between 1924 and 1955. His first play, *No. 17*, was produced at the New Theatre in 1925, when the actor Leon M. Lion 'made all London laugh' as Ben the tramp, an unorthodox amateur detective who became the most enduring of all Farjeon's creations. Rewritten as a novel in 1926 and filmed by Alfred Hitchcock six years later, with Mr Lion reprising his role, *No.17*'s success led to seven further books featuring the warm-hearted but danger-prone Ben: 'Ben is not merely a character but a parable—a mixture of Trimalchio and the Old Kent Road, a notable coward, a notable hero, above all a supreme humourist' (Seton Dearden, *Time and Tide*). Although he had become largely forgotten over the 60 years since his death, J. Jefferson Farjeon's reputation made an impressive resurgence in 2014 when his 1937 Crime Club book *Mystery in White* was reprinted by the British Library, returning him to the bestseller lists and resulting in readers wanting to know more about this enigmatic author from the Golden Age of detective fiction.

Also in this series

J. JEFFERSON FARJEON

Ben Sees It Through

COLLINS
CRIME
CLUB

COLLINS CRIME CLUB

An imprint of HarperCollins*Publishers*
1 London Bridge Street
London SE1 9GF
www.harpercollins.co.uk

This paperback edition 2016

First published in Great Britain for The Crime Club Ltd
by W. Collins Sons & Co. Ltd 1932

A catalogue record for this book is
available from the British Library

ISBN 978-0-00-815594-0

Set in Sabon by Palimpsest Book Production Limited, Falkirk, Stirlingshire

Printed by Clays Ltd, St Ives plc

MIX
Paper from
responsible sources
FSC **C007454**

FSC™ is a non-profit international organisation established to promote
the responsible management of the world's forests. Products carrying the
FSC label are independently certified to assure consumers that they come
from forests that are managed to meet the social, economic and
ecological needs of present and future generations,
and other controlled sources.

Find out more about HarperCollins and the environment at
www.harpercollins.co.uk/green

CONTENTS

1

The Cap That Started It

As England grew nearer and nearer, the deck rose and fell, and so did Ben's stomach; for Ben's stomach wasn't what it used to be, and it rebelled against all but the most gentle treatment. It rebelled against the coast that could not keep still, against the taff-rail that went down when the coast went up, and up when the coast went down, against the Channel spray that leapt into the air and descended over you like a venomous fountain, against the wind that sent you bounding forward again after you had bounded back to escape from the spray. Yes, particularly against the wind, for that attacked your meagre raiment, and sent the best piece flying! . . . Oi! . . .

As Ben's cap flew into the air, Ben flew after it. You or I, richer in earthly possessions, would not have followed it into the ether, but Ben's possessions had a special value on account of their rarity, and the departure of anyone spelt tragedy. Thus, starting from scratch, he lurched in the cap's wake, spraying out from the ship's side like an untidy rocket.

Then, fortunately, the head that had ill-advised this unwise adventure realised its mistake, and sent an urgent S.O.S. to the boots at the other end. The boots, responding smartly, hooked themselves round the taff-rail. There was a sharp wrench as boots fought Eternity. A moment later, Ben's head, instead of proceeding outwards, curved downwards, ending upside-down against a port-hole.

There followed a fleeting glimpse of a converted world. A chair grew down from a ceiling, and a suspended electric lamp grew up from a floor. Then the chair and the electric lamp shot in one direction while Ben shot in another. He felt his nose scraping upwards against the side of the ship. Finally came a bumping; a sensation like an outraged croquet-hoop; and momentary oblivion. When the oblivion was over, Ben found himself back on deck, with the man who had pulled him up bending over him.

'By Jove! That was a narrow shave!' exclaimed the benefactor.

'Go on!' mumbled Ben, as he came back to the doubtful gift of life. 'That ain't nothink ter some I've 'ad!'

'Feeling all right, then?'

'Corse! It does yer good!'

Reassured, the benefactor took out his cigarette-case. He was a tall young man, with a face that ought to have been pleasant but that somehow was not. He opened the case, and held it out.

'Have one?' he asked.

Ben rose unsteadily to his feet and considered the matter. He considered it cautiously. Was it wise to smoke on a stomach that was doing all the things his was doing and that was trying to do many things more?

I owe you some compensation,' urged the young man, 'for I'm afraid it was I who bumped into you.'

'That's orl right,' muttered Ben. 'I was born ter be bumped.'

The cigarette was gold-tipped, so Ben risked it. After all, you couldn't feel worse than you felt when you couldn't feel worse, could you?

'Thank 'e, guv'nor,' he said.

'Not at all,' responded the young man, amiably.

That ought to have been the end of it. Later, Ben wished devoutly that it had been. The young man seemed disposed to continue the conversation, however, and took up a position beside the piece of ragged misery who was smoking, somewhat anxiously, his first State Express 999.

'Been away from England long?' inquired the young man, amiably.

'Eh?' blinked Ben.

His mind was receiving slowly.

'I asked whether you had been away from England long,' repeated the young man.

'Oh,' said Ben. 'Cupple o' cenchuries.'

'And where did you spend the couple of centuries?' smiled the young man.

'Spine,' answered Ben. 'With Alfonzo.'

'That must have been terribly nice for him,' grinned the young man. 'Then you can speak Spanish, I suppose?'

'I can say *oosted*,' replied Ben, 'but I don't know wot it means.'

He wished the young man would go. He wanted to be quiet, so he could find out whether he was enjoying the cigarette or not.

'What did you do in Spain?' the young man persisted.

'Tried ter git 'ome agine,' said Ben.

'Didn't like the place, eh?'

'It ain't a plice, it's a nightmare. They does nothink but chise yer.'

'Really! Well—don't look so glum. You'll be 'ome agine very soon now.'

'That's right.'

'Where is your home?'

'That's right.'

'What?'

''Oo?'

'I said, where *is* your home?'

'Oh,' said Ben. 'I ain't got none.'

'Ain't got none,' murmured the young man, reflectively. 'I see. I see.'

The homelessness of Ben appeared to interest him. A sudden burst of spray interrupted the interest and sent them both back. But it did not separate them. When Ben returned to the taff-rail he found the young man still by his side. He seemed to have drawn an inch or two closer.

'No home,' said the young man, sympathetically. 'That's unfortunate. What'll you do?'

'Well, I ain't rightly decided yet,' answered Ben. 'They wants me in the Cabbynet.'

'In the Ministry of Repartee?'

''Oo?'

'Never mind. Don't let's start that again. But seriously— haven't you got a job?'

'Wot? Work?'

'You've been working on this ship.'

'Yus, I 'ad ter. On'y way ter git me passage 'ome, see. "Can you look arter a cow?" they ses. "Yus," I ses. That's the way ter git on, that is. Say "Yus," and 'ope. But I 'oped fer one cow, and they give me fifty. And forty-nine kicked me. Everyone bar Molly.'

The young man laughed, but Ben didn't. He was thinking of Molly. Molly had the nicest eyes, and he'd named her after someone he'd left behind him in Spain. Someone who had not been fortunate enough to get a job on a ship, but who was going to return to England somehow or other the moment she got the chance!

The coast of England continued to bob up and down. Only, for a few seconds, it ceased to be the coast of England, and became the coast of Spain. The long straight smudge that would presently materialise into Southampton changed temporarily into a mountainous outline, with dead men upon it, and bulging black moustaches, and daggers so long that they could go right through you and still have room for a couple more. But there was something else, also, upon that mountainous outline. Something that gave a queer beauty to the hideousness . . . something that made one almost regretful one had left it . . . companionship . . .

'If you want a job when we land, I dare say I could find it for you.'

Ben came to with a jerk.

'You've got to eat, I expect, like the rest of us, eh? And you can't get cake for nothing.'

'Wot sort of a job?' asked Ben.

'Well—how about that job you've dreamed of?' smiled the young man. 'Good pay and no work?'

'Go on!' said Ben.

The young man laughed. He grinned down on Ben, while Ben squinted up at him. Ben's head ended where the young man's chin began.

'I know a job like that,' remarked the young man. 'Maybe, for once in your life, you're going to be lucky!'

'Yus, but why should yer give it ter *me?*' demanded Ben, suspiciously. "'Oo's toldjer I've got the qualiticashuns?'

'What! To receive a couple of quid a week for doing nothing?' retorted the young man. 'You can hold out your hand, can't you?'

'Eh?' muttered Ben. 'Cupple o' quid?'

Forty pounds of chedder!

'And, after all, I owe you something, don't I, for bumping into you like that and making you lose your cap. By the way, I'll have to buy you another.'

So it was this young fellow who had made him lose his cap, was it? Well, the gust of wind had certainly seemed a bit solid, now Ben came to think of it! But, at the moment, there were more important things to think of. This job! Go on! Did he really mean it?

Ben did not like work. Not, at least, the kind of work he was given on the rare occasions when work came his way. You can't dream that all the figures in Madame Tussaud's are made of gorganzoler, or that you are hibernating in a hole in gruyere, while you are rubbing cows with a clothes-brush and trying to avoid their feet. But Ben realised that, as a general principle, you can't make money in this ill-managed world without being expected to do something for it—and two pounds a week for the simple operation of holding out one's hand was arresting.

'Wot'd I 'ave ter do?' he inquired.

'I've told you,' answered the young man. 'Nothing.'

'Yus, but I mean—ter *git* it?'

'Oh, just call at an address I'd give you.'

'Where?'

'In London.'

''Ow'd I git ter Lunnon?'

'Fare's included. And—as I mentioned—that new cap.'

'Go on!'

'I've gone on. Now it's your turn.'

'Look 'ere,' said Ben, coming to grips. 'D'yer mean ter tell me that orl I've gotter do is jest ter say Yus?'

'Yus,' nodded the young man. 'Provided my friend also says Yus.'

''Oo's 'e?'

'I'll tell you, if you want the job.'

Ben closed his eyes and thought hard. He always closed his eyes when he thought hard. When you think hard you have to push, like, against the darkness. Yet was there, in this case, anything to think hard about?

Life had made Ben suspicious of everything and everybody. The cow Molly, and the girl the cow had been named after, were the only earthly items he would recommend to God when asked for his opinion; the only items that hadn't got a catch in them somewhere. This young fellow beside him probably had dozens of catches in him! Just the same, with two quid a week and nothing to do—*could* one go wrong?

'I'm on!' said Ben, suddenly opening his eyes.

'Good,' answered the young man. 'Then I'll see you again when we're off the boat, eh?'

The next moment, he was gone.

Ben stared after him. When they were off the boat, eh? P'r'aps *that* was the catch!

But the future, on a heaving ship, is less vital than the present, and the disappearance of the young man brought thoughts back to one's stomach. A wave struck the ship's side with a hearty smack. 'Fust was right,' reflected Ben, as the spray showered down upon him. 'I didn't orter've 'ad that fag.'

Another figure approached. It was the petty officer who looked after the man who looked after the cows.

'Taking a little holiday?' he inquired, with good-humoured sarcasm.

'You gotter come up from cows sometimes,' Ben defended himself. 'They ain't vilette der parme!'

'That's all right,' nodded the officer. 'You look a bit green.'

'Put green by me, and you wouldn't reckernise it,' answered Ben. ''Ow long afore we're goin' ter stand on somethink that don't wobble?'

'We'll soon be in now,' smiled the officer, 'and I can't say *I'll* be sorry, either, after this dirty bit o' Channel. But, I say, you're not supposed to jaw with the nobs, you know!'

He glanced at the gold-tipped cigarette, as he spoke. Ben was still sticking it.

''E begun it,' replied Ben. ''Oo is 'e?'

'Not seen him before, eh?'

'Never set eyes on 'im.'

'Well, he's had his eyes on *you* more than once during the voyage. Supercargo. Came on board the same port you did. Hallo, what's happened to your top hat?'

'Gorn hoverboard, arter me yeller gloves,' answered Ben.

'Well, see you don't foller them!' grinned the officer, as the ship gave another heave. 'It's time you were getting below again.'

Ben nodded. After all, it didn't really matter. It was equally uncomfortable everywhere.

The cow Molly greeted him with friendliness. He swore

that she knew him, just as he knew her. Her mouth, and the tongue that came out of it to lick his fingers, was especially soft, and when the man and the animal stared wordlessly into each other's eyes, they understood each other. 'Life's not much fun,' said the cow's eyes. 'Mouldy,' replied Ben's. 'Frightening,' said the cow's. ''Orrible,' said Ben's. 'But *you* seem all right,' said the cow's. 'You ain't so bad yerself,' said Ben's.

Then he scratched the cow where cows like it, behind the ears, and then held out his hand to be licked. It was a very young cow, and Ben, despite his lines, had never really grown up.

Now, while the boat drew into Southampton Water, he stared at Molly for the last time, and a very queer sensation assailed him. If you had asked him whether it was sentiment or sea-sickness, he'd have tossed for it.

'I 'ope they're good ter yer,' he said. 'If they ain't, jest drop us a line.'

The cow looked back, solemnly. And who shall prove that, within the muddy mournfulness of its limited comprehension, it did not receive some fragment of Ben's message?

But the business of bringing a boat into port makes no allowance for either sentiment or sea-sickness, and before long Ben was busy with, not one cow, but fifty. They had to be examined. They had to be disturbed. They had to be shooed into new places where they belonged, and out of other places where they didn't; round a yawning hole; over a board flooring, down a gangway, into a fenced enclosure. Then fresh officials took charge, driving them into a waiting truck.

And so the fifty cows passed out of Ben's life, and at last he found himself a free man again.

9

A free man? Technically, yes. But, in a sense, he envied the cows as he stood on the dock with neither plan nor prospect. They, at least, had somewhere to go!

'Well—here we are again,' said a voice beside him.

It was the supercargo. In the midst of kicking cattle, Ben had forgotten him!

'Oh—you agine?' he blinked.

'Yes, me agine,' answered the young man. 'Have you got your discharge?'

'Eh? Yus.'

'Splendid! Then let's be getting along!'

Ben stared at the young man, incredulously. So it *wasn't* a catch, after all?

'Yer mean—that job?' he asked.

'Course,' nodded the young man. 'What did you take me for? I'm the sort that sticks to my word, I am. Step lively.'

He seemed in a hurry to be off. In such a hurry, in fact, that he suddenly seized Ben's arm, and began trundling him away.

'Oi! Are we goin' in fer a air record or somethink?' demanded Ben.

'We've got to find a shop before it closes, haven't we?' replied the young man. 'No, no! Not that way—this way!'

He swung Ben round a corner, and then round another corner. Ben began to gasp. Then a taxi loomed before them and Ben found himself shooting in. The door slammed. The taxi began to move.

'Wot's orl this?' panted Ben.

'I'm a hustler,' admitted the young man, 'when there's a reason.'

'Yus, but wot's the reason?'

10

The young man considered for a moment, then gave a reason.

'If we hadn't hurried, we'd have missed this taxi,' he explained, 'and if we'd missed this taxi we might have missed our shop.'

'Wot shop?'

'Where's your memory, man? I'm getting you a new cap, aren't I? And now suppose we stop talking, and try thinking? Thinking's so much more restful, isn't it?'

Ben subsided. Thinking was certainly more restful. The only trouble was, one didn't know quite what to think. The taxi made its way inland, and soon the docks were well in their rear. Narrow streets widened. The sense of ships grew less. Shops replaced blank brick walls, and chimneys funnels.

'Oi!' cried Ben, suddenly. 'There's 'ats!'

'Eh?' exclaimed his companion, jerked out of a reverie.

''Ats,' repeated Ben. ''At shop. 'Ats.'

The young man called to the driver to stop, and the taxi drew up by the curb.

'Wait here,' instructed the young man.

'Wot, ain't I goin' in with yer?' answered Ben.

'Wait here!' repeated the young man.

'Corse, the size don't matter!' observed Ben.

Apparently it didn't. The young man was already out of the taxi.

'Orl right, 'ave it yer own way,' muttered Ben, 'but 'ow's 'e goin' ter know if me 'ead's like a pea or a hefelant?'

He closed his eyes. An instant later he opened them again. The young man was back beside him.

'Well, I'm blowed!' said Ben. 'That was quick! Did 'e see yer comin' and toss yer one aht of the shop?'

11

'Don't be an ass!' retorted the young man. 'They were no good—didn't like the look of them.'

'Wot! Yer mean, yer went in?' exclaimed Ben. 'In that cupple o' blinks?'

'Shops have windows, haven't they?' growled the young man. 'Shut up!'

The taxi moved on. Ben noticed that the young man's forehead was dripping.

2

Two in a Taxi

If you had found yourself in Ben's position, you would very soon have ended it. You would not have submitted to the will of a strange young man who, however fair his promises, lugged you rapidly round corners, thrust you into a taxi-cab, invested the simple operation of buying a cap with queer significance, and burst, for no apparent reason, into sudden perspiration. You would have required some explanation of these things, or you would have contrived some means of leaving him.

But, after all, you could not have found yourself in Ben's position. As Ben himself would have told you, 'The kind o' persishuns I gits in ain't mide fer nobody helse!' And in this argument lies the reason of Ben's inactivity.

Things always happened to him. They always had, and they always would. If you tried to stop one thing, you'd only walk into another, so why waste energy? And, so far, Ben's present position was mild compared with others that lay behind him, and others that lay ahead of him.

Wherefore he did not comment upon his companion's

perspiration. He did not comment upon the speed with which they drove away from the hat-shop (the driver had clearly received an instruction to hurry), or upon the number of other hat-shops that were passed without pausing. And when, at last, the taxi made its second halt, he did not protest on receiving, once more, the injunction to stay where he was while fresh headgear was being obtained.

'I ain't payin' fer the cap,' he reflected, philosophically, 'so if I looks like a pea-nut hunder it, it ain't fer me ter compline!'

But he did wonder, when he saw the young man emerge from the shop with a small parcel, why the young man did not return immediately to the taxi-cab.

''E was in a 'urry afore,' thought Ben, as the young man walked leisurely round a corner, 'but time don't seem nothink ter 'im now!'

A minute went by. Two. Three. An unpleasant theory began to develop in Ben's brain. Was *this* the catch? Had the young man gone off, leaving Ben to pay the fare?

Apparently this theory was being developed also on the driver's seat. The taximan descended, and poked his head through the window.

'Where's he gone?' inquired the taximan.

'I dunno,' replied Ben.

'But you're with him,' objected the taximan.

'Then 'e carn't be gorn,' Ben pointed out.

This was beyond the taximan, who returned with a grunt to his seat. But after another three minutes had gone by, he descended again, and once more poked his head through the window.

'I suppose he *is* coming back?' he frowned.

'I s'pose 'e is,' replied Ben.

'Suppose he don't?' said the taximan.

'Then 'e won't,' answered Ben.

The taximan's frown grew, and focused itself directly on Ben.

'I'm going to get my fare,' he declared, with a hint of a threat.

'That's orl right,' nodded Ben. 'I'll sendjer a cheque.'

During the next three minutes the young man returned, and a crisis was averted. He gave an instruction to the driver, entered the taxi, and the journey was resumed.

'We thort we'd lorst yer,' said Ben.

'I had to go to another shop,' explained the young man, with no trace of apology, 'and while I was there I met a friend.'

'I see. And 'ad one,' replied Ben. 'And where are we goin' now?'

'To the station.'

Ben opened his eyes wide.

'Wot for?' he demanded.

'For the job,' answered the young man. 'There's a train at 6.22, and you can just catch it.'

'Me?'

'You!'

'Yus, but—' Ben paused. There was a rather disturbing sense in all this of being shoved about. 'Ain't you goin', too?'

'Never mind about me. Now, listen. The train goes at 6.22, and gets into London in a couple of hours. Waterloo. Do you know Waterloo? Your peculiarly pleasant accent suggests a knowledge of London. I hope you know your way about?'

15

'Wot! Lunnon?'

'Even so. Lunnon.'

'Without me,' said Ben, 'Lunnon *ain't* Lunnon.'

'Really! One of the sights?'

'Didn't yer know? When them Americans come hover, if I ain't there they turns rahnd and goes back agine.'

'Upon my soul, I'm honoured to have met you!' laughed the young man, and Ben found himself counting his teeth. 'I hope, in the circumstances, you won't feel above travelling third-class?'

'Well—jest fer once, like.'

'Splendid! Now, listen again. All this is very entertaining, but we mustn't forget that life's a serious matter—and especially,' he added significantly, 'when we're job-hunting. The fare to Waterloo is nine-and-tenpence. From Waterloo you will have to get to Wimbledon. Do you know Wimbledon?'

'That's right,' nodded Ben. 'That's where Tilden and me 'as our little knock-up.'

A slight frown appeared on the young man's face.

'I wonder,' he mused, gravely, 'whether, after all, you have too much humour for this job?'

'Don't you worry, sir,' Ben stuck to him. 'If it's wanted, I can cry like I got a fly in me eye.'

The young man weighed the information. He did not seem to find it immediately convincing. He studied Ben with a new interest and attention, and Ben felt that his fate was being decided. It was. The toss went against him, and the young man smiled again.

'Yes—after all, I think you'll do,' he said, 'although I'm afraid there won't be any tennis for you. The house you're going to is at Wimbledon Common. Are you good at remembering names?'

'Yus,' answered Ben. 'I can remember 'arf me own.'

'Yes, by the way, what is it?'

'Ben.'

'And you've forgotten the other half?'

'Yus.'

'Conveniently?'

'Wotchermean?'

'Oh, nothing. But sometimes people make a habit of forgetting their names. Well, so you won't forget this one—'

'Oo?'

'—the name of the house you've got to go to—'

'Oh.'

'Please don't keep on saying "Oo" and "Oh." It's getting a bit on my nerves. So you won't forget the name of the house you're going to, I'll write it down on a piece of paper, and you can stick it in your pocket. I suppose,' he added, looking at Ben's ragged suit, 'you've got a pocket?'

'You can put anythink in me anywhere,' Ben told him.

'Well, find a place where this will *stay* in,' replied the young man, as he took out a note-book.

He tore out a sheet and scribbled upon it. Then he handed it to Ben and asked whether he could read it.

'Corse I can!' retorted Ben, and held the paper hard against his best eye. '"Greystones," ain't it?'

'Splendid! Go on.'

'"Greystones,"' repeated Ben, to gain time. 'And the next is "North Lane." But where's the Common?'

'No need to write that,' responded the young man. 'You can remember Wimbledon Common, can't you? And if you lost that little piece of paper with the complete address on it, somebody else might find it and go after your job.'

'So they might,' murmured Ben, impressed.

'Now, I'm going to give you a pound,' proceeded the young man, 'and that will cover your expenses all the way.'

It would more than cover them. Ben kept very still, lest his companion should realise it.

'When you get to the house,' went on the young man, 'you will say that—Mr White sent you—'

'I'm bein' you, like?'

'—and you will hand over the piece of paper with the address on.'

'Yus, but 'oo—'

'I'm coming to that, now. The gentleman you will ask for, and hand the paper to, is Mr Lovelace—'

'Go on!'

'What's the matter now?'

'Nothink!'

'Then what did you say "Go on" for?'

'Well—Lovelice! I thort you was makin' the nime hup, like.'

'Try to think a little less when you get to Wimbledon Common,' said the young man dryly. 'If Mr Lovelace can stand your interruption and likes your face, he'll take you. If he can't and doesn't—' The young man shrugged his shoulders. 'Well, in that case you'll have had your fare to London, with a bob or two over.'

The taxi swung round a corner. A hundred yards ahead loomed the station.

'And that's orl?' murmured Ben.

'Yes—when I've given you your cap,' answered the young man.

He undid the little parcel. A dark brown cap of rough material bulged out of it.

18

'Have I suited your particular style of beauty?' asked the young man, as he put it on Ben's head.

Ben stared at a small mirror fixed in the taxi. The young man stared at Ben. Both were intent.

'Bit of orl right,' commented Ben.

'Good,' said the young man. He looked pleased. Then all at once he looked less pleased, for a blank expression suddenly replaced the self-conscious grin with which Ben had been regarding his face in the mirror. 'What's the trouble *this* time?' he demanded, sharply.

'Jest thort o' somethink,' muttered Ben.

'I advised you not to think,' retorted the young man.

'Yus, but—well, this is somethink I fergot, see?'

'All I see is that you'll have to go on forgetting it!'

And, as though to clinch matters and to end wavering, the young man whipped out his case and handed Ben the promised pound-note.

Ben clutched the note, but his soul was not soothed. The thing he had forgotten was important. More important, even, than a pound-note.

'It's a letter,' said Ben.

'Write it from London,' answered the young man.

'That might be too late, see,' replied Ben, doggedly. 'It might miss the person.'

'Who is the person?' asked the young man.

Ben hesitated. He didn't feel inclined to admit that the person was a girl he had left in Spain, who wouldn't know where to connect up with him when she got back to England unless she found a note waiting for her at Southampton Post Office. Such an admission, besides treading on sacred ground, would reinforce the young man's proposal that the note should be sent from London, since it was hardly likely that Molly Smith would reach Southampton hot upon Ben's heels.

'Yus, but she *might*,' reflected Ben, 'and I ain't takin' no charnces! Lunnon's a long way orf, and while I'm 'ere I'm 'ere!'

So he told the young man that the person was a bloke wot owed him a fiver and that he wasn't going to waste no time in getting after it.

This story, coupled with the queer doggedness by which Ben occasionally got his way at unexpected moments, produced a halt of two minutes outside a small stationer's shop. In these two minutes, while the young man waited in the taxi, Ben bought a sheet of paper and an envelope and a penny-halfpenny stamp, borrowed a pen, wrote: '*Dere Molly i'm ere graystones north lane wimbledon Common,*' stuffed it in the envelope, addressed it to '*Miss Molly Smith, Post Orfis, Southamton,*' thumped on the stamp, and posted the lot in a pillar-box.

''Ow's that fer quick?' he exclaimed, as he got back into the taxi.

The young man made no reply.

'Oi! I ses 'ow's that fer quick?' repeated Ben.

The young man still made no reply. Suddenly, Ben looked at him.

As a rule, Ben moved slowly. His motto was that you never got nowhere, so why 'urry? But, at chosen moments, he moved with a rapidity that baffled logic. He could get down three flights of stairs in two seconds, and round two corners in one. He had never got down stairs or round corners, however, with half the rapidity at which he now got out of the taxi. The driver was still in first gear, driving a dead man to a station, while Ben was legging it four blocks away.

And on Ben's head was a cap, and in his pocket was a pound-note, which the dead man had given him.

'Now, you!' exclaimed a voice in his ear.

A hand grabbed his coat. With a yelp, he wrenched himself free. And, as he did so, he wondered why Fate never gave him a decent deal, and why the hand he had wrenched himself away from was not an ordinary hand, but bore a livid red scar.

3

Flight

Ben did not possess many accomplishments, but he could run away, probably, better than anybody else in the world, and since he spent half his life running away he was never out of practice. This gave him an advantage over the owner of the hand with the livid red scar, and before the hand could make a second grab at him there only remained thin air to grab at.

In the next sixty seconds Ben knocked three people over. Two of them were men and the other was a small boy. The two men had to pick themselves up, but Ben risked life and liberty to replace the small boy in a standing position, and he also made a funny grimace in the hope that this would restore the small boy's faith in a somewhat violent world. He always had a fellow feeling for small boys because to him, as to them, everything looked so big.

Then followed sixty more successful seconds. He improved his steering, and all he bumped into was a lamp-post. Even that proved helpful, in a way, because he bumped into it at such speed that he bounced off round a corner without the trouble of turning.

Then he paused. You have to after a hundred and twenty non-stop seconds. You pause to find out whether you are still alive—to discover whether all the pumping and thumping inside you is going on in this world or in the next. If you're dead you stop and wait for an angel. But, if you're not, you probe your bursting brain to remember what you are running away from. You see, you've been running so fast that you've forgotten. And then, when you remember what you are running away from, you start off again for another hundred and twenty seconds.

Ben ran away for considerably longer than he had any immediate need for, and he might have gone on running away indefinitely if it had not suddenly occurred to the remnants of his brain that he did not know in what direction he was running, and that, for all he could say, he might be running back again. Then he sat down on a post to think about it.

For several seconds, however, thought was impossible. He felt sick, felt better, felt sick, was sick, and felt better.

After which sequence of emotional events he wiped his clammy forehead, shoved his new cap back on his head, and endeavoured to work out his geographical and spiritual position.

Fust, where was 'e?

He gathered from the road's loneliness that he was somewhere in the outskirts of Southampton. That was good! And when he was out of the outskirts, that would be better! Southampton, recently a Mecca, was now an inferno. Ben desired most keenly to shake the dust of the port for ever from his holy boots.

'Meanin', o' corse, with 'oles in,' he told himself.

Away to the right lay the city he was flying from. Gloaming cloaked, blessedly, the road. There was no sight of Southampton's activity from this peaceful spot, no throb of its distant sound. The only sounds were immediate sounds—of wind blowing in fitful gusts as it played hide-and-seek with itself round corners, of dead leaves indignantly awakened by the game, of a little dog barking behind a wall, of a sign creaking somewhere. Each of these sounds was capable of striking terror into any soul, for the heart of sound is its association; but, to Ben regaining his breath on his post, the sounds were sweet, because they had nothing to do with dead men in taxi-cabs and hands with livid red scars.

In front of him was the wall beyond which the little dog barked. It divided Ben from a thousand other stories, even the little dog's, but Ben was only interested in his own. To the left, a faint light glimmered, contending for supremacy against the waning day. The sign creaked above it. That meant a drink.

Well, this was where he was. Now the next question arose. What was he going to do?

Ben worked on this for a long time. Longer than, during the actual inoperative process, he realised. He only began to realise it when he found himself sitting on the ground and wondered how he had got there. Apparently, instead of working on the question, he had worked off the post.

All right. Stay where you find yourself. That was as good a motto as any. Ben did most of his thinking from the bottom level.

But, after another lapse of time, he discovered that his thinking wasn't leading anywhere. So he cut the question into two—(1) what should he do presently in a general way, and (2) what should he do now in a specific way— threw the former, more difficult half over the wall to the dog, and concentrated on the second, simpler half. The second half was simple because its solution was clearly indicated by the creaking sign.

'Yer brine's no good while yer throat's arskin' fer it,' he decided.

Whereupon he rose, and, having removed himself from the road, he proceeded to remove the road from himself. More particularly from the latter portion of himself. He didn't want no clues on his trousers.

And then he heard a car coming along the road from Southampton. It came in the middle of a big gust of wind, and he did not hear it until the gust had died down. Then his heart began to increase its pace. Not that a car was anything to be afraid of, but his heart was behaving as unreasonably as his brain, and was just as anxious for that drink.

'Go on! Wot's a car?' he chided himself.

As the car approached he adopted an attitude of excessive unconcern and decided to whistle. You can't whistle when you're worried, so if he whistled it would prove he wasn't worried. The only snag in the theory was that he found he couldn't whistle.

Only one car in ten thousand would have stopped on seeing Ben. This proved to be the one. The brakes were applied sharply, and there was an unRollsroycian squeak. Now Ben did not even try to whistle.

What was the car stopping for? Perhaps the driver wanted a drink, too? Thus Ben clutched at his straw. But the straw slipped away in his hand. The driver wanted Ben.

'Hallo, there!' he called.

Ben's stomach turned over with relief. It was the petty officer whose duty on board a ship lately arrived at Southampton had been to look after a man who looked after cows. The future will be simplified if we admit that the officer's name was Jones.

'Hallo, there! Not a bad distance for Shanks's pony,' cried Jones. 'Where are *you* heading for?'

'Anywhere,' replied Ben, noncommittally.

'Well, that's as good as anywhere else,' grinned the officer. 'But you're not going to tell me you were going to pass that pub?'

'Eh?'

'Say, have you ever counted how many "Eh's" you say per day? It must be somewhere in the thousands. However, I've something more int'restin' to talk about. Have you seen a blood-thirsty Dago anywhere about?'

Ben's heart jumped. On the point of another 'Eh?' he altered it to ''Oo?'

'Eh, 'oo, 'ow and oi—that's about all the bright conversation you've got! Dago! A murdering Dago! He's around loose somewhere. Have you seen 'im?'

'Wot for?' murmured Ben.

'Well, not for pleasure, I'd imagine! I say, what's up with you? You look as green as cabbage!'

'Go on!' retorted Ben, slowly fighting back. 'Anybody'd turn green, 'earin' abart a murderer, wouldn't they?'

'Murderer's right,' nodded Jones, with a frown. 'And now you can get ready to turn a bit greener. Who d'you s'pose he's murdered?'

'Wot—did '*e* do it?' gasped Ben.

'Hallo!' cried Jones, sharply. 'Do what?'

26

'Eh?'

'Oh, shut that! What do you know about this?'

'Me?'

'No, Ramsay MacDonald, of course! Buttons and braces, have you *ever* been known to answer a question properly? What do you *know*?'

'Nothink.'

'Then what did you say "Did 'e do it?" for?' pressed Jones. 'What did you mean by "it"?'

'That was the murder.'

'Well, go on?'

'You sed 'e done a murder, didn't yer?'

'Yes.'

'Well, that's the one I'm arskin' abart,' said Ben. Jones gave it up.

'The chap who's been murdered,' said Jones, 'is our supercargo.'

'Go on!' muttered Ben. And then suddenly added, 'Well, if 'e done it, it'd let anybody else aht, wouldn't it?'

'Not an accomplice,' answered Jones, 'and he's believed to have had one. It's a queer business altogether. You see, the fellow was killed in a taxi-cab, and this other bloke seems to have bunked out of the taxi immediately afterwards. However, don't ask me for details,' he added. 'All I know is that the police are after both of 'em, and that I wouldn't care to be in either of their shoes. Like to jump in and join in the hunt?'

Ben gulped, and shook his head.

'Why not? Free ride!' urged Jones. 'You've got no other appointment!'

'Yus, I 'ave.'

'Oh! What?'

'Gotter see a man abart a helefant.'

'Blamed fool! About a drink, you mean! Hallo, where did you get your new cap from?' He stared at Ben, and then suddenly swung his head round. 'By Jove!' he cried. 'Hear that? Police whistles!'

In a flash he was turning his car. Not far off, shrill blasts pierced the gloaming. A second or two later, the car vanished back along the road.

Ben stared after it. Had he been a fool? 'Arter orl, *I* ain't done nothink!' he told himself. But he had been blamed for hundreds of things he hadn't done. And he had to admit that, in his fright, he had acted suspicious, like. And when you act suspicious, like, people aren't apt to believe you, like.

So he resisted a momentary impulse to go after Mr Jones, and decided that the best plan was to keep right out of it.

The next instant, however, he was right in it. Someone slipped out of a shadow and laid a hand on his shoulder. He had only seen the hand once before in his life, but he recognised it the moment it touched him. And, this time, he was unable to wriggle away.

4

Diablo!

If you can move, move quickly. If you can't, keep quite still. Such was Ben's motto in the horrible moments of life. This was a horrible moment, and he kept quite still.

The owner of the hand that was pressing on his shoulder with fingers that felt like hot sharp knives also kept quite still. Utter immobility seemed to be a mutual need while the police whistles sounded fainter and fainter in the distance, and until they finally died away. But when silence reigned again, the owner of the hand moved; and, to his surprise, Ben found himself moving, too.

The hot sharp knives were propelling him and directing him. They propelled and directed him into the long shadow of the wall, and they kept him in the long shadow until the wall took an unexpected, narrow turn. Now Ben was between two walls, and there was nothing whatever but shadow. He felt as though he were being marched along a black plank, with a drop into further blackness at the end of it.

Then, suddenly, the unpleasant journey concluded, and he was jerked into a halt. Behind him, in a low fierce whisper, sounded the voice of his captor.

'Now, say!' the voice commanded. 'Who are you?'

'Wotcher mean, 'oo am I?' muttered Ben. 'That won't 'elp yer!'

'Answer!'

'Well, tike yer 'and orf me neck—'

'Sst!'

'And don't spit!'

'Diablo!' hissed the man behind him, and Ben's heart gave a jump. Diablo! He'd heard that before! Diablo was Spanish for 'Bother!' . . . 'Answer, as I say!'

'Corse, it's heasy ter tork when yer 'avin' yer gullet choked,' retorted Ben. 'But if yer want it, me nime's Ben, and me At 'Ome Day's fust Fridays.'

'Ben, eh?'

'Yus.'

'Si!'

'That's right. Jest come orf it.'

'No more that!' The voice grew more menacing. 'Now say again. Say why you run?'

''Cos yer was arter me.'

'Arter?'

'Arter. Chise. Try ter catch.'

'Oh! So I try to catch you?'

'Yus.'

'And so—you run?'

'Yus.'

'But before I try to catch you?'

'Eh?'

30

'You still run? Say, now! Why you run before I try to catch you?'

Ben thought he would try to run again, but as he gave a lurch the fingers tightened on his neck and his breath began to go. 'Oi! Stow that!' he gulped. 'I won't be no good to yer flabby!'

'Dios meo!' rasped his captor. 'Speak what I say, and no more! *Why you run away?*'

'Gawd, yer worse'n a cop!' murmured Ben. 'Why was I runnin' away? Well, I reckon you knows that as well as I do . . . Orl right, orl right! I was runnin' away 'cos—'cos a chap wot I was with died sudden, like.'

'Died?'

'Ain't I tellin' yer? If you don't comprennez the langwidge you orter've stayed at 'ome—'

'Who is it that die?'

'I've toljer!'

'Who?'

'Chap I was with.'

'Diablo!'

'That's right.'

'But who were you with?'

'Chap wot died. Eh? Well, 'ow do I know. I on'y jest met 'im.'

'Si, si! You meet him and you say "Buenos dias," and he die!'

'I never tole 'im ter dias—'

Then the whole Spanish dictionary descended upon Ben, and he felt something prick his back. He recognised that prick. It was a part of the Spanish Constitution, and in a panic he poured out particulars.

''Is nime was White. Leastwise, that's wot 'e sed. 'E got torkin' ter me when we was on the boat, see, and then 'e got torkin' ter me when we got ashore, see, and then—'ere, stoppit, I'm goin' as quick as I can, ain't I?—and then 'e got torkin' when we was in the cab, and so, well, we got torkin'—'

'But what you talk about?' interrupted the Spaniard.

'Eh? Orl sorts o' things,' replied Ben. 'Weather. Price o' bernarners. You know.'

'I do *not* know! But I get to know! You tell me! Quick! Yes?'

The prick was reborn in Ben's back.

'Lummy, wotcher want me ter tell yer?' yelped Ben. 'Me bloomin' ige? He tells me abart a job, see—'

'Job?'

'Yus. Persishun. Tells me if I goes along I can 'ave it—'

'Where?'

''Oo?'

'Where, where?'

'Oh! Where did 'e tell me ter go?'

'Si!'

''E tells me ter go ter the plice where the job is.'

The Spaniard swore. Ben swore back. The Spaniard swore again, and won.

'Wimbledon,' muttered Ben. 'Wimbledon Common.'

'But the house?' pressed the Spaniard.

'I've fergot it.'

'Then how you go there?'

'It's on a bit o' piper.'

'Piper?'

'Yus. 'E wrote it.'

The Spaniard's eyes gleamed, but Ben did not see as the eyes were behind him.

'Show me,' ordered the Spaniard.

'Yus, and 'ave 'im follerin' me,' thought Ben. 'No blinkin' fear!'

'Show me!' repeated the Spaniard, and his voice grew more tense.

'Carn't,' replied Ben. 'I lorst it.'

'You lie!' threatened the Spaniard.

'Wot, me lie? There's a thing ter say!' protested Ben, and then suddenly jumped. ''Ere, tike yer dirty 'and aht o' me pocket! I tell yer I lorst it—it ain't there.'

'But something else is there, eh?' retorted the Spaniard, while his bony fingers felt around Ben's middle. 'This dead man! This White. He give you *something else*, eh?'

Something else? Lummy! Was the Spaniard after his pound?

Urged now by the financial aspect, it is possible that Ben would have continued his protest and, by so doing, would have ended his uneasy life in a narrow passageway on the outskirts of Southampton. But the Spaniard suddenly stiffened. A moment later, a policeman came round the corner.

The policeman was a smart fellow. On this occasion, however, he was not quite smart enough. He did not realise that he was face to face with a couple of speed kings. While the Spaniard used his legs, the Briton used his arms, and unfortunately for official prestige the constable's face was within the circuit of the arms. Caught in the first whirling of the human windmill, the constable fell to the ground; and, when the human windmill stopped whirling, the constable was still trying to come back to earth from a confusion of distant stars.

Ben, of course, had not intended to knock the policeman

down. He respected the law even while the law refused to return the compliment. Confronted with a situation that refused to reveal any immediate solution, he had merely obeyed the self-protective instinct of endeavouring to transform himself temporarily into a danger zone, and any man whose arms are revolving at the speed of fifty revolutions per second is a danger zone.

But now, his energy spent, the late human windmill stared down at the policeman's recumbent form, while the enormity of his offence percolated into his steaming brain.

Previously, Ben had run away from the menace of suspicion. Now he would have to run away from the menace of fact. It is not an offence to be with a man when he is murdered, provided you are not one of the main parties, but it is an offence to knock a bobby down. The only bright spot in the miserable situation was that the Spaniard had gone, and that a yellow hand with a red scar upon it was no longer groping about Ben's underfed person.

'Thank Gawd *'e's* 'opped it!' reflected Ben. 'And now *I'm* goin' ter 'op it!'

Hopping it was fast developing into his normal mode of progress.

But, before Ben hopped it, he took a risk. He paused and stooped over the policeman's prostrate form to ascertain that he still lived. 'It'd be jest my bloomin' luck,' he thought, 'if I'd killed 'im.'

Happily for both of them, the policeman was not dead. Indeed, as Ben peered down, the policeman began to show such obvious signs of life that Ben abruptly reared himself erect again, and lost no more time in hopping it.

Once more he sped. He sped in a circle. It was a very

large circle and a very fast circle. Possibly an astronomer on Mars spotted it and reported a ring round Southampton, reviving an extinct theory that the earth was inhabited, but Ben himself did not know it was a circle until he had completed it, and found himself once more under a creaking sign.

You or I might not have recognised the creaking of the sign. Ben, however, did. He was a creak expert, having more or less lived with creaks all his life. The creak of the stair, the creak of a ship, the creak of a door, the creak of a boot—he knew them all. He knew the difference between the creak that preceded a sudden rush and the creak that was merely investigatory, between the creak courageous and the creak cautious. Once, during an unusually long sojourn in an empty house, he had learned the creaks so well that, for the sake of convenience, he had numbered them. No. 3 was the back door. No. 6 was the hall window. No. 9 was the boot-cupboard. No. 17 was the loose stair on the way to the attic. He himself performed No. 17 while escaping from No. 9.

After this, inn-signs were child's-play!

And thus Ben recognised that the sign now creaking above him, almost invisible in the increased gloaming, was the sign that had creaked near by when the Spaniard had laid an unwelcome hand upon his shoulder.

It was a depressing discovery. He had run five miles, and they had got him nowhere! But even more depressing was a discovery that dawned a few moments later, while he stood hesitating and wiping his forehead with his cap.

Voices were sounding from the road along which he had come.

As with creaks, so with voices. Again Ben was an expert, and he did not need to know their words before he knew their temper. These voices, experience told him, were panting voices. Indignant voices. Excited voices. Official voices. Determined voices . . .

'Along here?'

'Quiet, now!'

'D'you think he stopped?'

'What about that pub?'

And then a figure suddenly materialised close to him. It materialised in a startling flash. The voices had not sounded so close!

In a flash no less startling, Ben entered the inn. There seemed no alternative. The figure barred the way ahead, and the approaching voices barred the way behind.

He found himself in the public bar. His mind was so confused that he could not have told you at the moment whether the bar were full or empty. His whole being was concentrated on the figure that had sent him diving into this dubious sanctuary, and he stood stock still in the expectation that the figure would follow him.

But the figure didn't follow him, and all at once his mind switched galvanically back to the voices. They were now much closer. Just outside, in fact. Where the figure would be . . .

'Come on!'

'You think he's in there, then?'

'Bet he's popped in a barrel!'

A reply from the door-step, however, dissolved this picturesque theory.

'Are you after a run-away? If you are, he's just gone along that road there towards Southampton,' came the amazing information. 'Yes, and the brute knocked me clean down in his hurry, he did, so I hope you catch him!'

The pursuers shouted thanks. Feet turned, and hurried away. But Ben remained motionless. For the voice that had turned the pursuers' feet was the voice of Molly Smith.

5

Drama in a Bar

Molly Smith! Molly! Not in Spain! *Here!* . . .

The room began to jerk about, and through the gymnastics swam a face. A large, red, fat face, that seemed to be propelled by its two fin-like ears. The eyes in the face were pale blue, and they stared.

'Feelin' queer?' asked the owner of the face.

'Wot's that?' murmured Ben, mechanically.

'Are you feelin' queer?' repeated the owner of the face.

Did suspicion lurk in the pale blue eyes? If so, Ben was not in a condition to combat it. He merely stared back, while the suspicion appeared to grow.

'You've been runnin'!' The statement was more like a challenge. 'And where's your cap, mate? Lost it?'

'No, here it is,' chipped in another voice.

And Molly Smith entered, cool as a cucumber, and with the cap in her hand.

'Lying on the door-step,' she said. 'Did that chap they're after barge into you, like he did into me?'

She held the cap out to Ben. Automatically, he took it, while their eyes met. They might have been strangers for all the recognition she showed. Lummy, what a kid she was, when it came to a tight corner!

'I tell you, I was frightened proper!' she ran on, producing a shiver. 'And *you* look as if you'd had a bit of a scare up, if you don't mind me saying it. Did *you* dodge in here to get out of the way, too?'

'Tha's right, miss,' answered Ben, catching at the cue.

Her quick, keen mind was like a rope thrown out to him in a raging sea.

'Well, I don't blame you!' she exclaimed. 'All these Bolshies and bag-snatchers—it doesn't seem safe to be out! But what's this one done? Nothing to do with that murder in the town, is he?'

Another cue! She was letting him know that she knew! Yes, and how *much* did she know? P'r'aps more than he did!

Now another voice joined in. The voice of the barmaid this time.

'Nothing to do with it?' she exclaimed, polishing a glass which had lately been bathed in her fair breath. 'I'd say he'd everything to do with it! Wouldn't you, Joe?'

The red-faced man, addressed as Joe, nodded solemnly, and continued to stare at Ben.

'We was just talking about it, wasn't we, when *you* popped in,' continued the barmaid, nodding towards Ben. 'There's two of 'em. One's from Spain or somewhere, so they say, and the other's a sailor what's come off a ship.'

'The sailor's the one *I* saw!' interposed Molly, quickly. 'Six foot, if an inch!'

'I heard he was little,' said Joe.

His tone was that of a man who objects to discarding a theory. Molly, however, stuck to her point.

'Little be boiled!' she retorted. 'That only shows what stories get around!'

'She's right there,' agreed the barmaid. 'What *I* was told was that he was little and had a yeller tooth sticking out like a tusk! But, there you are! What are you to believe? Is it true,' she added, turning to Molly, 'that he was in the taxi when they heard the scream, and that this sailor fellow popped out of one door while the policeman popped in at the other?'

Just in time, Ben prevented himself from denying that there had been any scream,

'Out he jumps,' the barmaid ran on, 'with his knife still in his hand and the blood dripping on the pavement, there's no sleep for *me* tonight, and into a house, and then escapes off the roof! And then, just when they think they've got him, along comes this foreigner—'

'Spaniard, Spaniard,' interposed Joe, irritably.

'Spaniard, was it? They're all the same. And he knocks a policeman out, and off they bolt together.'

'Wot, tergether?' blinked Ben.

'That's right. They was both in it. It's my belief the sailor done it, and then passes the pocket-book on to this Spaniard. Well, anyhow, let's hope they're both caught. Ain't anyone going to drink to it?'

'Pocket-book, eh?' murmured Ben. 'Was there a pocket-book?'

'Well, I didn't say a coal-scuttle, did I?' retorted the barmaid. 'Easy to see *you* don't know nothing about it!'

'Ay, and mebbe *you* don't know quite as much about

it as you think,' observed the red-faced Joe, tartly. Six feet!'

'*I* never said nothing about six feet!' returned the barmaid, with equal spirit. 'P'r'aps it's getting time you used your *two*!'

Joe looked at her with a scowl, then looked at Ben again.

'Mebbe it is,' he said. 'Mebbe it is!'

And, abruptly draining his glass, he placed it on the stained counter, planked down the payment, and strode out of the inn.

Ben and Molly exchanged glances. The barmaid laughed.

'Don't you worry about *him*!' she exclaimed. 'Loony, that's what he is! Well, what'll you have?'

'Three penn'orth o' champagne,' replied Ben, making an effort to hide his intense uneasiness at the red-faced man's abrupt departure.

'My! Aren't you a wag!' smiled the barmaid. 'And the lady? Ain't you going to treat her for picking up your cap? And a new one, too, ain't it?'

Sometimes, for no apparent reason, one's mind will be diverted from a main issue to a trivial one. Ben's mind, now, was diverted to his cap. Queer how often his cap cropped up in the conversation! Of course, it was all quite natural, really, but . . .

Mechanically, he adjusted and completed his drink order, but his mind still flitted vaguely around his cap, or his cap flitted vaguely around his mind. Meanwhile, Molly was drawing casually closer, till her lips were within a few inches of his ear.

'Drink it quickly,' whispered the lips, 'and go!'

Ben donned an expression intended to convey the

response, 'I get yer.' To anyone else it would merely have conveyed that he had suddenly got a fly in his eye.

'Go to the right,' whispered the lips again. 'I'll follow.'

Ben repeated his expression. He now looked as if he had got two flies in his eye.

'And leave your cap behind you,' came the final whispered injunction.

'There yer are,' thought Ben. 'Cap agine. Funny!'

He approached the counter, took his glass of three-penny champagne, and held it aloft.

''Ere's wot,' he said.

'Buenos dias,' answered Molly.

'That's a new one!' commented the barmaid. 'Russian, ain't it?'

'No, Chinese,' smiled Molly. 'It means "Good luck and we'll meet again!"'

Ben grinned, and shoved his cap so far back on his head that it fell to the floor.

'Well, I 'ope we do,' he nodded, 'becos' now I gotter be orf.'

He drained his glass, and made for the door.

'Oh, and where are you off to?' inquired the barmaid.

'Mothers' Meeting,' answered Ben, 'ter knit socks.'

The next moment he was gone. The barmaid stared after him, and laughed.

'Talk about lightning,' she observed. 'Bit of a hurry, wasn't he?'

'Yes, and he's left his blessed cap behind!' exclaimed Molly, suddenly. 'I'd better go after him.'

And, hastily emptying her own glass, she picked up the cap and made an equally hurried exit.

For about ten minutes the barmaid's life became dull

again. She yawned, breathed on glasses, wiped, yawned, breathed, wiped, in dreary but philosophic sequence. Then life brightened once more, the door was pushed open, and a police officer entered.

Behind came Joe, redder than ever with a kind of crimson triumph.

'What did I say?' he cried.

As a matter of fact, he had not said anything; he had merely thought. But when your thought proves right, it is human to assume that you have spoken.

The inspector silenced him with a sharp motion. Then he addressed the barmaid with even greater sharpness.

'Where's the couple who were in here just now?' he demanded.

'I'm sure I don't know!' replied the barmaid, her eyes popping.

'When did they leave?' barked the inspector.

'Ten minutes ago!' gasped the barmaid. 'You're never going to tell me—'

'Know which way they went?'

'No.'

'Did they leave together?'

'No! Yes—'

'Which? Which?'

'Well, I'm all of a fluster! The man went first, and the girl went a few seconds after.'

'Aha!' exclaimed Joe, his triumph increasing. 'Aha!'

The inspector rushed out of the bar, gave an order, and rushed in again.

'Now, then!' he said. 'How long were they in here, and look lively!'

'I can't look lively when you make me so breathless!'

returned the barmaid. 'Three or four minutes, I should think.'

'What did they do?'

'He came in first, and she came in afterwards—'

'Yes, yes, I know that. She came in after spilling a red herring! What happened when *he* left?'

He jerked his thumb towards Joe.

'Nothing happened,' answered the barmaid.

'Think again!'

'Well, nothing happened that was anything, if you know what I mean. They had drinks—'

'Drinks!' cried the inspector. 'Where are the glasses?'

'Washed up.'

'Damn! You've washed off their finger-prints!'

'How was *I* to know—'

'Yes, yes, all right! Did they seem in a hurry?'

'*He* did! Tossed it down quicker than you talk! I thought to myself, "You've got a throat a mile wide, or you'd choke," I thought. And then out he goes, leaving his cap behind.'

'Cap, eh?'

'That's right.'

'Good! Where is it?'

'She took it out after him. Naturally I thought—'

'What you were intended to think,' interposed the inspector, disappointedly. 'A put-up job, of course. Otherwise she'd have come back, wouldn't she? And you can't think of anything else, eh?'

'I can describe 'em,' answered the barmaid, combatting an unjust sense of failure. 'The man was a funny little fellow—'

'In a greasy coat and a new cap,' interrupted the inspector,

44

'and the girl was small, too, but trim and neat, pretty and with brown hair.' He glanced at Joe. 'I've got their descriptions.' He glanced back at the barmaid. His head moved as sharply as his tongue. 'Well, if that's all you can do for us—'

'No, I can do a bit more!' exclaimed the barmaid, suddenly recollecting. 'They come from China!'

'China?' repeated the inspector, staring.

'Yes! I know, because when she drank she said Buenos Aires or something, and it meant "Good luck and we'll meet again."'

'Why, that fixes it!' cried the inspector. '"Good luck to our escape and we'll meet again outside!" You've been treated to a nice little bit of acting, miss! But your Buenos Aires don't sound exactly Chinese to me.'

'Well, she *said* it was,' frowned the barmaid.

'And the next time you see her, if she says she's eating kippers you can bet your life it's haddock! I suppose you can't get any nearer that foreign toast?'

'I'm sure of the Buenos, but the Aires don't sound right. Would it be Dairies? No, that's cows, and this made me think of a donkey . . . Ah, I've got it. Buenos Dias! Funny how things come back all of a sudden. Buenos Dias—'

'And if that isn't Spanish, it's damn like it!' interposed the inspector, with another quick glance at Joe. 'Now, you see, they're all *three* tied together. The sailor knocks a policeman down while the Spaniard makes his get-away, and the girl puts a drink down while the sailor makes *his* get-away. And the girl speaks Spanish, so is obviously thick with the Spaniard. The circle's complete. Well, we'll have 'em all three under lock and key before bedtime tonight, or I'll take up knitting!'

Upon which he swung round and left the pleasantly fuggy bar for the cheerless night outside.

'There you are,' said Joe.

'Yes, and he couldn't stop thanking you, could he?' retorted the barmaid.

The retort hit Joe bang in the middle. Joe preferred recognition even to service. He looked pensive.

The barmaid also looked pensive.

'Them two!' she murmured. 'Would you have believed it?'

6

Sanctuary in a Barn

This time Ben did not run in a circle. He found himself piloted by someone who preferred zizags. In Ben's best moments he also preferred zigzags, but he had not had many best moments since he had left the ship, and he found it exceedingly restful, even while he panted, to act under orders again.

He realised, of course, the motive of this hastily resumed flight. The red-faced man was the motive. Those unpleasant pale blue eyes had never lost their suspicion, and it had been quite obvious that the fellow had not left the bar to go home. He had left the bar to return to it with company, and neither Ben nor Molly was in a mood for any company saving their own.

So they zigzagged ingeniously through dark and windy lanes. The darkness hid their forms and the wind drowned their gasps. But Molly, the pilot, was taking no chances. Elements might assist, but it was wit that won in the end, and when they came to forked roads she suddenly whispered, 'Wait!' and darted up one of them.

Ben waited. He endured with wavering fortitude a score of lonely seconds. The wind blew his cap off, and he only just saved it from sailing over a hedge. If he had not saved it, the whole course of his immediate future would have been changed.

'I 'ope she ain't goin' ter be long!' he thought, fixing the rescued cap more tightly on his anxious head.

She reappeared an instant later, materialising out of the blackness like a happy ghost. But it was a ghost with only one shoe.

'Where's it gorn?' asked Ben.

Perhaps he would not have noticed the absence so soon if the unshod foot had not been so pretty. Neat, it was! But then she was neat all over. Lummy, she could tell some o' them toffs off when it came to looks! Neat as a pin—and as sharp, too, when she liked, as she now proved.

'I've lost it,' she smiled.

'Yus, and I nearly lorst me cap,' said Ben. 'We'll go and find it.'

'No fear!' she answered. 'We'll let a bobby find it. Ever heard of a false trail? Come on!'

And, seizing his arm, she started him off again up the other fork of the road.

They ran for another ten minutes. Then,

'How's your breath?' she whispered.

Hers seemed unimpaired.

'Gorn,' he gasped.

'Stick it for just a minute more,' she urged.

She took his arm and guided his tottering feet round a corner into a narrow, rutted lane. Fifty yards up the lane she suddenly stopped and pulled him towards a clump of trees. Under the trees was a big black shadow. It was a barn.

A few seconds later they were in the barn, and Ben lay panting on a little mound of hay.

Molly sat beside him. When he tried to speak, she put her fingers on his mouth. Ben yielded gratefully to the silent injunction, and slowly gasped back to life.

'Now, then,' said Molly at last, 'let's try and straighten things out a bit. Only we must speak low, or we may be heard from the road. You didn't *really* have anything to do with that murder, did you?'

'Don't be silly,' answered Ben.

'Of course you couldn't have,' she nodded. 'You've been white ever since I've known you. Which is more than I can say for myself!'

'Now, don't start that, miss,' replied Ben. 'There ain't nothink wrong with you!'

'Oh, no! I only pick pockets.'

'Go on! You've give that up, ain'tcher?'

'Ses you! Well, p'r'aps. But we won't worry about that just yet. I want to hear things.'

'Sime 'ere! 'Ow did yer git ter England?'

'Like you.'

'Eh?'

'On a boat.'

'Yus, but—'

'Your boat started first, I know. But mine was a bigger boat, and we raced you.'

'Go on!'

'It's true. I've been in Southampton two days.'

'I'm blowed!'

'Well, try and blow a little less loudly!' she warned him. 'We're not out of the wood yet!'

She crept away from him as she spoke and groped her

way to the barn door. Then she came back again, and reported all clear.

'If you was 'ere afore me,' said Ben, who had been thinking, 'why wasn't yer on the dock ter meet me?'

'Oh, I've not been in easy street,' she answered, cryptically. 'I would have met you if I could have. As it was, I got there just too late, and then I had to pick up the threads.'

'Yer mean clues, like?'

'That's it. And they weren't nice clues! When I heard about the murder, and that a sailor had jumped out of the taxi and disappeared—well, I guessed by the description that it was you. They've got you tabbed, Ben! We'll have to do something about it.'

'Yer mean, me descripshun's aht?'

'I'm afraid so.'

'But I ain't *done* nothink, miss!'

'Wasn't it Molly last time?'

'That's right.'

'Well, there's no need to go back on a good thing! No, Ben, you haven't done anything, but your whole trouble, ever since I've known you, is that you get mixed up with other people who *have*. You've got mixed up with this Spaniard—'

'Yer mean, Don Diablo?'

'That's a good name for him! Yes, Don Diablo! And you're mixed up with me—'

'Now, look 'ere, miss—Molly,' interposed Ben, seriously, 'we ain't goin' ter 'ave none o' that. You ain't doin' no more pickpocketin', see, and wot you done afore weren't your fault.'

'Oh? Then whose fault was it?'

'The fault o' the street yer was born in.'

'It's a nice idea! But—were *you* born in Park Lane?'

''Oo?'

'Your street didn't turn *you* into a thief!'

'Well, yer see—I comes from Nelson,' mumbled Ben. He hated any kind of washing, even white-washing. 'Any'ow, we ain't thinkin' o' the past, we're thinkin' o' the fuchure—'

'When we ought to be thinking of the present,' interrupted Molly. 'How did you come to be in the taxi with—with the man who was killed?'

'Yus, that was a funny bizziness right from the start, miss—'

'Molly!'

'Eh? Oh! Molly.' He liked her little interruptions. They kept things warm, like. 'Well, 'e ses he can find me a job, and so 'e arsks me ter come along with 'im, see, but fust 'e buys me a new cap—'

'Why, did you lose your old one?'

'Yus. It's gorn ter see Father Nepchune.'

'But why should he buy you a new one?'

'Well, 'e was with me when the old 'un went. Barges inter me, and so 'e ses 'e must git me another. And we gits in the taxi, and 'e buys me the new cap—'

'The one you've got on?'

'That's right. Bit of orl right, ain't it? And then, jest as we're goin' ter the stashun, I suddinly thinks of you, like, and that letter I was goin' ter 'ave waitin' fer yer at the Post Orfice, so aht I nips ter send it orf, and I sends it orf, givin' yer the address o' that job I was goin' ter, and then—blimy, I gits a shock proper.'

'What happened?'

'No good arskin' me!' muttered Ben, sepulchrally. 'It

'appened while I was writin' that there letter. I—I gits back inter the cab, see, and I ses "Ain't I bin quick?" and 'e—'e jest stares back at me from the nex' world, like. So I jest thinks, "Oi," and 'ops it. Well, I arsk yer?'

'I can guess what you felt like,' she answered, with a little shiver. 'And then?'

'I told yer.'

'What?'

'I 'opped it.'

'But the Spaniard? Don Diablo! You mentioned him.'

'Oh! 'Im!' Ben gulped at the memory. ''E's a proper nightmare, *'e* is! Fust time I bumps inter Don Diablo 'e ketches 'old of me with a blinkin' 'and wot 'as a scar on it—funny thing, if a 'and 'as a scar on it, it jest mikes fer me!—but I gits away, on'y the nex' time I *don't* git away, see, and 'e arsks me a lot o' questions, like wot was I doin' with the deader, and did I know 'is nime, it was White, and did 'e give me hennythink, and wot was the address of the plice I was goin' ter for the job. Lummy, tork abart a woman! Old Diablo'd beat a dozen. And then 'e begins to feel in me pockets, and me born ticklish, and then a bobby comes up, and 'e scoots, and I 'its the bobby, and then I scoots—'

'Sh!' whispered the girl, suddenly, and gripped his arm.

Ben stopped abruptly, with his mouth still open. Footsteps were sounding along the road.

For a few seconds they listened in strained silence. The footsteps grew closer, and as they grew closer they also grew slower. Molly slid suddenly to the barn door and began feeling about in the dimness.

Ben knew what she was feeling for. A bolt, or a crossbar, or some contrivance that would secure them from outside.

Her search was unsuccessful.

The footsteps had now stopped. Then, all at once, the dead stillness was broken by a welcome little sound. A match was being struck. They even caught a momentary glow of the light as it flickered into brief life on the other side of a crack. A few moments later, the footsteps were resumed, grew fainter, and died away.

'Aren't we a couple of mugs?' whispered Molly, returning.

'Well, two's better'n one,' murmured Ben.

The words were hardly complimentary, but Molly smiled. She understood the meaning behind. Then the smile faded, and she became thoughtful.

Ben found himself staring at the vague silhouette of her figure as she stood before him. It occurred to him that another lady he'd heard of called Venus de Smilo or something wasn't in it with Molly Smith. This superior silhouette just a few inches away from him wasn't only pretty. It was companionable. Matey. And prettiness wasn't really no good unless it was matey, too. When you thought of the darkness outside, and of the unfriendliness of it, and of the size of it—it stretched as far as the stars, with nothing in between— it sort of frightened you. But you only had to hold out your hand an inch or two and touch that silhouette, and— well, then everything was all right, wasn't it? . . .

'You know, Ben—we haven't got it all straightened out even yet,' said Venus's superior. 'Tell me! What did—old Diablo want? Was he trying to get that address when he started on your pockets, do you think?'

'I dunno wot 'e was arter,' answered Ben.

'You believe it might have been something else?'

'Lummy, it's a riddle! See, e' arst if the chap wot was dead 'ad *give* me somethink—'

'And did he?'

'Wot?'

'The man who's dead—you said his name was White, didn't you?—*did* White give you anything?'

'No!'

'No! But Don Diablo *thought* he might have! Look here, Ben, how does this sound to you? Do you suppose Don Diablo killed White—never mind for the moment how he did it—do you suppose he killed him because he wanted something White had on him? And, as you were with White, Diablo now thinks that *you've* got it on *you*?'

'Got wot?'

'What Diablo thinks you've got?'

'Wot's that?'

'Oh, Ben! How've you lived all this time?'

'Eh?'

'With no one to look after you?'

'People don't look arter me—they runs arter me!'

'And now this beastly Spaniard's joining in the chase!'

'Yus. Corse, there was that pocket-book that barmy barmaid talked abart, but 'e didn't give me no pocket-book, orl 'e give me was this cap, and if yer arsk *me*,' added Ben, as his mind harped back to the inn, 'that barmaid 'eard more'n wot 'appened, and then said more'n wot she 'eard. There's some folks turn a pea inter a mellon afore yer can say Jim Crow!'

'Yes, yes, but we're not *getting* anywhere!' sighed Molly. 'You know, Ben, I think I'm right—I think Don Diablo *does* believe you've got something that he wants! P'r'aps it's only the address White gave you—the address of the job, you know—though what he could want with that I don't know. It may be something else. By the way, what *is* the address?'

'Eh? Oh! I've fergot.'

'But wasn't it written down—'

'Oh, yus, that's right. In me pocket. 'Ere it is.'

He groped in his pocket, while she watched him. He groped in all his pockets.

'Well, I'm blowed!' he muttered. 'Where's it gorn?'

But now she wasn't watching him. Footsteps again resounded in the lane outside. Tottering, staggering footsteps.

'Funny,' thought Ben, ''ow nothink can go right.'

A moment later, something fell with a thud against the door.

7

Wanted, an Address

A thud is not a subtle sound. It is crude and blatant; but the very blatancy gives it a special distinction of its own. A footstep may be a murderer or a sweetheart. A creak may be a policeman or a child. A bell may be a creditor or a rich uncle. But a thud, in nine cases out of ten, eliminates all pleasant possibilities. It is a call to the listener that something has gone wrong.

And now the two inmates of the lonely barn knew that something had gone wrong on the other side of the barndoor. The question presented itself, should they risk their security by attempting to right what was wrong?

The question lingered only in the muddy mind of Ben. Molly, residing closer to the full range of her reactions, needed but a second to find the answer. The second over, she crossed swiftly to the door and flung it open.

On the coarse grass that separated the barn from the lane lay the crumpled figure of a man.

As Molly stared down at it, her silhouette now more distinct against the background of lane and evening sky.

Ben roused himself from his momentary stupor. Lummy, you couldn't let a slip of a girl face whatever she was facing all by herself! That was hardly in line with the best traditions of St George and the Merchant Service. No matter what your stomach was doing (and these things always hit you first in the stomach, just in the space that was waiting for food), you had to go and face it with her! That was right, wasn't it?

So, before Molly had finished staring, Ben joined her and added his startled eyes to hers. And, having roused himself to this extent, he went farther and produced the first comment.

'Dead, miss, ain't 'e?'

In such moments of tension habit came on top, and the pleasant intimacy of 'Molly' was forgotten.

The girl did not reply. The words that expressed her own unspoken fear whipped her into action, and she stooped suddenly to examine the figure more closely.

'Go 'way!' murmured the figure.

She jumped up, in surprised relief. The surprise shot her back into Ben, for the Merchant Service, despite its good resolutions, had kept behind, guarding the rear, like. Now the Merchant Service toppled down on its own rear, like, and murmured shakily from the ground,

'Wot did 'e say?'

The information was supplied by the other figure on the ground.

'Go 'way!' repeated the recumbent intruder. 'Go *way*!'

The advice seemed excellent. Just the same, it had to be thought about.

''E's drunk,' reported Ben in a whisper, as he reassumed the perpendicular.

'Dead,' nodded Molly.

'Eh?'

'Dead-drunk.'

'Oh! Well, it's 'is licker, not our'n. Let's 'op it!'

'Where to?'

'Eh?'

'Another barn?'

'We'd better leave 'im this 'un. S'pose 'e starts singin'?'

'Yes, he's rather spoilt this little Conference Hall,' agreed Molly, frowning, 'but when we move *this* time, Ben, we ought to know where we're moving to.'

'Yer mean, we 'adn't decided, like,' answered Ben.

'That's right.'

'If you tush me again, you dirty bit o' Sothershen Europe,' babbled the tipsy one, 'I'll—'

The threat ended ineffectively in the grass.

'Barmy!' muttered Ben, and suddenly noticed Molly's expression. It was odd. 'Wot's up?'

'Buy British!' burbled the barmy one.

The girl withdrew a little way into the barn, pulling Ben back with her. She looked anxious, and Ben's heart missed a beat. Anxiety is catching.

'Did you hear what he said?' she asked.

'Yus,' replied Ben. 'Buy British.'

'I mean before that.'

'Eh? Oh! 'E tole yer not ter touch 'im agine—'

'Me?'

'— and then called yer somethink I'd give 'im a swipe for if 'e was sober.'

'He wasn't referring to me.'

'Go on!'

'Can't you guess who he was referring to?'

58

Ben thought, and guessed.

'Some'un helse,' he said.

'Someone else who he said was a dirty bit of—'

'Sothersomethink Europe.'

'Suppose he meant Southern Europe? That might be Spain, mightn't it?'

'Blimy!' said Ben.

The sudden vision that sprang into Ben's mind was confirmed a moment later.

'I'll teach dirty Spaniard talk to Englishman!' came the tipsy fellow's voice from outside. 'Who foun' it? *I* foun' it, an' findin's keepin', hic. An' what business ish it yours *where* I foun' it? Hic?'

Happily the remarks were addressed not to solid substance but to thin air. They were, however, quite disturbing enough. The tipsy fellow had obviously met the Spaniard, and the meeting had been sufficiently recent to remain embedded in his muzzy consciousness.

'We must go!' exclaimed Molly, quickly.

'Yus, but wot did 'e find?' gulped Ben.

The answer was revealed when he followed Molly's gaze. Already she had moved again towards the door, but she had paused to stare at the odd sight of the tipsy fellow, now sitting up, kissing the tip of a lady's shoe.

'Findin's keepin',' repeated the amorous one, fatuously, 'an' 'spretty shoe. Now all I got to fin' 'slady!'

Molly Smith's record was far from blameless. She had picked pockets and had committed other offences of equal demerit. But she had her standards, odd though this may have seemed in her particular circumstances, and her womanhood could be affronted. It was affronted now at the spectacle of a tipsy man saluting her shoe.

Indignation was assisted by a dexterity she had often utilised in less worthy cause. In a flash she was out of the barn and had whipped the shoe out of the tipsy man's hand. In another flash she had sped up the road with it and was round a corner. The reasons why the tipsy man did not see her, and imagined that invisible fingers had relieved him of his trophy, were firstly because she had adopted the pickpocket's ruse of tapping him on one side before doing her work upon the other, and secondly because he was really too blind to see anything that was not immediately before him, and that was not held tight.

It was only through the second reason that Ben, less dexterous, was able to make his own escape without becoming a coherent memory. Subsequently the tipsy man was merely able to record that, after the avenging angel had snatched the shoe away in heavenly indignation, there had been a short, swift rush of wind and thunder. At the moment, however, he was himself indignant, and bellowed his wrath to the world.

Round the corner, Ben and Molly heard him.

''E'll bring along the 'ole of Southampton,' muttered Ben.

'Then the sooner we're off again, the better,' answered Molly, as she stopped and slipped on her regained shoe.

'Wot! More runnin'?'

'Got to be, hasn't it?'

'Jest run and see wot 'appens?'

'We must sleep *somewhere*, Ben.'

'That's right.'

'Where we won't be disturbed.'

'There ain't no such plice!'

'And where we can decide where to go afterwards. Oh, Ben, are you *sure* you've lost that address?'

'It's gorn, miss. Molly, that is.'

'And you can't remember it?'

'Not more'n Wimbledon Common.'

'Think hard.'

'Yer carn't, not with a sorft brine.'

'But you said you'd written it in that letter to me!' exclaimed Molly, suddenly. 'It's there waiting for me, Southampton Post Orfice!'

'So it is,' murmured Ben. 'On'y *we* ain't at Southampton Post Office!'

'No—but I could still *go* to the Southampton Post Office! Couldn't I?'

'What for?'

'For that letter—and the address.'

Ben stared at her. Out of sight, the tipsy man was still audible. He was no longer shouting, however. He was singing.

'Look 'ere, miss,' said Ben, very solemnly. 'Ain't we a couple o' mugs standin' 'ere like this and torkin' abart goin' back ter Southampton?'

'Weren't you once a mug in Spain, Ben,' responded Molly, just as solemnly, 'when you took a long and dangerous journey because you thought a girl was in danger?'

'Eh? That was dif'rent,' muttered Ben.

'You'd say so,' answered Molly.

'Well, p'r'aps the gal's in danger now!' he challenged.

'P'r'aps you are, too,' murmured Molly, musingly.

She seemed to be weighing things in her mind.

'Oh, I'm uster it,' retorted Ben. 'It's you I'm torkin' of jest now.'

'Bless the man! Aren't I used to danger, too!' exclaimed Molly. Then her voice suddenly dropped again. 'But you know, Ben, I'm wondering whether somebody *else* isn't in even greater danger than either of us?'

'"Oo?'

'The person at that house on Wimbledon Common you were going to—and whose address is lost!'

'Lummy!' murmured Ben.

Now he, too, started weighing things in his mind.

'Yer mean—the dainjer of Don Diablo, eh?' he said. 'Don Diablo might 'ave fahnd the address?'

'What do *you* think?' she inquired.

'That's right. 'E might. And we orter git ter 'im furst—that hother Wimbledon chap—and warn 'im, like?'

'It'd be decent. Especially if Don Diablo has really got the address from *you*.'

'Yus,' nodded Ben. 'From *me*, not from *you!* Wot's this got ter do with you, any'ow?'

'Don't you see, I'm the only one who can get the letter at the Southampton Post Office,' she said. 'And besides, why shouldn't I stick to you, as you've stuck to me?'

Ben swallowed. It was nice, her saying that. Just the same . . .

'Look 'ere,' he said, suddenly, 'I ain't 'eard nothink abart *you* yet! Orl you've told me is that yer've bin in port a couple o' days. Do you know anythink more abart orl this? 'Cos, if yer do, now's the time ter spill it.'

'I know something more about—Don Diablo,' answered Molly, after a little pause. 'You see, we came over on the same boat.'

'Go on!'

'If you want me to tell you his life story, I can't—'

'Leave out wot yer can't. Wot *can* yer?'

'I can tell you this, Ben. There are just two things in his mind at this moment. One's murder. And the other's—love. Ugh! Or what a beast like that calls love.'

'Yer mean, 'e's got a sweet'eart?' inquired Ben.

'He'd like to have one,' she answered, and suddenly turned her head away.

Round the corner, out of sight, the tipsy man's voice rose again.

'Why—if it isn't Mr Spaniard!' it cried. 'Now, lishen, Mr Spaniard—I've not *got* the shoe! Angel from heaven—hic—just snatched it away.'

8

Largely Concerning Ben's Clothes

For the fourth and last time that memorable evening Ben found himself running. But this time he knew in advance that he would lose the race.

For breath doesn't last for ever. After forty million miles it gives out, and you need a rest of forty million years to get it back again. The world won't let you rest, however, so you start borrowing on your prospects; and since lungs object to paying interest the borrowed breath presently gives out, too. Then you become breathrupt. Ben, now, was breathrupt.

Still, with that queer reversal of logic which made him a potential museum exhibit, he managed to run for just a little while. He made strange noises as he ran. One was a sort of dying whistle. Another reminded him of a small boy sucking lemons against time. He ran because he knew that if he didn't his companion wouldn't, and her need to run was even greater than his own.

Once, she half-paused, even though their pursuer could be heard quite plainly in the distance, and he had to gasp 'G'arnm'ere.' Correctly interpreting this as Ben for 'Go on,

I'm here,' she went on, oblivious to the fact that Ben would not be here much longer.

Ben, on the other hand, was supremely conscious of the fact. His race was lost. The only question that troubled him was, how could he ensure that he lost it alone?

A couple of seconds later, that question was answered. Molly, a few feet in advance, darted up a side-lane expecting him to follow. He caught a momentary glimpse of her clambering over a stile before a mess of shadows swallowed her up. Then he tottered on, continuing along the main lane out of which she had turned.

The next few seconds were nightmare seconds. This was partly due to the circumstances and partly to his condition. When you are running after you can't, things get a bit distorted, like.

The lane was distorted. The trees on either side were distorted. The sounds of the pursuit were also distorted. Time itself was distorted.

''E's nearly up ter me,' thought Ben. 'I'll stop now.'

But he didn't stop. In order to lengthen the chase and to give Molly a longer advantage, he veered off the lane and staggered into a wood. The undergrowth rose up and clawed at him. Branches shot out at him. Each shadow concealed a panting animal. And then he found himself down among the shadows, and one of the animals was panting above him.

It was an animal called Don Diablo.

'Orl right, let it come,' said Ben, meekly.

It came in the form of a flashing fist. Don Diablo had no objection to hitting a man when he was down.

The wood vanished. So did Don Diablo and everything else. When the wood reappeared, after a lapse of time that might have been a minute or an hour for all Ben could judge, Don Diablo did not reappear with it.

Where had Don Diablo gone? Why wasn't he still here? Was he still hunting for Molly. And, if so, would he find her? These and other questions revolved round Ben's mind; but since he had no possible means of solving them he reverted at last to the question of himself.

Though the Spaniard had gone, probably he would come back again. In that case it would be wise to shift one's quarters. One couldn't shift them far, because the shifting process involved too many aches and pains, but by inventing a new dance called the crawl-step one could remove oneself slowly over the undergrowth till one reached a declivity down which one could roll . . .

It was a longer and a swifter roll than Ben had anticipated. It seemed in the darkness to carry him down a mountainside, and a trickle of water made him fear at one moment that he was going to end in a torrent. But he ended in a prickly bush. Ben was now quite fifty yards from the spot he had started from, and it was exceedingly unlikely that anybody would discover him before sunrise. Thus the prickly bush had its virtue.

So he stayed where he was, and listened fearfully to shifting branches and snapping twigs. Twice he believed that, somewhere far above him, a figure was moving. He could not be sure. It is impossible to be certain of anything when you are lying on a prickly bush trying not to protest. He would have betted all his remaining brace-buttons, however, that at one crucial moment he had seen Don Diablo's eyes gleaming down upon him from the heights.

The moment was crucial because he was trying not to sneeze into a spike . . .

''Allo! Wot's this?' thought Ben.

The wood was transformed. It was no longer dark. Grey light filtered through it, revealing for the first time the spot on which Ben lay and had miraculously slept.

The bush which held him was only a part of the way down the slope. The rest of the slope was considerably steeper, and the steeper portion began just a few inches away from his left boot. It was punctuated with rough slabs and jutting points, and as Ben stared down at the precipice, on the edge of which he had passed the night, he realised that the bush had been an even better friend to him than he had imagined. It had saved him from destruction below as well as above.

'Jest ter think,' he muttered, 'I might 'ave woke hup orl hover the plice!'

Then he stopped looking downwards, and looked upwards. There, now, his salvation lay. A poor salvation, certainly, but better than the precipice! Question was, could he climb up and reach it?

He managed, somehow. The bush was considerably less prickly when he left it because he brought most of the prickles up with him. Half-way up the slope he came upon his cap.

'Well, I'm blowed!' he murmured. 'You and me carn't lose each hother, can we?'

He picked the cap from the branch on which it hung, blew it, and stuck it on his head. Then he completed his laborious journey to the top.

He came over the top cautiously. A small animal got a fright. The fright was shared. But you get over frights quicker in the morning than at night, and a minute later Ben was standing in the lane from which on the previous night he had made his frenzied lurch.

The lane was deserted. Ben stood and puffed. Then a car came round a corner, and the driver pressed on his brake.

It wasn't a Rolls-Royce, and the driver hadn't a collar. The driver, in fact, was only a couple of rungs higher up in the social ladder than Ben. That may have been why he applied his brake.

'Want a lift?' he called, good-naturedly.

'Where to?' replied Ben.

'Downton and Salisbury,' said the driver.

'I'll 'ave 'em both,' answered Ben.

For he had been thinking while he had ascended the slope, and his thoughts had run something like this:

'Corse, it's nex' mornin', ain't it? Lummy, wot's 'appened ter me neck? Nex' mornin', and if I stays arahnd 'ere I'll be caught proper. It's got twisted. If it ain't the Spaniard, it'll be the perleece. Where's me swaller? No good lookin' fer Molly—she'll 'ave 'oofed it. Will she? Well, wouldn't she? That's funny, one lump's gorn and another's come. Oh, no, 'ere's the old 'un, they're both 'ere. This is wot she'd do. She'd look fer me, but she'd know she couldn't find me, and so she'd stop lookin' fer me, and then she'd say, "'Ow can I find 'im," sime as I'm now sayin' 'ow can I find 'er, like. Gawd, me knee-cap's busted. And then she'd say, "Well, if I goes back ter Southampton and gits that letter, it'll give the address of that there 'ouse at Wimbledon Common, and p'r'aps 'e'll remember the address orl of a sudden, like, sime as one does, and then we'll meet agine, but even if 'e don't go there," this is wot she'd say, "*I* must go there," she'd say, "'cos I gotter give that there warnin', see?" Wot's this in me marth? I must 'ave bin chewin' leaves in me sleep. Well, orl I can do is ter go ter Lunnon, too, an' watch the trines come in.'

That was as far as thought had carried him when the car came along.

'Well, jump in,' said the good-natured driver, with a grin. 'You look as if you could do with a sit down. Bin makin' a night of it, mate?'

Ben climbed in. There was just room for two. The car began to move forward again.

'Sort of,' answered Ben.

'Lookin' for work?' came the next question.

Ben wasn't ready with a reply this time, and the man ran on.

'Well, there's plenty of others doin' the same, mate. I've two brothers and an uncle—all out. And so'll *I* be nex' month unless, mebbe, this Medway Bill goes through!'

''Oo's 'e?' asked Ben, not in the least interested. He did not know that he was making the acquaintance of a name soon to be intimately interwoven with his own.

'What's that?' exclaimed the driver.

'Medway Bill,' repeated Ben. 'I've on'y 'eard o' Buffalo.'

'Medway! Joseph Medway—the bill 'e's bringin' in this week!' answered the driver. 'The bill that's goin' to make England what she was and all the other countries what they used to be!'

'Never 'eard of it.'

'Never heard—?' The driver stared at Ben incredulously. 'Where've *you* been lately, mate?'

'Eh?'

'Jest come out of a Rip Van Winkle sleep or something?'

'Oh! I git yer. I'm jest orf a boat.'

'Oh, I see! Sailor?'

'That's right.'

This was a mistake. A sailor was being sought in Southampton! But the driver did not make any disturbing comment.

'And 'ow long 'ave you been on the briny, mate?' he inquired.

'More'n 'arf-a-minit,' replied Ben, relieved but cautious.

'You must of. Why, Medway's the big noise. Of course, there's some say he goes too far, but there's others say he don't go far enough. Regler war on about it. Well, let 'em fight it out—all I care about is my own little bit of bread and cheese.'

'You 'aven't got a bit on yer, 'ave yer?' asked Ben.

'Well, I don't carry it about in my pocket!' retorted the driver, and suddenly stared at Ben in the growing morning light. 'Say, who's been knocking you about?'

'That ain't a knock, that's nacheral,' answered Ben.

After this, conversation dragged. Ben wasn't interested in politics, and he was reticent about himself; and the driver did not appear to be interested in any other subjects.

Perhaps the driver was a little disappointed in his passenger. The driver was a talkative soul, and Ben was somewhat monosyllabic. You can't expect to pick plums from the roadside, however, before breakfast, and there was some consolation at least in getting the daily Good Act over so early. One can always recognise a good act by the discomfort it causes.

Ben, on his side, was glad of the silence. He wanted to go on thinking. He wanted to convince himself that he was not moving in the wrong direction and that he should not really be moving towards Southampton instead of away from it. He might have changed his

policy, asked the driver to stop, got out, and walked
back, but for the practical certainty that Molly would
have left Southampton if she'd been there before Ben
reached it if he got there.

'Corse, I ain't really got a brine,' he told himself, miserably. 'It's jest a bit o' cotton.'

That was what it felt like.

The driver made two more essays at conversation. The
first essay was,

'Is Salisbury where you live, mate?'

''Oo?' answered Ben.

The driver considered this a rotten answer. He did not
know that he had struck Ben at a bad moment. Ben's mind
was now absorbed in Ways and Means, and he was feeling
for the Means. In other words, he was feeling for the pound
note the dead man had given him, and the note seemed
to be as dead as the donor. His fingers, fumbling in his
best pocket, could not find it.

But Ben's garments were as full of holes as gruyere, and
after some intensely anxious moments the fumbling fingers
discovered that even a best pocket can err. He found a
hole he had not suspected. It brought the total up to forty-
nine. The fingers slipped through, and touched *two* bits of
paper. And the driver chose this instant for his second essay
at conversation.

'What part have you come from, mate?' he asked. 'Ameriky?'

This time he was even more unlucky, for Ben did not
reply at all. For one of the bits of paper he had brought
out of his latest hole was twenty shillingsworth of green,
white and pale blue, with a red 'L82 714067' in the top
right-hand corner, and it makes you a bit emotional when
you find a pound you thought you have lost.

And the other bit of paper was something else he thought he had lost. A bit of paper on which was written: '*Greystones, North Lane.*'

'Strewth! 'E '*adn't* lorst it . . .

'Oi! Where's this we're comin' ter?' he asked, suddenly.

'Downton,' the driver told him.

'Is there a stishun?'

'You're lookin' at it.'

'Then, if yer don't mind,' said Ben, 'I'll git out.'

'I don't mind a bit,' answered the driver.

The car stopped. Ben got out. It occurred to him he ought to make a speech.

'Thank yer,' he said.

'It's been a pleasure,' replied the driver. 'I ain't enjoyed a conversation more for years. Hey! Don't you want your cap?'

9

'Where's the Sailor?'

At ten minutes past eleven a train drew in at Waterloo station, and at fourteen minutes past a porter prodded the only passenger who had so far shown no inclination to leave it.

'Going to stay there all day?' inquired the porter.

'Git orf me!' murmured the passenger.

The passenger looked not unlike a sleeping scarecrow. His face was dirty, his hair—or what could be seen of it beneath a capacious cap—was tangled, and bits of countryside were sticking to his clothes. In the circumstances, this was not the way for him to speak to a respectable London porter.

'Now, then, now, then, wake up!' said the respectable London porter.

To assist the operation the porter laid his hand upon the scarecrow's shoulder, and the effect was as though he had pressed an electric button. The scarecrow left his seat with a bound.

'Hi! What's the matter with you?' cried the porter, backing indignantly.

"Oo?' replied the scarecrow.

By which response we recognise the scarecrow as Ben. For this was Ben's most frequent remark on earth, and would form his most appropriate epitaph when under it.

The porter, lacking our advantages, did not recognise the scarecrow, and regarded him merely as an annoyance in the daily round. Consequently his attitude became a trifle menacing, and as Ben had had enough of menace during the past eighteen hours, he removed himself hastily from the porter's daily round, slid from the compartment to the platform—the porter swore subsequently that he slid through his legs—and, so to speak, shuffled shorewards.

The shore was the barrier. The barrier is a station's tide-mark where collect the flosam and jetsam cast up by the line. Until you have passed the barrier you are still under control of the official tide; only when you have passed it are you a free entity again.

Ben had some little difficulty in becoming a free entity. The official at the barrier insisted on seeing his ticket. Ben knew he had bought a ticket, because another official at Downton had made him do so just as the up-train was coming in. In his pocket was the eight-and-sixpence he had received at the Downton booking-office in change for his pound note. At least, the sixpence was in his sock, having travelled thither via the perforated tunnel of his trouser-leg, but the rest was in his pocket . . . No, was it? Now a shilling, rendered mobile through agitation, suddenly slid coldly down Ben's thigh to join the sixpence.

One-and-six below and seven bob above. The sock was gaining!

'Where've you come from?' barked the ticket collector, as Ben fumbled.

Being busy, Ben did not reply.

'What class?' came the collector's next sarcastic inquiry.

'Pullman,' answered Ben.

He answered two inches from the ground, for he was peering at the bottom of his trousers to see whether they had a turn-up. He remembered that the last trousers he had possessed, ten years ago, had had a turn-up, because he had once found a black-beetle in it. These trousers, however, didn't have a turn-up. They concluded their descent thinly.

The search, nevertheless, proved productive. As Ben stooped his cap fell off, and the little ticket suddenly winked up at him from a convenient crevice of the cap's material. He quickly brought his boot down on the ticket, lest it should run away, and a moment later he was triumphantly handing it to the collector.

'Think I was aht ter cheat yer?' he demanded, secure in his righteousness.

'Well, I've known it happen,' returned the collector, dryly.

'Yus, but not with me,' retorted Ben. 'I never cheats the railway hor the hincome tax.'

Then he was permitted to pass the barrier, and became once more a free man. As free, at least, as Ben could ever be.

He stood for a few moments in the vast, grey space fed by its platform tributaries. He looked for a clock. Seventeen minutes past eleven. How long did it take to get from Waterloo to Wimbledon Common?

People moved about him. He didn't matter to any of them, and none of them mattered to him. Funny, how one mattered to oneself! Smoke hung about. Or was it fog? He wouldn't know till he got outside. Stations hatch their own atmosphere.

All at once, through the smoke, or the fog, or both, he got a shock. His eyes fell on a poster, and the poster asked a question. The question ran:

'*Where's the sailor?*'

The next moment, the sailor was somewhere else.

But the change of location merely brought Ben up against another poster asking the same question. Lummy, wasn't there *no* way of getting away from it?

Southampton had followed Ben to London! Turning from the second poster he came face to face with a third: '*Murder in a Taxi.*' It was a relief to find, after this, that one editor preferred politics to police news and contented himself with '*Medway Bill This Week;*' but the relief was short-lived. In the next ten seconds Ben came upon three more posters each asking in fierce type where he was.

The entire world appeared to be hunting for him. Because of this, and because he felt that every official was looking at him suspiciously, he discarded his original intention of getting a bite and a gargle inside the station. Also because of this, he did not learn that he could have got to Wimbledon from Waterloo. His one desire was to quit this unpleasant review of glaring posters and staring porters! There would, of course, be posters outside, but not perhaps such a conglomeration of them! Moreover, as he passed from the roof of the station to the more distant roof of the street, he discovered that fog did indeed exist outside, and that its concealing cloak was very comforting . . .

Well! Here he was, back in London again! He had left it as a fugitive. As a fugitive, he returned. But in spite of its associations—in spite of the kicks and the hunger and the poverty it had meant for him, and the fear it still held for him—there was something homelike in its oppressions, something queerly sweet in the fog that stifled his eyes and nostrils. Out of the foggy metropolis Ben had been conceived! He had learned his very accent in it. If you were going to be tortured, it was something to know that your torturer would understand you when you said, 'Wot cheer!' . . .

A smell brought him to a standstill. A smell of coffee. He turned aside and tracked it, through what looked like a hole in a wall, to its source.

He found himself sitting at a cheap, stained table. A large figure materialised out of a dimness that appeared to have been hatched by human nature rather than by the elements. From this large figure Ben ordered a cup of coffee, which he hoped would be equally large, and a lot of bread and butter.

'A 'ole loaf,' said Ben.

He hadn't had any breakfast.

'I s'pose yer can pay for it?' inquired the proprietor, impolitely.

His answer came rattling out of Ben's left trouser leg. A shilling emerged on to the floor.

'Wot's this?' exclaimed the proprietor. 'A slot-machine?'

'That's right,' answered Ben. 'On'y yer gotter put corfee in me marth ter mike me work proper.'

The proprietor laughed, picked up the shilling, paid himself out of it, and brought the coffee. Financial doubts appeased, he lingered to chat.

''Ow d'yer like this weather?' he asked.

'Rerminds me o' the Sarth o' France,' answered Ben, swallowing.

'That's good, that is,' grinned the proprietor. 'But there

77

won't be no more South o' France for England, I reckon. 'Ollerdays at 'ome now, ain't it? I wonder what the South o' France thinks of Medway?'

'Medway? Wot's orl this abart Medway?' mumbled Ben, chewing.

'Go on!' exclaimed the proprietor. 'Medway's goin' to bring England up to the top again, ain't 'e?'

'Up ter the top? Ain't we always up at the top?' retorted Ben, spitting. 'I don't know wotcher mean.'

The proprietor tried a new tack.

'Well, p'r'aps I could get up to the top if I could find that sailor they're after,' he chuckled. 'Fifty pounds'd look just nice in my bank balance.'

'Eh?' jerked Ben, now ceasing all operations.

'So I've 'eard. Fifty pounds for catchin' 'im. It ain't given in the papers, yet, but I got it from my brother-in-law, whose cousin's in the Force.'

He paused, to mark the effect. But Ben was struggling to conceal the effect.

'Well, I 'ope somebody catches 'im,' went on the proprietor. 'We don't want no Chigargo 'ere! Sticking the knife right through the feller's stomach! It's enough to make yer sick.'

It nearly made Ben sick.

''Corse, wot we're waiting for is a proper offishul discripshun,' said the proprietor. ''Allo! There's a boy callin'. P'r'aps there's some more news.'

He went out of the shop. When he returned, his customer had left. Before opening his paper, the proprietor stared at the empty seat for quite a considerable time.

And, while he stared, the late occupant of the seat continued on his anxious, foggy way.

At first Ben concentrated solely on the object of putting

as large a distance as possible, in as short a time as possible, between himself and the shop where he had begun but not finished his late breakfast, but presently he realised the need of a more constructive policy. You cannot run away for ever. There must, eventually, be some place to run to. Where was this place?

Was it Greystones, North Lane, Wimbledon Common, where the mysterious Mr Lovelace lived? In the circumstances, that spot now seemed as unhealthy as any he could choose! Yet, anomalously, there was no other spot that called him. If Molly had acted in the manner he had surmised—if she had gone back to Southampton, collected the letter, and decided to carry out her intention of warning Mr Lovelace—it was towards Wimbledon Common she would be journeying at this instant!

She wouldn't be there yet. That was impossible, without an aeroplane! But, at some moment of the day, she would present herself at Greystones, and wasn't it unthinkable that she should present herself alone?

'Yus,' decided Ben.

Then his mind ran on:

'But orten't I 'ave wited at the stishun? 'Ave I bin a blinkin' idjit?'

He decided, after careful reflection, that he had not been a blinkin' idjit. Firstly, how did he know what train she would travel on? Secondly, he might easily miss her in a station crowd. Thirdly, with all those platforms, two trains sometimes came in at once, and then where were you? Fourthly, to hang around in the middle of all those posters, drawing greater attention to himself as each minute went by, was more than heart could stand or brain advise. Fifthly, there mightn't be time to go back now, anyway.

No, he had not been a blinkin' idjit.

And thus Ben decided to stick, after all, to his plan, and made a decision upon which hung issues bigger than any he dreamed of.

And thus, by devious routes through the fog-bound south of London, he found himself at last standing in a cold, white mist, staring at a little strip of metal on a derelict wall bearing the words, 'North Lane.'

10

Incidents in North Lane

As Ben gazed at the two words he had been groping for through miles of mist, trying to persuade himself that they were just ordinary words and not in the least uncanny, a figure approached from the left.

Was this figure, as yet only an indistinct blur, the mysterious Mr Lovelace—the man to whom Ben had been despatched to offer himself for two pounds a week? There was no special reason to suppose it, for Mr Lovelace did not comprise the entire population of Wimbledon Common, nor was it likely that he had a monopoly even of North Lane; but while Ben had been drawing closer and closer to his destination, Mr Lovelace had grown and expanded into an obsession that stretched spiritual tentacles over the whole of Wimbledon Common with the embracing completeness of an octopus!

The approaching figure did not turn out to be Mr Lovelace. The indistinct blur materialised, rather surprisingly, into an attractive outline. For an instant Ben thought it was Molly, and his heart gave a bound. Then the attractive outline defined itself into a girl some inches taller than Molly, though with the same willowy slenderness.

Ben, close against the wall, was to her left as she approached. She did not see him because her head was turned slightly to the right, and her eyes were fixing themselves on an object which appeared to interest her unusually. The object was an ordinary red pillar-box.

She paused for an instant, regarding it. Then she advanced again, reached the pillar-box, and paused again. Ben, watching from the wall, vaguely expected that she would post a letter, but no letter was forthcoming, and she continued to regard the letter-box as though it were some oriental curiosity.

'I'm blowed!' thought Ben. 'Ain't she never seed a piller-box afore?'

Perhaps ten seconds went by, during which neither of them moved. The pillar-box fascinated the girl, and the girl fascinated Ben. Then she turned her head, and looked back along the lane from which she had come . . . North Lane. . . .

Very little of the lane could be seen. The mist blotted most of it out. Somewhere in a region beyond the mist a dog barked. The bark became a whine, and the whine suddenly ceased. Ben found himself shivering.

Now another sound caught the girl's ear. Ben didn't know what this sound was. Perhaps he had made it himself. On the other hand, perhaps he had not. The girl turned abruptly, and the movement put Ben to flight.

'Why am I runnin'?' he asked himself, as he felt North Lane swallowing him up. ''Abit?'

He consoled himself with a possible reason. After you've been watching a person, well, you don't want to be spotted, do you, not even if you haven't meant no harm? Ben didn't want a nice girl like that to take him for a bag-snatcher!

It wasn't a very good reason, but it would have to do, and anyway she was blotted out behind him now and he had more important things to think about. He'd got to find a house called Greystones. Yes, and how was he going to do that in this fog?

He stopped running, and, lost in a maze of space, felt his way towards the right-hand side on the lane. Once he only just saved himself from stepping into a ditch that wasn't there, and another time he all but bumped his head against a non-existent post. But at last, after walking a distance that seemed about a mile, he found himself kissing a hedge, so concluded that he had arrived somewhere.

Endeavouring to be a little less intimate, he followed the hedge for several yards, lost it, found it, and lost it again.

'Oi! Where are yer?' he asked.

The dog answered him. Its bark sounded closer. And, as before, the bark dwindled into a plaintive whine and suddenly ceased.

'Wunner if I'll go on?' reflected Ben.

But he went on.

The hedge, rediscovered, became a fence, the fence became nothing, nothing became a tree, the tree became a hedge again, the resuscitated hedge became a wall. There was a bit of everything barring the one thing he was looking for—a gate.

'Ain't there no 'ouses nowhere?' he wondered.

Then his guiding hand slithered along a bush and touched wood. A gate, at last!

Now, was there a name on the gate? And, if there wasn't, would he have to pass through the gate and make inquiries?

There was a name on the gate. You could just see it if you stuck your nose close. The name was 'Greystones.'

''Ome!' muttered Ben. 'I *don't* think!'

Well, home or not, here he was! And now, what? Just go in and say 'Allo?

Ben made a few decisions in his life, but Fate made most, and if the decisions of Fate were not too agreeable, they at least saved trouble. Fate decided now what Ben's next step was to be by selecting this moment for the passage of a policeman through North Lane.

Even an unskilled ear can generally identify the peculiar acoustics of a policeman's boot, and Ben's ear was far from unskilled. As soon as the familiar tread resounded on the invisible road, he knew its origin. It was hardly likely that a chance meeting with a policeman in a London fog would lead to an arrest for a murder in Southampton, but Ben had the wit to realise that this was the last spot on earth where it was advisable for him to be seen, even foggily, by official eyes. The house outside which he stood was connected in some strange way with the murder in Southampton. It stood at the other end of the chain. With posters shouting, 'Where's the sailor?' the most dangerous path for Ben, obviously, was along that chain!

So he opened the gate swiftly and jerked himself through, his immediate object being less to call upon Mr Lovelace than to avoid being called upon by a constable.

The gate swung to behind him with a clank. To Ben the clank sounded deafening. Had the constable heard it? The cessation of the constable's footsteps suggested that he had, and also that he had paused . . . Well, what of that?

Darting a few steps to one side, so that there could be no possible view of him from the gate, even if the sun suddenly came out, Ben waited for the footsteps to continue. Presently, they did continue. They came towards the gate.

When a policeman comes nearer, you go farther. That is one of the vital principles of lower life. Ben began to go farther. But all at once his retreat was impeded by an unpleasant sensation at his feet. They had touched something soft. He stopped, and at the same moment the unseen policeman stopped. The obstacle in the policeman's way was, apparently, the gate.

A vague amber warmth appeared in the mist. It moved about in the indecipherable region between the policeman and Ben, illuminating filmy outlines and revealing wraiths. The wraiths slithered slowly in fantastic shapes. They were the population of the mist. Some were definite. A dog with a glowing head. A snake with three curling tongues. A skeleton, swimming. But others were merely half-formed, offering themselves for completion to the sculpture of fevered imagination. Thus among the white population appeared a Spaniard with a dagger in his mouth, and a pale young Englishman, still and flabby . . .

Had the policeman realised the visions his light was helping to create, his interest would have increased.

With Ben's sense of sight disturbed by these unpleasant visions, and his sense of feeling tortured by the soft thing his feet had touched, his sense of hearing might have been given a holiday. But Ben's senses were not designed for rest. A new sound fell upon his ears. The sound of gravel crunching.

Well, when you're surrounded and know you can't get away, you don't try. You just stand still and dispose of your earthly property. Ben left all his to Molly, thereby enriching her to the extent of seven shillings and sixpence, a third of a cigarette, a bone penknife with most of one blade and the place where the other blade had been, a handkerchief of rare vintage, and clothes containing forty-nine holes and three pending.

Meanwhile, the gravel continued to crunch.

It crunched from the direction where the house assumedly was. All you can do in a mist is to assume. If it stopped crunching it meant grass and Ben. If it went on crunching it meant the gate and the policeman. It went on crunching. Perhaps Molly wouldn't get the forty-nine holes just yet awhile, after all?

There came a brief moment when the white wraiths were obliterated by a large dim shadow. The shadow itself looked shapeless, but as the crunching came from immediately beneath it, it obviously had substance, and as though to support this contention a wisp of white hair gleamed for an instant in the amber glow. Then the shadow vanished. There were about half-a-dozen more crunches. Then they, too, ceased.

'Anything wrong?'

The voice was high and shrill. It fitted into the wisp of white hair.

'No, sir—not if nobody's slipped in through your gate.' This voice fitted into a dark blue uniform.

'Nobody has,' replied the first voice, very definitely. Then added, 'Why, constable? Are ye looking for somebody?'

'Well, there's all sorts about this weather,' answered the constable, non-committally.

'I see. Protection's in the air, and you're doing your bit, eh?' The humour sounded acid. 'Much obliged to ye for giving me my moneysworth. But nobody's come in! Nobody!'

The constable did not act immediately on the information.

'I thought I saw someone run in through this gate,' he persisted, rather heavily. He had to explain himself. 'Seemed as if I heard the gate bang, too.'

'Well, would that be a thing to write to Scotland Yard about?' retorted the other. 'I wish *I* had as good sight and hearing as you in a fog!'

Still the constable hung on.

'And I thought I heard somebody cry out, sir,' he remarked.

Ben gulped. Observations of this kind are peculiarly unsavoury after your feet have just come into contact with something soft on the ground. He moved away from the soft thing, and came into contact with another part of it.

'The somebody was a dog,' said the owner of the wisp of white hair. 'Yes, and if there's anything wrong here, the dog is the first to report it. Satisfied, constable?'

'If you are, sir,' responded the constable. 'Good-afternoon.'

The silence that followed was broken only by the constable's boots as they turned from the gate and departed with slow and measured tread. The measured tread grew fainter and fainter. It ceased to sound . . .

'And now,' said the voice, inside the gate, 'where *are* you?'

11

Hunt the Corpse

When a person asks you where you are and you do not
want him to know, you stay where you are if you think
he doesn't know, and you move if you think he does.
Something told Ben that the old man who had just turned
back from the gate knew. Wherefore, Ben moved.

The object of the move was to find some spot about
five million miles from the gate, but unfortunately there
were about five million obstructions. As he turned first
this way and then that, bushes bounced him back again,
and branches dealt him uppercuts. Only the ground beneath
him remained kind. Being grass, it muffled the acrobatic
perigrinations of his feet.

In a very few seconds he had lost his bearing utterly. He
did not know whether he faced north, south, east or west.
Whether the gate were in front of him or behind him, or
to the side of him. Whether his unseen pursuer, whose
footsteps, like Ben's, were muffled, were a mile away from
him or an inch. Once, by mistake, he left the sanctuary of
the grass, and his boot struck the gravel with a thunderous

scrunch. In his anxiety he added a lightning 'Oi' to the thunder, and the storm continued in his soul. He put his head down and ran till it hit something. It hit something hard.

He examined the hard thing he had hit. It was wood. Then he examined the thing he had hit it with, and found that another bump was in the agony of birth on his already well-populated forehead. 'Fifty hup!' he muttered. Even in his most poignant moments Ben kept inventories.

He stood still and listened. He was in a world of white silence. Surely this was not London? Go on! It was more like a desert!

But now the silence was broken by a tiny sound. It came from a long way off. Softly and faintly. Tick—*tick*. Pause. Tick—*tick*. Pause. Tick—*tick*.

'So long as it don't git no closer,' decided Ben, 'it's a brarnch. So long as it don't git no closer,'

Branches sometimes did funny things. They rubbed against each other, or cracked, or offered little complaints about the weather. Tick—*tick*. Pause. Tick—*tick*. Tick—*tick*.

In the act of examining the wood again, Ben suddenly changed his mind. The last ticking had lacked its little pause! And then came another tick, and another, and another, and the theory of the branch was replaced by a less pleasant theory of tiptoes. For here there was no grass; and if you cross gravel delicately, on tiptoes, you can avoid the scrunching of the heel.

In a dense fog, a light is often invisible until you are within a few inches of it. Sound can be similarly cloaked. Ben was still developing this theory of the distant tiptoes when suddenly, without warning, they became ten times as loud. They were no longer distant; they were disconcertingly close. Much too close for comfort. He put his head down again, and ran.

He ran nine inches, and this time his head hit something soft.

'Got you!' said a voice equally soft. 'Don't move! Kicking won't help!'

'Lemme go!' yelped Ben.

'Hardly!' replied the voice.

'Lemme go! You ain't got no right ter keep me 'ere—'

'On the contrary, I've a perfect right to keep you here till I learn why you've *come* here. Oh, very well—if you *won't* stay still!'

Ben felt his arm being whipped behind him by a deft movement. In response to the necessity of retaining some connection with his arm, his body swung round and he found himself facing the wood again. He knew by this time that the wood was a door.

'Now, then,' remarked his captor. 'Let's hear you talk!'

'Orl right,' muttered Ben. ''Ow are yer?'

'I wasn't referring to polite conversation.'

'No, *I* can see yer ain't the perlite sort.'

'Then suppose you act upon your knowledge?'

''Oo's that?'

'Of course, my man, if you *won't* speak sense—'

'Well, let go me arm! 'Ow can a feller speak sense when 'e's tied hup in a blinkin' knot? *You* couldn't speak sense not if yer helbow was trying ter scratch the back o' yer neck!'

'But if I let go, you'll run away again.'

'That's right.'

'Is it?'

'Wot?'

'This fellow is the world's congenital idiot,' said the old man, to the mist. 'Listen! If I let go your arm, *will* you run away?'

'Corse, you'd let me!'

'But you would if you could?'

''Oo wouldn't?'

'Guilty conscience, eh?'

'Guilty me 'at!'

'Indeed? H'm! Do you remember that policeman I was talking to just now?'

'Yus.'

'Weren't you running away from him?'

'Yus. No.'

'Meaning?'

'No. Yus.'

'You know, you ought to have brought an interpreter along with you. The balance between positive and negative is still unaltered. Does "No, yus," mean no, you were?'

'Yus, I wasn't,' explained Ben.

'Very amusing, I'm sure,' commented the old man, dryly. 'Just the same, I think we'll cut the comic stuff, and have the truth.'

A sudden pain darted up Ben's imprisoned arm.

'Oi! Wotcher doin' of?' he gulped. 'I *am* tellin' the troof. And, look 'ere, if yer thort I was runnin' away from the bobby, why didn'tcher tell 'im I was 'ere? Oi! Stop that! Think me arm's a corkscrew?' Driven by pain, as the pain was designed to drive him, Ben continued unwisely, 'Yus, and I'll tell yer why yer didn't want the perlice in 'ere! It was becos' o' that there corpse—'

He stopped abruptly. His twisted arm had been suddenly released, and now it fell limply to his side while the old man peered closer into Ben's perspiring face.

'Corpse?' he inquired, quietly.

'Yus,' growled Ben. It was clear to him, from the old man's grim expression, that a denial would merely revive the livecoal joy-riding along his funny-bone.

'A corpse!' murmured the old man, thoughtfully.

'Say it agine,' suggested Ben.

'I probably shall, though it's not a pretty word. And where is this—corpse supposed to be?'

'Yer don't need *me* ter tell yer that!'

'Oh! Why not?'

'Well, seein' as 'ow it's in *your* garden!'

'Believe me, my man, that increases my desire that you shall tell me! Yes, yes—now I'm beginning to see things a little more clearly. So *that's* why the policeman was after you, eh?'

''Ere—!'

'Quick, now! Where is this corpse?'

'Look 'ere, guv'nor, it ain't nothink ter do with me—'

'Quiet, quiet! We'll see about that,' the old man chipped in. 'And don't raise your voice so much! You're speaking too loudly. Once more, I ask—where *is* this corpse of yours?'

'Near the gate.'

'Near the gate? Right! And you can take me to it?'

'Wot—in this fog?'

'If I take you first to the gate?'

On the point of continuing his objections, Ben paused. Take him to the gate, eh? Something in the idea after all!

For if the old man took him to the gate, biff—bang—bunk, and Ben might be over the gate!

'Well, p'r'aps I might be able ter find it,' answered Ben, non-committally.

'Then come along!' exclaimed the old man, briskly. 'You won't mind if I take hold of your arm, will you? The fog, you know—it would be so easy to lose each other!'

Whether Ben minded or not made no difference. He was swung round again the next instant, and felt himself being piloted along the gravel way.

En route, he made one protest.

'Yer ain't goin' ter put it on *me*, so doncher think it!' he declared, defiantly. 'I got *proof*, see?'

'What proof?' demanded the old man, pausing.

'Why, if I'd killed 'im, I wouldn't 'ave bin the mug ter mention 'im to yer, would I?' explained Ben. 'There yer are!'

'If you didn't kill him, how do you know he was dead?' inquired the old man.

'Eh?'

'*Do* you know he was dead?'

'Yus.'

'Are you sure he is dead?'

'Yus.'

'How?'

'There's—somethink abart 'em. Yer can *tell*!'

'I see,' mused the old man. 'I see. Well, now we won't talk any more. Loud voices might bring that policeman back, mightn't they? And we wouldn't like that, would we?'

It appeared that they wouldn't, for from now until they reached the gate, only their feet talked upon the gravel.

All at once the gate loomed up out of the mist. It looked unnaturally large and black. Ben regarded it speculatively, while the old man regarded Ben speculatively.

'I don't think I'd try,' said the old man.

'Try wot?' jerked Ben.

'What we're both thinking of,' replied the old man, and swung Ben round towards the grass on their right. 'You were somewhere over there, weren't you?'

'Owjer know?' inquired Ben.

'I heard you arrive.'

'Oh! Didjer?'

'I've said so. Let me see you walk to the spot.'

Ben hesitated. Escape was impossible. Perhaps it would be better to go through with it.

He took his bearings. He remembered just how he had come through the gate, and just how he had turned. That's right—he'd turned just where the old chap was pointing. In quick; up the path; back again; bump into post—yes, there was the post—on to the grass—that's right, just along there—and then . . .

The mist grew momentarily thinner. A branch stretched towards him. The end of it hung loose, almost detached. It was a branch he had convulsively seized when his boot had touched the soft thing at his feet . . .

Where was the soft thing?

'Well?' queried the old man.

'It was—'ere,' muttered Ben.

'Was?'

'Yus.'

'But isn't!'

94

'Yus.' He stared at the spot. Mist curled over it. It became obliterated.

'Are you sure it *ever* was?' inquired the old man.

Ben was quite sure. There are some things you know just because you know. But was it going to help him if he insisted on his knowledge?

Still staring downwards at vacant space and endeavouring to dispose of its depressing similarity to his mind, Ben strove to work things out, while piercing eyes watched him from beneath white eyebrows. If he insisted on the existence of the corpse, and they found the corpse, the old man would say that Ben had had something to do with it. Every murder committed within a four miles radius of Ben came home to him! Of course, Ben hadn't had anything to do with it. Somebody else had had something to do with it. But the old man would say he had . . .

And suppose it was the old man himself who had had something to do with it? Would that make him any fonder if Ben insisted that he had seen a corpse?

'P'r'aps I was mistook,' murmured Ben.

'That may well be the happiest thing for us both to assume,' replied the old man, slowly. And then added, after a pause, 'One *can* make queer mistakes in a fog, you know. Eh?'

Ben nodded.

'And if this *wasn't* a mistake, it might be pretty awkward for you, mightn't it? You see, then I would *have* to go to the police about it. Yes, I'd have to. So—for the moment— for the *moment*—we'll leave it. But I'm still waiting—since you say it wasn't to avoid the police that you came here—to know *why* you came?'

Ben hesitated. Should he give the real reason? And, if

not, what plausible alternative could he invent? His mind became vacant again. Because he could not invent a good lie, he spoke the bad truth.

'I—I bin sent 'ere arter a job,' he said.

Something leapt into the old man's eyes. At the same moment, a faint moan came from the direction of the house.

12

The House of Dimness

The moan that had risen in the mist sank back into it. Silence followed. Then, suddenly, the old man spoke.

'Confound that dog!' he exclaimed sharply. 'Let's be getting back to the house.'

He laid his hand on Ben's arm, but Ben drew away quickly. He did not want to go back to the house.

'What's the matter?' demanded the old man.

'I'm—I'm wonderin' if I'd suit yer,' faltered Ben.

'You can leave me to judge that!'

'Yus, but—'

'Now, listen!' interrupted the old man, and now Ben found his arm gripped again. There was no mistaking the determination behind that grip. 'I've had enough of your nonsense! You come to my house blabbing about corpses that disappear, and about jobs that you want one moment and don't want the next. Do you think you're out of the wood yet? Not by a long shot, my man, not by a long shot! You'll come to the house, as I say, and when you get to the house you'll do as I tell you. Is that clear?'

It was quite clear. Even if the words had not been, the grip on his arm was painfully so. Ben gave way. The next moment they were returning towards the house along the gravel path at a pace that, in Ben's case, far exceeded zeal.

'What are you lagging for?' asked the old man.

'Thorn in me boot,' mumbled Ben.

The answer appeared to amuse the old man. He laughed softly. But he did not accept the explanation.

'Sure it wasn't the thought of my dog?' he inquired.

'Oh! Dog, was it?' murmured Ben.

'Of course! Didn't you hear me say so? What else?'

Ben offered no alternative theory.

Soon, they reached the house. It loomed up suddenly, as had the gate, and appeared to rise as high as heaven. There was a clink of a key. The wooden door against which Ben had bumped his head swung inwards. Ben was shoved inwards, after it.

Then the door closed, and something else clinked. Ben had his back to the door, but he turned round quickly. The second clink had sounded very like a bolt.

'What's the matter with you, my man, what's the matter with you?' demanded his host, irritably. 'All jumps and jerks! I never knew such a fellow!'

Ben glanced beyond the speaker. There wasn't much light to see by. The thick white mist outside, combined with the beginnings of gloaming, rendered the visibility bad in the hall, and the old man showed no immediate intention of providing artificial illumination. In the heavy, cold whiteness, Ben studied the door.

'Have you never seen a door before?' came the sarcastic question.

'Yus, but ain't it bolted?' answered Ben.

'Certainly, it's bolted,' nodded the old man. 'That's to prevent you from achieving a similar condition.'

Then, for the first time, the old man appeared to hesitate, and to be at a momentary loss. He glanced rapidly round the hall, and Ben's eyes followed his. There was no sign of any other presence. The only sound came from a clock on the wall. The clock had a jerking, uneven tick, as though it were trying, without success, to prove a new theory about Time.

The hall was a spacious one. Large and square. The only two visible doors were on the left and right, near the front of the hall, but there was a sense of other doors in the shadows at the back, out of which also grew the dim outlines of a wide ascending staircase. A casement window gloomed opaquely above the staircase where it turned. White forms wreathed outside it, pausing every now and then to peep in.

'Where can I put you,' considered the old man, 'while I see to that dog?'

'Ain't he in a kennel?' replied Ben.

'Why shouldn't he be in a kennel?'

'Well, we're in 'ere.'

'We are certainly in here.'

'Oh, I see. Yer goin' aht agine?'

'As a matter of fact,' the old man informed him, with a smile, 'I am *not* going out again. And you were quite right—the dog is not in a kennel. The dog is upstairs.'

'Wot for?'

'It is ill.'

'Wot's 'e got? The jim-jams?'

'That may be the untechnical name. Personally, I think it may be going mad.'

'Eh?'

'And that's why I've brought it in. Are you fond of dogs?'

'Not mad 'uns!'

'What kind?'

'Little 'uns.'

'Before they have teeth?'

'That's right.'

'Well, this one has plenty of teeth. And, though ill at the moment, it is not too ill to use them. I think—yes—that room. Step this way, will you? I'll join you again in a moment.'

He opened the door on the right. Ben entered in obedience to a push. Before leaving him, the old man stood in the doorway and delivered a short speech.

'You will wait here until I return,' he said. 'I shall be gone for less than a minute. If you behave like a sensible fellow all will probably be well with you. But, if you don't—well, you mustn't blame me for any little accidents.'

Then he stepped back into the hall, closed the door, and locked it.

'Dog mad?' thought Ben, desperately. 'Wot abart *'im*?'

He ran to the door and listened. He heard his host's footsteps ascending the stairs. When they ceased to resound all was silent again, saving for the spasmodic ticking of the clock with wrong ideas.

Turning away from the door, Ben gazed round the room. Like the hall, it was large. Also like the hall, it was unilluminated. The heavy whiteness that hung about seemed to possess a malevolent spirit. There was something dirty about it.

A heavy piece of furniture blocked most of the front window, cutting off the natural light by half, but it made a good platform for examining the window, and, suddenly realising its potentialities, Ben was on it with a cat-like bound.

It was not an attempt to escape. It was an attempt to investigate position. During that little walk to the house from the gate Ben's muddy mind had been moving slowly, and things seemed to be shaping in the mud. That corpse—that dog—that moan—would the Merchant Service expect him to turn his back upon them? And then too, even if he escaped, he could not escape far. He saw that now. Molly was making her way towards this spot, and there could therefore be no thought of leaving the spot finally until he could do so in her company.

'Yus, but didn't I orter be ahtside, ter warn 'er like?' thought Ben, as he mounted to examine the window. 'She didn't orter come in 'ere, did she? Yus, didn't I orter—'

The condition of the window decided his point for him. It was not merely closed and latched. It was nailed.

'Lummy, '*e* don't like fresh hair!' thought Ben.

He heard a sound in the hall. He nipped down from the window in a panic. True to his word, the old man had not been away more than a minute. The door opened a second after Ben had reached floor level again, and the unpleasant monarch of this house of dimness entered the room.

'Well, have you been good?' he asked, ironically.

'Cherub,' answered Ben.

'And, like all cherubs, have been trying to fly to heaven?'

The old man glanced at the window. Ben said nothing. It might have been a chance shot of the old man's. Anyhow, it didn't matter. If you nailed windows down, you must have been born suspicious!

'Now, to resume our conversation,' said the old man. 'Sit down.'

'I'm orl right standin',' replied Ben.

'Sit down!'

Ben sat down.

'That's right,' nodded the old man. 'Good servants should always obey their masters, and, of course, you won't get this job you're after unless you're a good servant. Do you know my name?'

'Eh?'

'I asked you if you knew my name? Since somebody sent you here, I assume you were told my name. Somebody *did* send you here, I take it?'

'Wotcher takin'?'

'Somebody sent you here?'

'Yus.'

'And told you my name?'

'Yus.'

'Good! Then, at long last, we have established our point! What is my name?'

'Lovelight, ain't it?'

The old man's lips quivered.

'Not quite,' he said. 'Try again.'

Ben thought, and remembered.

'Lovelice,' he corrected himself.

'That is, perhaps, near enough,' nodded Mr Lovelace. 'And now for yours?'

'That don't matter—'

'Forgive me, but it does.'

'Ben.'

'Ben what?'

'Ben nothing. Horphen.'

'I see. Orphan. That's interesting. No one to take any interest in you, eh? No one to inquire about you?'

'On'y the King.'

'I see. Well, well! That's two of us named. And now for the third.'

'Eh?'

'Yes. The man who told you of this job. The man who met you at Southampton. The man who sent me a telegram that you were coming—'

'Wot! Did 'e?'

'—just after, so I understand, buying you a new cap?' Mr Lovelace took a step closer to Ben, and fixed him with gimlet eyes. 'What about *his* name?'

The atmosphere in the room suddenly tightened. Ben struggled against a return of panic. When panic returned to Ben, it never had far to travel.

'Oh—'is nime?' muttered Ben.

Now they were coming to it.

'Yes! Sharp!'

'It was White, sir,' answered Ben. '"Tell 'im as Mr White sent yer," 'e ses ter me.'

'Mr White,' repeated the old man, softly. 'Yes—Mr White. But—I'm interested, Ben,' he went on, after a short pause, during which the gimlet eyes grew more and more piercing. 'Why do you say—*was*?'

'Eh?'

'Why not *is*?' And while Ben was gulping, he added, 'Yes, Ben. Tell me this? Why did you kill Mr White?'

103

Ben started violently, and backed. As he backed, Mr Lovelace advanced. The bent form appeared to rear and grow bigger.

'Kill 'im?' gasped Ben. 'I never killed 'im!'

'No?' replied Mr Lovelace, raising a hand and pointing towards Ben's head. 'Then where, may I inquire, is your cap?'

13

The Attraction of Pink

Twenty-four hours ago, Ben had been presented with a new cap.

He had dropped it outside an inn. He had caught it in a lane just as the wind was lifting it from his tangled head. He had deposited it unconsciously on a spike while rolling down a hill, and had found it still on the spike when, considerably later, he had crawled up the hill. He had left it in a motor car, and had had it tossed after him. Surely, in these circumstances, some special God of Headgear was preserving it for the culmination of his strange journey to the house of Mr Lovelace on Wimbledon Common!

Yet now for the first time Ben realised that he had reached the end of his journey without his cap, and as the realisation became revealed on his countenance an exceedingly unpleasant glint departed rapidly and mysteriously from Mr Lovelace's eye. In fact, when Mr Lovelace spoke again, breaking a silence beyond Ben's capacity to break, his voice was almost friendly.

This sudden transition to the amicable eased, but did not clarify, Ben's bewildered mind.

'You didn't *know*, then, that you had lost your cap?' inquired the old man.

Ben shook his capless head.

'I see. I see. But—well, you remember when you last had it?' continued Mr Lovelace.

'Me cap? When did I larse 'ave it?' muttered Ben. 'When *did* I?'

'That's what I want to know,' nodded the old man, encouragingly.

'I 'ad it afore I got in the trine.'

Why all this to-do about his cap? It was Ben's loss, not Mr Lovelace's . . .

'Oh—you got in a train,' said Mr Lovelace. 'Yes, naturally. And when you got *out* of the train?'

Ben frowned. Something was worrying him, and he didn't know what it was. It was like a tickle that you can't find. You scratch your chest and it hops away to your stomach. You scratch your stomach, and it runs round to your back.

'Yes—and when you got *out* of the train?' repeated Mr Lovelace, patiently.

Another thing. Why was the old man so patient all of a sudden? Did *that* have anything to do with the tickle?

'It don't matter, guv'nor,' said Ben. 'I'll git another aht o' me wages.'

That was an attempt to scratch the cap right away. It was not successful. Mr Lovelace continued to press his point.

'It *does* matter, it *does* matter!' he retorted with odd definiteness. 'I can't have my servants catching cold! And are you always asked questions three times before you answer them? This is the third time. Did you have your cap when you got out of the train?'

Ben closed his eyes, to concentrate. Then he opened them, and having seen himself leave the train with his cap on, reported, 'Tha's right.'

'You did have the cap?'

'Tha's right.'

'And when you got here? When you reached my gate? Did you have the cap on *then*?'

Ben closed his eyes again. This time he only saw a large circular space with little black things wriggling about.

'Dunno,' he said, opening his eyes.

'Think, man, think!' commanded Mr Lovelace, becoming less patient.

'Yer carn't think when yer carn't,' answered Ben.

'But surely you can remember being at the gate!'

'Yus. But there was a mist, weren't there?'

'You don't have to *see* a cap to know it's on your head, idiot!' rasped Mr Lovelace, the patience now evaporated. 'You *feel* it, don't you?'

'Well, if yer do,' retorted Ben, 'yer don't keep on sayin' ter yerself, nah it's hon, nah it's orf, nah it's hon, nah it's orf! Yer gits useter to it like, doncher? Once a 'eavy trunk fell on me. It 'urt the fust hour, but arter six hours I didn't notice it and went ter sleep.'

'I am much obliged to you for this little glimpse of personal history,' remarked Mr Lovelace, dryly, 'but when the trunk was removed I expect you noticed it?'

'Yus.'

'And so you might have noticed the removal of your cap, despite the fact that a cap is lighter than a trunk. However, you don't appear to have noticed it. Your head is probably too thick. Well, Ben, we will continue this conversation later. You and I have quite a lot to talk about. But, for a little while, kindly excuse me.'

The interview ended with startling rapidity. Before Ben realised it, the old man was out of the room again, and the door was locked upon him.

''Ere, wotcher lockin' me in for?' he shouted, in sudden rebellion.

Evidently Mr Lovelace did not take the rebellion seriously, for he paid no attention to it.

Running to the door, Ben stuck his ear to the keyhole and listened. He thought he heard the old man moving quietly about, but he could not be certain. He thought he heard a door open somewhere, but he could not be certain. He thought he heard a door close somewhere, but he could not be certain. In this gloomy, unsatisfactory house, one could not be certain of anything.

'Corse, I'm 'aving a luvverly time,' he informed himself, as he removed his ear from the key-hole and substituted his eye. 'When I leave this blinkin' world, I'll cry meself ill!'

The eye was even less successful than the ear. You can see through a key-hole, but not through a key.

Ben left the door, and stood in the middle of the room, thinking. Was he just going to wait there and do nothing? He was sure Molly would not have waited and done nothing! She always had an idea up her sleeve, she had. She always found a way out, she did. Sheer brain, with a pretty face round it, she was!

''Allo—wot's that?' he muttered suddenly.

Whatever it was, it was outside the window. He slipped to the sideboard (that being the nearest name he could give to the massive piece of furniture that blocked the window's lower portion) and climbed on to it. Lummy, the mist was thick!

But you could hear the noise through it! Backwards and forwards, backwards and forwards, backwards and forwards . . .

'Some'un walkin' hup and dahn,' decided Ben. ''Oo is it? Wish they'd git a bit closer, so's I could spot 'em!'

Then a dazzling idea came to him. It was so dazzling that it almost dazzled him off his perch. Was it Molly?

Gaining the top of the sideboard, he prepared to tap cautiously on the glass, but just before he could do so the pacer outside drew momentarily closer and came into view. It was Mr Lovelace, walking with head bent low.

Ben did not tap on the window. He slithered hastily to the floor, and felt slightly sick.

The door he had heard close, then, had been the *front-door*, and Mr Lovelace's abrupt necessity had apparently been to interview the fog!

'Wot's 'e doin' aht there?' Ben wondered. 'And all doubled-up?'

The more Ben thought of Mr Lovelace, the less he liked him. The less he liked him, the more he wanted to get away from him. But the more he wanted to get away from him, the less anxious he was to get away without Molly. Thus in his mind was completed the vicious circle.

'I s'pose I'll 'ave ter wite 'ere till 'e comes back from 'is little walk in the sunshine,' he thought.

He sat down in a chair. After all, there was no sense in standing all the time, was there? He chose the chair nearest the large fireplace. There wasn't any fire, but even the memory of a fire warms you, and the memory existed in the grate, in the form of ashes, bits of burned-out coal, and scraps of half-charred paper.

There'd been a fire there yesterday. Probably there'd be a fire there tomorrow. Today had been missed, because Ben was calling.

'Ain't there no servants?' he wondered, with his eye on one of the half-burned scraps of paper. 'And if there ain't, why ain't there?' The scrap of paper couldn't tell him. 'Yus, why does 'e live alone 'ere? Jest 'im and the dawg, eh? Dawg wot's goin' mad!' A notion came to him. 'P'r'aps dawg's wot's goin' mad sahnds like 'uman bein's wot ain't?' He hoped so. It would explain that human-like moan he had heard. Even a mad dog was better than that! 'So long as the dawg don't come dahn 'ere,' he added the provision, 'I don't want me best trahsers rooined!'

As he went on thinking, he kept on eyeing the half-burned piece of paper. Why? And why did his thoughts gradually join his eyes, and give the eyes intelligence? What had the scrap of paper to do with it all?

Perhaps it was the colour of the paper that first translated it from a mere focusing point to an object of interest. The colour was pinkish. Even in the fading white light the pinkish colour revealed itself, whispering up from its bed of ashes, 'I'm pink—I'm pink! Look at me! *Pink!*'

Well, what if it *was* pink? Why should that provide it with significance? Why should that make it more important than, say, the poker—a nice, useful-looking poker—or any other object in the room? Lots of things were pink! Roses, cheeks, pink sweets, pink dresses, pink anything, blotting-paper, kid's writing-paper, yes, sometimes that was pink, he'd had a pink letter once, strawberry-ices, telegrams—

"Strewth! Telergrams!' muttered Ben.

Yes, but why all this excitement about a telegram?

"Cos 'e sed 'e'd *'ad* a telergram,' Ben replied to the question. 'Abart *me*!'

Thus, with labour, Ben at last tracked his growing interest to its source.

He rose from the chair, glancing furtively towards the window as he did so. All clear there! Then he dived down towards the grate, and seized the pink paper. The charred edges crumbled as he touched them, but his hand came away with a considerable prize.

He lowered his face till it was close to the paper. He was always polite to his reading and his food, meeting them half-way. The big, protruding mantelpiece, however, cut off what light there was, and after bumping his head he turned and risked the window.

Near the window the light was better, and he made out a bit of a word. The bit was:

'. . . *outhampton.*'

'Sarthampton!' he murmured. 'There y'are! That's where it come from. Sarthampton!'

He searched diligently for other words. For a while he found none, but this was because in his emotion he had turned the paper over and was searching the wrong side. Turning it back to the right side, he was rewarded with a consecutive string of three words and a bit. The bit started it:

'. . . *ool calling himself Ben* . . .'

'Ben's me!' he blinked. 'But wot's 'ool?'

He knew his alphabet up to F for Food, and he tried it as far as he knew.

'A, nuffink. B, bool. Wot's that? C, cool. That's wot it is

111

in 'ere. D, dool. That's when two blokes git fightin'. E, nuffink. F, fool. Eh?'

He referred to the string of words again. He prefaced an F. His face grew dark.

'Fool!' he growled. 'That's wot it is. A Hef!'

Odd, how one often accepts big things while little things rankle! If the writer of the telegram—it was the last telegram he ever wrote—had whipped out a dagger in the taxi and held it over Ben's face, Ben would just have opened his mouth and taken it like a lamb, but when he called Ben a fool, not to his face, like, but behind his back, like, it raised a storm of indignation. The fool decided, while he began searching for more words, that he would prove the writer wrong! Yes, and Mr Lovelace, too! *And* the mad dog!

He only found one more word, but it was an immensely interesting word. It was:

'. . . *cap.*'

Cap! So *that* was why Mr Lovelace was out in the garden! That was why he was all doubled up! He was looking for the cap that Ben had lost—the cap Mr White had insisted on buying him—after Mr White had bumped into his back and sent his old cap flying . . .

Something clicked at the door. Ben whirled round, instinctively closing his fingers over the paper in his hand. Mr Lovelace stood in the doorway, regarding him.

'Are you being a good boy?' inquired Mr Lovelace.

Ben did not reply. He was thinking too much. Mr Lovelace seemed to be thinking, too.

'Lost your tongue, eh?' the old man asked, after a pause.

'No, it's still 'ere,' answered Ben, making an effort, 'but wotcher want me ter say? "Yus, Daddy"?'

Mr Lovelace smiled faintly.

'Well, go on being good,' he said, 'and then perhaps I'll give you that job. I'll be back again, very shortly.'

'Oh, yer ain't back yet fer keeps, then?' queried Ben.

'I'll be back—for keeps—in a minute.'

'Then wotcher come in this time for?'

'Just to keep an eye on you.'

'Oh! I see! Thort I'd steal the ceilin'! Well, s'pose I don't *tike* the job?'

'Why not?'

'A bit lonely, like, ain't it? If there ain't no hother servants?'

It was a leading question, but Mr Lovelace did not avoid it.

'There are no other servants, Ben,' he responded. 'You and I will be here entirely alone.'

'Oh!'

'Yes. To tell you the truth, I usually have some difficulty in keeping servants here.'

'Why?'

'They say this place is haunted.'

''Aunted?'

'No. Haunted. A silly idea, isn't it? But I shall keep you, Ben! Oh, yes—I shall keep *you*!'

He slipped from the room as he spoke. And, as before, he locked the door after him.

Ben stood motionless for a minute. Then he raised a hand to his forehead, in order to set it going. The piece of paper he had been concealing in the hand fell to the ground. It was now a scrunched ball, and in stooping to regain it he slipped and kicked it towards the fireplace. It rolled into the wide hearth.

Ben went after it as though it had been a Rajah's ruby. He ducked at the big protruding mantelpiece, and came up beyond. He found his head in the lower end of the chimney, and he was surprised to discover the chimney's roominess. He glanced upwards . . . and then, once more, he heard the moan.

It came from above, and there was no mistaking its source this time. It was the moan of a girl.

14

The Mysterious Caller

Technically speaking, there is only one way out of a room, and that is by the door. In emergency, however, there are alternatives, these being in order of preference, the window and the chimney. The chimney is the least popular.

But, in the present case, the chimney bristled with favourable arguments, and the first argument was that the door and the window were impracticable. The door was locked, and the window was nailed. Of course, you can always smash a window with your fist or with a poker, and a poker was here for the purpose; but the noise of breaking a window is liable to bring more than glass upon your head! It was hardly likely that Mr Lovelace would fail to hear such a noise.

Moreover, even if Ben escaped successfully into the maze of mist outside, how would that avail him? The girl's moan had come from *inside*, and it was the girl he had to reach!

Now the chimney, as has been said, was large, while Ben, as has been shown, was small. This convenient reversal of the usual state of things was another argument in favour of the chimney. Squinting up the shaft, Ben spotted further arguments, in the dim form of vague irregularities and protuberances. These would assist ascent towards the spot from which the cry had come—and the spot from which the cry had come was, of course, the biggest of all the arguments.

Still, it takes a good deal to make a man shinny up the inside of a chimney, and the final argument was supplied a moment later. A sudden sound in the hall implied that Mr Lovelace was now returning 'for keeps.' That settled the matter.

As the key turned, Ben leapt upwards.

Then followed some of the most uncomfortable moments of Ben's uncomfortable life. He was fortunate in finding that one of the protuberances was a bit of iron to which he could cling, and he clung to it with all his soul, but it was not high enough to elevate his legs to the desired point of invisibility and to destroy a view from the doorway resembling a comic Christmas card unless he curled his legs up under him like a spider when touched. Therefore, as he leapt, he also curled. His rapidly rising knees made many contacts as they rose—direct, unclothed contacts with bricks that selected his holes and enlarged them—but, just as Fortune had given him something to cling on to with his hand, so it now gave him in his new crisis a cleft to wedge into with his boot.

The position Ben found himself in was not fit for heroes to sleep in, but he knew he was out of sight, though not out of mind, and he was grateful for the smallest crumbs. All he had to do now was to stay still, stop breathing, and pretend that a little bit of soot had not descended on his nose with the express object of tickling it.

When you are intensely interested in a scene, you can

visualise it even while you cannot see it. Thus, in the utter blackness of sooty walls, Ben visualised Mr Lovelace standing in the doorway and discovering an empty room. He visualised him turning towards the window and discovering it intact. He visualised him gazing round the room, and resting his eyes on the fireplace.

He visualised him beginning to move, softly and silently, towards the fireplace.

Now Mr Lovelace would be half-way across the room. Now three-quarters. Now by the chair in which Ben had sat. Now pausing for the last little lap, and regarding the poker—the poker that had been designed to poke fires, but that was quite capable of poking other things.

Then, in a sudden flash, the picture vanished. Something tore it to bits, dissecting it and rearranging it in the form of a Cubist abortion, where vases and sofa-legs establish strange unions and eyes peer out of sleeves. Somebody was knocking on the front-door.

Now it may be possible to convey some sad idea or diseased philosophy in a dissected and distorted picture, but it is not possible to carry on a coherent story by such means, and since we are following the present story through Ben's eyes there is nothing to relate of the next few seconds beyond the agony of a jig-saw. But by the end of these few seconds two definite things had happened. Mr Lovelace had reached the front-door; and Ben, without any recollection of it, had ascended a couple of feet farther up the chimney. His chin now rested on what appeared in the darkness to be a sort of wooden ledge . . . Though what would a wooden ledge be doing up a chimney?

From below came Mr Lovelace's voice, as he called from the hall,

'Who's there?'

Apparently his voice was not heard outside, for the knock was repeated, this time more loudly.

'Bet it's that bobby!' thought Ben suddenly, and wondered whether he wanted it to be.

'Who is there?' called Mr Lovelace again. Also more loudly.

"*E's* takin' no charnces!' reflected Ben.

'Please let me in!' came the faint response. 'I've lost my way.'

Bobby? That wasn't no Bobby! That was a gal! One above him, and now one outside. Two of 'em!

The front-door opened. Ben could hear it distinctly, even though it was opened cautiously. Mr Lovelace had not closed the intervening door.

'Where do you want to get to?' inquired the old man's voice, none too kindly.

'Where am I?' replied the girl's.

It was what Ben described as a high-class voice. Rich and refined. The kind you said 'Miss' to immediately, without having to think about it.

Then something happened that beat Ben's capacity to interpret. It was muffled and indeterminate, and seemed to increase in his direction. He did not know that the girl had swayed forward, had tottered towards the open doorway, and, apparently by the sheer volition of weariness, had entered the room. But in a few moments he learned that she was in the room, even though he did not know how she had got there, for her voice soon sounded below him again in apology. It was now considerably closer.

'I'm—I'm sorry,' murmured the girl. 'I thought I was going off that time.'

'Are you ill?' asked Mr Lovelace.

He had followed her in. His voice had not increased notably in kindliness.

'No—just a little faint,' she answered.

'Just faint, eh?'

'Yes. I thought I'd better get near a chair. May I sit down for a moment?'

'Eh? Of course. And, while you're resting, I'll tell you the way to wherever you want to go.'

'Thank you. You're very good. I wonder if I could have a glass of water?'

'Water? Certainly. Just wait a minute.'

He darted out of the room. Ben heard the door close after him.

Then Ben heard other sounds. He heard the little slither of a chair that has suddenly been left. He heard quick, soft footsteps. He heard a girl who was supposed to be half-fainting moving swiftly around the room. He heard a faint noise as of a desk-flap being opened and then closed again. He heard a drawer pulled out. He heard a sharp exclamation, a rustle of paper, and the quick return of the drawer.

Then silence, broken in a few moments by the return of Mr Lovelace.

'Here's the water,' said Mr Lovelace, abruptly, 'and how are you feeling?'

From his tone, he might have been saying, 'How soon can I get rid of you?'

'Not too bad,' came the weary response. 'I'll be all right in a minute. It really was too silly!'

'But what was it made you so dizzy?' demanded Mr Lovelace. 'Are you often taken this way?'

'Never before! I think the fog upset me.'

'Nothing more?'

'Well—there *was* something more,' she admitted, after a pause.

'What?'

'A sort of a tramp.'

'Oh!' The exclamation came sharply. '*You've* seen him, then, too?'

'What! Has he been here?'

Now Mr Lovelace paused. His answer, when it came, was non-committal.

'Well, you can't really say anything definite in a fog. But—maybe I've seen the fellow about. And, when next I catch him, he's in for a bad time!'

'You think he's a bag-snatcher?'

'Do you?'

'I don't know. He—just frightened me.'

'Did he do anything to you?'

'No.'

'Where did you see him?'

'By a pillar-box.'

The simple statement nearly caused Ben to loosen his chin-hold on the ledge, and to fall down into the grate with a ton of soot. The pillar-box! Lummy! So *that* was the girl, was it? The one he'd seen at the pillar-box!

'Yus, but I didn't frighten 'er!' he thought. 'Wot's she wanter put up that yarn for?'

Meanwhile, the girl's statement appeared to be having some effect below. Mr Lovelace was murmuring, 'The pillar-box, eh? The pillar-box!' as though he found the word unusually interesting.

'And nothing actually happened?' queried the old man.

'No,' the girl answered.

'That was all that worried you?'

'That was all. And now, please, I think I'll be going. It's awfully good of you to have let me come in. Where *is* this house?'

'You're on Wimbledon Common.'

'Yes, but what road is this? And where exactly—'

'Don't worry. I'll see you to the gate. Maybe a step or two beyond. Well, shall we be starting?'

The voices ceased for a few moments. The conversation was resumed at the door.

'But I really mustn't take up your time,' the girl said, a note of anxiety in her tone.

'Don't mention it—it's a pleasure,' answered Mr Lovelace, in a tone of contrasting complacency. 'Besides, you won't be taking up *much* of my time. I shall be back here again very soon—very soon indeed. You see, I've got to find that tramp you mentioned, haven't I, for we can't have bag-snatchers frightening people in lonely lanes! Yes, I'll find him, I'll find him—and make the rascal sorry he was ever born!'

But Ben was already that as he heard the key turn in the door for the umpteenth time.

15

Down Agine

In the uncomfortable darkness Ben began to count up things. Among the units in his impossible sum were a malevolent old man, a missing body, a missing cap, a girl who pretended to be faint with the object, apparently, of examining other people's drawers, and another girl whose distressed condition was less open to question. There were, of course, further units lurking in the fog outside, but those already enumerated were enough to go on with and to confuse a more astute mathematician than a simple sailor.

The unit of most immediate importance, however, was the chimney. Was Ben to stay in it, or to get out of it? And if which, how?

He re-examined his position. He was not sure where his legs were, but his chin was still resting on the ledge, and this was due, he gathered, to the ledge's generous proportions. It was indeed a rather remarkable ledge, and when you were able to get your hand upon it as well as your chin, and to grope about it, you discovered that it

obtruded from a small wooden partition. The ledge was
at the bottom of the partition. This was proved by another
sudden and startling discovery. A cold, horizontal line that
had vaguely distressed the lower latitude of Ben's face
turned out to be a draught emanating from a crack beneath
the partition.

'Blimy, it's a door!' thought Ben.

A door to the room above—to the room from which
had come the moans!

Yes, but how could the door be manipulated unless you
untied your elbow from your knee-cap? From Ben's
present cramped and restricted position he could only
feel the lower portion of the door. The upper portion was
unattainable Mecca! He might attain it by elevating his
own upper portion a few inches, yet here again there
were difficulties. The chimney, wide below, was narrow
above. There was not much farther up that even a little
man could go.

Ben went up the rest in a sudden, disastrous lurch. His
head reared roofwards in response to an effort he never
thought could be fruitful; and, meeting converging bricks,
it stuck. Now Ben felt like the nut in the nut-crackers.

How long he stuck there he did not know. The abrupt
narrowing of the shaft had dislocating consequences. But
all at once a sound fell upon his ears that produced a fresh
burst of convulsive energy. The moan was repeated, and,
in this new proximity to its source, it came to his ears in
startling, recognisable form.

The nut-crackers opened as fresh energy came to the
imprisoned nut, Ben shot abruptly downwards, and a
moment later found himself once more on the floor,
warding off a shower of soot.

He also found Mr Lovelace peering at him through the shower.

'Thank you,' said Mr Lovelace, in tones of unconcealed sarcasm. 'You have saved me from the trouble of going up.'

There were several reasons why Ben did not reply. The least important was that his mouth was full of soot.

'Don't hurry,' continued the old man. 'Recover from your journey. There's plenty of time.'

'I ain't goin' ter 'urry,' Ben told himself. 'I gotter think.'

'And, if I may suggest it,' the old man proceeded, 'one should never fall down chimneys with one's mouth open. Strictly speaking, one shouldn't be in chimneys at all.'

'Wot about lyin' doggo,' thought Ben, 'and then jumpin' hup sudden like and givin' 'im a bit o' Kid Berg?'

'Of course, I knew you were up the chimney,' said Mr Lovelace. 'Never having seen you perform at Maskelyne's Theatre, I assumed you couldn't penetrate a locked door, or escape through a nailed-up window without breaking it. Why did you go up the chimney, may I ask? What did you expect to find there?'

As Mr Lovelace put the question, and his eyes glinted with piercing inquiry, Ben suddenly realised his policy. There must be no physical encounter—yet. He was not equipped for it. He must meet subtlety with subtlety, quell the old man's suspicions, and then . . .

'Bird's nest,' replied Ben.

'I see! You thought you heard—sparrows up there?'

'That's right.'

'Suppose we stop being funny, and grow serious?'

'Suits me, guv'nor.'

'Really? I'm relieved. Hitherto you have religiously concealed your more sober requirements!'

'Me wot?'

'Never mind. Pick yourself up. You'll find it easier to be serious on your feet.'

'I can't be nothink till I've 'ad a drink,' retorted Ben, as he rose.

'There's half-a-glass of water on the table,' answered Mr Lovelace. 'You know who took the top off, don't you?'

Faithful to his new policy, Ben admitted that he did, while he prepared to deal with the bottom.

'That gal,' he replied.

'Yes. That girl,' nodded Mr Lovelace. 'Our recent visitor who stated that you frightened her. You heard what she said, of course?'

'Yus.'

'Well, what's *your* version?'

'Wot's that? Poetry?'

'No, no! Your story! What happened when you met her at the pillar-box?'

'Nothink.'

'She said you scared her?'

'I can't 'elp that.'

'No. Scarecrows can't be choosers. But what did you think of her story, while you were up the chimney?'

'Yer can't think up a chimney.'

'Then why did you go up the chimney?'

'Ter git away from you,' replied Ben, hoping that his frankness would prove acceptable. 'Yer lock me in a room, and yer nail hup the winder, and when I come fer a job yer asks me why I killed a bloke wot I didn't! If yer want me ter love yer, guv'nor, yer goin' a funny way abart it!'

The little outburst had its effect. Mr Lovelace's expression became a little more hopeful as he gazed at the indignant individual before him.

'I'd almost forgotten! You came here for a job,' he observed.

'Corse I did!' answered Ben.

'And you still want the job?'

Heroically swallowing his hesitation, Ben responded, 'Corse I does!'

'Well, maybe you'll get the job if you behave yourself in the next few minutes.' Ben strove to look delighted, and resembled a sweep pretending hard that he had not eaten lobster salad. 'So you had nothing to do with the murder of our mutual friend, Mr White?'

'I've toldjer.'

'What happened, exactly?'

'I've toldjer that, too. 'E knocks off me 'at and 'e gits me another, and we're goin' ter the Stashin in a taxi, see, and I gits aht fer a minute—'

'Why did you get out?'

'Eh?'

'You've not told me *that!*'

No, and he didn't particularly want to. The old man saw his hesitation, and added sharply,

'You ask me why I've locked you in this room? Do you realise, my man, that the police would be delighted if I handed you over to them? Perhaps *that's* why I've locked you in? Till I could make up my mind about you!'

'Yus,' thought Ben, 'and is that why you nailed the winder hup, too? I reckon the police'd like ter see the pair on us?'

But he kept the thought to himself.

'So—once more—*why* did you get out of the taxi?'

'Ter send orf a letter.'

'Whom to?'

'Oh—chap in Cannerder,' lied Ben. He wasn't going to be first to mention Molly.

'Chap in Canada,' murmured Mr Lovelace, disbelievingly. But he passed it over. 'Well, and then?'

'I gits back ter the taxi, and finds 'im dead.'

'And then?'

'I 'oofs it.'

'And then?'

'Eh?'

'I said, "And then?"'

'Oh. I goes on 'oofin' it.'

'Even though you had nothing to do with the murder?'

'Go on! If a feller nex' ter yer steals a sorsidge, yer both 'as ter run, doncher?'

'Do you? Well—have you any idea who stole *this* sausage?'

'Corse I 'ave!'

'Who?'

'A Spanish bloke!'

'Yes—I was wondering when you were coming to him,' murmured the old man. 'You know, of course, that the newspapers are connecting you together?'

'Well, they can just *hun*connect us agine,' retorted Ben, ''as we *ain't* together, see?'

'But you've been seen together.'

'So's a birch and the plice where yer uses it. Lummy, yer don't suppose I'd tike hup with a bloomin' Spaniard, do yer? It's t'other way abart. 'E's bin tryin' ter tike hup with *me*.'

'Indeed?'

'Yus. I bin tryin' ter shike 'im orf, see? But 'e's stuck

127

closer'n a postage stamp. I'd 'ave sed 'e wos arter me money if I 'adn't fergot wot money was.'

'Perhaps he was trying to help the police, who were also after you!'

'Go on! 'E was 'oofin' it, sime as I was!'

'H'm!' murmured Mr Lovelace, contemplatively.

'Then your theory is that this Spaniard poked his head into the taxi while you were out of it—and killed Mr White?'

'Yus.'

'And then chased you?'

'Yus. We was both runnin' away, like.'

'But in the same direction?'

'Yus.'

'And you've no idea *why* he chased you?'

'Barrin' 'e might 'ave liked me fice,' suggested Ben.

Then Mr Lovelace turned away and made a casual remark; but he kept Ben in view through a mirror while he made it.

'The lady who has just left,' he observed, 'told me outside that you had no cap on when she saw you at the pillar-box.'

Lummy! That cap! Had Don Diablo been after it, too!

Ben just saved himself from exclaiming at this thought, but he did not control its reflection upon his sooty visage. Through the little mirror, Mr Lovelace marked the reflection.

'Was she correct?' asked the old man, quietly.

'That's right,' muttered Ben.

'Then you must have lost your cap between the time you left Waterloo Station and the time you reached the pillar-box?'

'That's right,' agreed Ben.

'Have you seen the Spaniard since leaving Waterloo Station?'

'No.'

'Sure of that?'

'No.'

'Meaning?'

'Yus.'

'Yes, you're sure?'

'No, I 'aven't.'

'Lucid as ever,' murmured Mr Lovelace, and all at once shrugged his shoulders. 'Well, it's a pity about your cap, but I expect we'll have to let it go. Unless, of course, you can tell me of any place you visited on your way here? That is, you know, between Waterloo and—the pillar-box?'

This question, the apparent casualness of which did not deceive Ben, suddenly raised two questions in Ben's mind.

First—he *had* visited one place on his way here. He had visited a restaurant from which he had subsequently bolted, leaving his meal half-finished. Was it at this restaurant that he had left his cap? Second—if Ben mentioned the restaurant to Mr Lovelace, would Mr Lovelace go and seek the cap there, leaving the coast clear at this end for Ben's investigations?

A difficult problem had to be decided in a flash, at a moment when hesitation might destroy the assumption of genuineness that Ben was striving to build up. For some urgent reason quite beyond his ken, Mr Lovelace wanted Ben's cap. Was it wise to set a man of Mr Lovelace's doubtful quality on the right road? Even though the prize would be an opportunity to find the girl in the room upstairs?

'If that cap is lined with di'monds,' decided Ben, ''e can 'ave it.'

For Ben had learned, in his last moment up the chimney, that the girl in the room above was Molly Smith.

16

Quadruple-Crossing

Half-an-hour later Ben sat in the kitchen, staring at a brown tea-pot. On the table, also, were a neglected cup of tea, a well-hacked loaf of bread, a pat of butter that looked as if the loaf had sat in it, five lumps of sugar on a paper-bag, and a fork all dressed up and nowhere to go. This was Ben's idea of the way to set a tea-table.

A somewhat similar selection lay on the table of the front-room in which he had spent the first portion of his visit; and there Mr Lovelace sat with as little interest in the tea as Ben was showing himself. He, too, was staring at his tea-pot. Each man seemed to be listening for the other.

Following upon Ben's effort to locate the restaurant in which apparently his lost cap resided—an effort that had been encouraged by the old man with considerable enthusiasm—this preparation of tea had formed Ben's first office in the service of Mr Lovelace at two pounds a week, paid surprisingly in advance. It really seemed as though a point had been reached where Mr Lovelace was as anxious to appear friendly to Ben as Ben was anxious to appear friendly to him; and because Ben knew his own friendship was sheer pretence, he wondered whether his new employer's amicable advances were also being actuated by some ulterior motive.

'*I'm* waitin' fer 'im ter go aht arter my cap,' reflected Ben, as he gazed at the pot, 'but wot's '*e* waitin' for?'

Two points had surprised Ben while he had been trying to locate the restaurant under Mr Lovelace's expert guidance. The first was that, largely owing to the latter's complete knowledge of the vicinity of Waterloo, it had been comparatively easy to reconstruct Ben's first gropings through the fog and to reduce the possible restaurants to two. The second was that the idea of camouflage did not occur to him until it was too late. After all, why should Ben not have invented a restaurant, and so defeated the old man's end while gaining his own? But by the time this brain-wave occurred to him it was too late to adopt it, and he consoled himself with the reflection that he might not have made his story convincing if he had not built it on reality.

'I 'ope 'e goes orf soon,' thought Ben, despairingly, as the minutes dragged by. The house was getting horribly on his nerves, and he longed to satisfy the instinct of St George and then be off. 'Wunner if 'e'd pop orf quicker if I pertended ter go ter sleep?'

The more he thought of this idea, the more he liked it. It was, he considered, a distinctly brainy idea, and he couldn't quite understand how he had thought of it. Perhaps it was because he all at once discovered he really did feel a little sleepy!

'Yus, lummy, if I ain't careful, I'll go orf proper!' he blinked, sitting up with a jerk.

Thus reality trod on the heels of pretence, casting disturbing doubts on the ruse of dissimulation. *Was* it such a good idea, after all? Suppose he both feigned sleep and found it!

'I'll 'ave a little drink while I 'ave a little think,' he decided, turning to his neglected cup. 'P'r'aps the warm inside me'll 'elp.'

As he took up the cup he noticed that the surface was half an inch below the rim. This vaguely surprised him, because he had poured it out right up to the slop-over—he always did this, to avoid wasting any—and he didn't remember having taken a sip.

'Must 'ave done it while I wasn't lookin',' he thought. 'That's a pity.'

You can't enjoy food and drink properly if you don't concentrate.

He raised the cup to his lips, and was about to pour it down his mouth, also to the slop-over, when a bell rang and something clicked above him. He jumped up, giving the floor a drink as he did so, and replaced his cup on the table. Then he noticed that the thing that had clicked was an indicator, and that the word 'Drawing-room' was wobbling in a glass-topped wood box on the wall.

'I hexpect that's fer me,' he frowned. 'It's a come-dahn, bein' a 'ousemaid!'

He left the kitchen and went into the room misleadingly described as a drawing-room. Ben would have described it as a Morgue, if that was right for where you kept dead people. But Mr Lovelace was very much alive when Ben entered to inquire.

'Yus?'

Mr Lovelace regarded him keenly. Then ordered,

'Pull the blinds down.'

'Oh,' answered Ben, and walked to the window.

'Had your tea?' asked Mr Lovelace's voice behind him.

''Avin' it,' replied Ben.

Looking out, he noticed that the fog was thinner.

'Well, I hope you're enjoying yours better than I'm enjoying mine,' observed Mr Lovelace. 'You've introduced a wonderfully tinny taste into it. Do you make your tea with nails?'

One doesn't reply to remarks like that.

'Still, I hope you're surviving?' continued the old man. 'Feeling all right, eh?'

'Yus,' said Ben, and suddenly added, 'but a bit sleepy like.'

Subtle, that!

'Well, if you're tired, you can take a nap afterwards, Ben,' responded his employer—with equal subtlety? 'There'll be nothing more for you to do till dinner. Don't forget that little side window. By the fireplace. Where are my cigars? Ah—I remember—in the next room.'

He darted out of the door. He returned just as Ben was pulling down the blind of the little side window.

'Capital!' he exclaimed, approvingly. 'You're excellent at blind work!'

Back in the kitchen, Ben pondered over the remark.

'Blind work, eh?' he murmured.

He turned to his cup once more and raised it. So far he had had one-eighth of the contents and the floor had had one-quarter. He prepared to make sure of the balance.

'Blimy, it *does* seem tinny!' he agreed as the lips established contact. 'I s'pose it *was* tea I put in the pot, and not tacks?'

Then, suddenly, he put the cup down again. A dozen things were shouting to him warningly, turning his forehead damp. One was the taste of the tea—that wasn't no *tin*! Another was Mr Lovelace's deliberate reference to the taste—to put Ben off his guard, like? Another was the slight drowsiness Ben had already experienced—imparted by a one-eighth dose? Ben recalled that during the tea preparations, Mr Lovelace had entered the kitchen once to tell him where the second tea-pot was—and maybe to put something into the second tea-pot! Another was the bell—to see whether Ben was capable of answering it? Another was the lightning dash just now for cigars. More likely for a peep in the kitchen and an increase in the dope?

And another was that remark, 'You're excellent at blind-work.' *Blind,* eh?

Ben was only being saved from blindness at the eleventh hour! He'd been blind to think that Mr Lovelace would dream of leaving the house while Ben was free to roam about in it! He'd been blind to imagine the old man quite as big a fool as that!

Yes, but wasn't the old man making an identical mistake about *Ben*? And, if so, could not Ben profit by the mistake?

Swift as the proverbial arrow, Ben darted to the sink and poured his cup of tea down the plug-hole. Then he darted back, and replaced the now empty cup on the table. Then he darted to the sink again, and turned on a tap to make the tell-tale tea-leaves flow away. Then he returned to the table, sat down, leaned forward, and closed his eyes. Then he waited.

He waited an interminable while.

'Strewth!' he thought, presently. "Owjer know if yer pertendin' or not?'

135

He believed, on the whole, he was pretending, because you can see flapping objects and crawling crabs even when you're awake; but he had to convince himself periodically by counting thirty and then opening his eyes, and for a few minutes you could almost have told the time by Ben. But presently, he stopped counting at fourteen . . .

In the distance, some eight thousand miles away, a bell was ringing. At first he didn't pay any attention to it. It was only a black man in Australia eating a tambourine. Tambourines always make a tinkle as they go down. Just listen to it tinkling in his stomach. Silly, to gulp 'em so fast. It made 'em ring louder, and louder . . . and louder . . .

He jumped up suddenly. The black Australian vanished. It was Mr Lovelace ringing again. Lummy, he must go! How long had he been ringing?

Then, in another jerk of memory, he remembered the whole of the situation, and not merely half of it. Lummy, he *mustn't* go! He must get back to his chair double-quick before Mr Lovelace came along! He must go on pretending to be asleep!

The bell rang again. He bolted back to the chair and resumed his Rip Van Winkle attitude. Then he heard a door open quietly in the hall, and soft footsteps approaching.

A terrible fear swept over him, a fear that under scrutiny he would not be able to sustain the deception. Suppose he gave himself away? Suppose Mr Lovelace submitted him to some test which proved Ben's duplicity? With Ben's duplicity would also be proved his knowledge of Mr Lovelace's duplicity, and then all the cats would be out of all the bags and there could be no further chance of deception on either side. Ben would be drastically dealt with, and Molly upstairs could wait in vain for St George!

136

As Mr Lovelace approached, Ben now tried to go to sleep in earnest, just as previously he had tried not to. He was unsuccessful. He remained painfully awake, and tortuously aware of his surroundings as the old man passed into the kitchen and came straight to his chair.

He felt him pause at the chair. He felt him lean over the chair. He heard the ticking of the old man's watch as the owner's waistcoat brushed his left ear. He prayed that no breath would tickle the back of his neck. A gale he could stand, but the gentle tickle of human respiration below where you shave and above where you finish your swallow was Ben's personal notion of Chinese torture.

But his very terror assisted him. It produced at last a semi-swoon. And when he came out of it, Mr Lovelace had examined the empty tea-cup as well as the empty head lolling beside it, and was softly retracing his steps to the hall.

'I 'ope 'e gives the front-door a good bang when 'e goes!' thought the motionless figure he had just left. 'If 'e don't, I'm 'ere till Christmas!'

A long, disconcerting silence followed. It was broken occasionally by vague sounds. One of the sounds came, disturbingly, from above. Had Mr Lovelace gone upstairs?

But at length came the sounds for which Ben's ears longed. A click in the hall, a sense of outdoor things, and a soft, definite slam.

''Ooray!' thought Ben. 'Now orl I gotter do is ter count five tharsand!'

You see, Mr Lovelace might come back. He might have forgotten something. Or he might be playing a trick. You weren't really safe with a man like him till five thousand!

After seventy, however, Ben risked the odd four thousand

nine hundred and thirty and raised his head. The kitchen swam for a few moments as he opened his eyes. When it stopped he rose and swam himself out into the hall.

A key clicked in the front-door lock. Ben bolted for the hat-stand and dived behind a coat. A moment later the front-door opened, and Mr Lovelace's hand stretched towards the coat. The coat developed a palpitating heat.

Then the hand came away with a pair of thick gloves, extracted from a side-pocket of the coat. The door slammed again. Mr Lovelace's footsteps faded up the gravel path.

'Corse,' thought Ben, as he emerged from the hatstand, 'when yer *do* die it's orl over!'

Then he moved towards the staircase and began to ascend.

17

Secrets Behind Doors

With the sensation that he was exploring new country, Ben ascended the staircase at the back of the hall, while the clock with the irregular tick sent its spasmodic whispering through the dimness.

Ben might have dissipated the dimness which Mr Lovelace had refused to dissipate by switching on a light or two, and in theory he certainly preferred light to darkness. He was afraid, however, that illumination might draw unwelcome attention to the house and his presence in it, and for the time being he deemed it best to work in the semi-dark. So up the stairs he went, closing his eyes to shadows, and trying to convince himself that, with Mr Lovelace out of the house, there was nothing now to worry about.

He reached the top of the stairs, and found three doors to choose from. One straight ahead, the other two on the right and left. Not a sound came from behind any of them.

The door on the left, he calculated, would lead to the room over the drawing-room. That was the door he wanted. He turned towards it.

A sound crept up the stairs after him. He jerked round, forgetting his theory that with Mr Lovelace out of the house there was nothing to worry about. Then he muttered, 'Mug!' The sound was merely the clock. The door had taken his mind off it, and when the clock's whisper had returned to his consciousness he had failed to recognise it. The failure was assisted by the circumstance that the ticking was now below him, whereas previously it had been above him. The clock, which was of the large grandfatherly variety, stood on the half-landing of the staircase.

Turning back to the door, and determining to be diverted by no more noises, Ben placed his hand upon the knob.

'Miss!' he called softly, before turning the knob. 'Oi! Molly!'

There was no reply, so he turned the knob. Of course, the door was locked.

He knocked on the door and called again.

''Allo!' he said. 'It's me!'

Even that information failed to stimulate vocal activity on the other side of the door.

Well, never mind! He was *going* to get in! It was just a question of how.

An idea occurred to him. His brain appeared to be clearing. Perhaps it was the reaction from that one-eighth dose of whatever-it-was he had imbibed in the kitchen? Perhaps it was the proximity of another brain which, when permitted to function, was perpetually clear? Molly Smith was a wonderful stimulant!

But before he put his idea into practice he called once more through the dividing wood, just in case she was able to hear though she could not speak.

'Doncher worry!' he called. 'Heverythink's goin' ter be

140

orl right, see? 'E's gorn, and I'll be with yer afore a cat can spit!'

Then he turned towards the other doors.

His idea was to find a key in one of the other doors that would fit this one. Sometimes key-makers lacked variety, and a key designed for one door would occasionally unlock two. He knew this was so because the year he had taken a bath he had found the bathroom door locked, and had opened it with the key of the coal-cellar. He had always remembered it, because he had found the landlady in the bath reading Edgar Wallace. So why shouldn't one of the keys from one of these other doors fit the door of Molly's room?

Worth trying, anyway!

The first door he tried was also locked, with the key absent, but the second door, though no key protruded outside, yielded when he turned the knob, and opened. And—yes, there was a key on the inner side. Good! A bit o' luck!

Ben whipped the key from its rusting socket, and as he did so he caught sight of a black silent object in a corner.

'Gawd! Wot's that?' he thought, feeling suddenly less lucky.

It was a dog.

Ready to run, Ben stood fascinated. The dog held him as a snake holds a rabbit. Its very stillness added to its potency. If it had moved, he would not have remained an instant.

So—there *was* a dog, after all! And this was it—this crouching, motionless, silent thing! Ben recalled that before he had reached the house he had heard a dog yowl from the road—yowl and then suddenly whimper and

141

stop. He had heard it more than once. And here the creature was! Lying in a shadowed corner like a low black tree-trunk!

Why didn't it yowl now? Why didn't it leap up at the intruder? Surely that was the reception one would expect from a mad dog! Why did it lie there, as though it were dead?

And then Ben realised that it *was* dead.

For a moment this realisation wiped out all thought of Molly. Some men can hold a dozen thoughts in their minds and a dozen emotions in their bodies at the same time. Ben could only encompass one, which explains why he was apt on occasions to move so slowly towards his main object. D'Artagnan, hearing a lady moan while concealed in a chimney, would have run half-a-dozen men through and been at the lady's side in a trice; but Ben, whose simpler structure reacted to each immediate obstacle, and became absorbed by each, journeyed to his crowning acts through devious delays and by-ways, and could even forget a face that meant his only comfort while contemplating the carcase of a dog.

'Did that there dawg die nacheral?' he asked himself.

And, if not—?

Again, in imagination, he listened to the dismal yelping and to the sudden softer whining. He visualised the possible aspect of this very room while the yelping and whining were going on. The dog was alive in its corner then. And the old man would be standing by it, eh? With a stick or something. Lummy, no! Not a stick! *An iron hammer!* For there *was* the iron hammer . . .

Yes—but *why*?

Well, the fact remained, if the reason evaded. Mr Lovelace

had killed his dog. Killed it while Ben had been groping his way towards the house.

Now hatred as well as fear entered into Ben. Kill a bloke, if you like! The bloke might turn the tables on you, see? But—a dog!

He went to the corner and touched the limp mass. It was not yet cold. He returned to the door, walked out into the passage, and crossed to Molly's door.

Disappointment awaited him here. The key did not fit.

He found and tried four more keys. None of them fitted. He began to despair. Then all at once he remembered the chimney.

'Mug agine!' he thought. 'Corse—the chimbley! That's the ticket, ain't it?'

He knocked on the unresponsive door, to pass the news on.

'If you 'ear me goin',' he called, 'it's on'y becos I'm comin', see, and don't git a shock if I comes aht o' the fireplace!'

Then he turned, to put his latest brain-wave into execution.

Down the stairs again, past the sentinel clock—the ticking sounded queerer than ever now; had a mouse got inside?—across the large hall, with its unpleasant memory of the hat-stand, into the bleak 'drawing-room' once more, where the remains of Mr Lovelace's tea still waited to be returned to the kitchen, and across to the capacious fireplace. A mound of soot formed a conspicuous reminder of his last ascent.

''Ere goes!' he muttered, as he crept into position.

To his surprise he found the climb comparatively easy. He had time now to pick and choose his bricks, and to mount from one foothold to another with deliberation.

He approached the ledge with caution, manipulating his arms so that they could continue to function, and watching for the narrowing of the shaft that had previously imprisoned his head.

Now his groping hand touched the wooden door. He felt for a knob to turn, but evidently the only knob was on the other side, for he searched in vain. The door, from its unyielding tightness, seemed to be locked. A little slit, suggestive of a key-hole, strengthened this view.

'Orl right—'ere goes!' grunted Ben, grimly.

He stuck his head over the ledge, directing it towards the door like a battering-ram. He raised his waving feet behind him till they crouched with a light pressure against the bricks at his rear. Then, suddenly, he increased the pressure by violently straightening out.

His head shot forward, meeting the door with the impact of a bullet. For a few moments, during which the heavens split and the stars came tumbling out, Ben did not know whether the door or his head was broken; he simply knew that one of them was; but when the stars ran back into heaven and the celestial split was sewn up—or maybe remedied with a zip-fastener, it was so quick—Ben found that his head had won, and that the conquered door was flat off its hinges.

He did not waste time in personal triumph. Beyond the prone door was a chair, and on the chair, bound and gagged, was Molly.

Her eyes were open, and as they met the eyes of Ben he needed no greater reward for the bruise on his head and the soot on his face. For such a glance he would have been willing, at any time, to negotiate the tallest chimney in America.

''Ere I am!' he gurgled, foolishly. 'Toldjer, didn't I?'

She did not reply for the obvious reason that she couldn't.

He rose from the ground—for he had not won standing—and dived towards her. His trembling hands groped at her cords, and tore at the cloth tied so cruelly round her mouth. How she had managed to moan was a mystery! It must have been a superhuman effort produced by dire necessity . . .

But now she was free, and staring at him limply.

'Oh, Ben!' she murmured. 'Ben!'

He stared back at her. He couldn't think of anything to say. Call him a fool or an idiot, and he'd a dozen retorts ready. But call him 'Ben' like that, in a tone that almost made the name sound Biblical, and he just crumpled up.

Then Molly crumpled up. Her eyes closed, and she collapsed like a pricked balloon. Ben saw her collapsing, and dived forward to catch her. He was just in time to save her from the floor.

There was a bed in the room. Somehow or other he got her on to it. She lay like a closed flower, so quietly that for a moment Ben thought she was dead, and decided to die, too. Then she sighed faintly, and Ben decided that he needn't die after all. He'd stay alive to get her a cup of tea.

The door to the passage was, of course, locked, and the tea would have to arrive by the same channel as had delivered Ben himself.

Do not ask me how Ben managed to bring a cup of tea up a chimney without spilling more than three-quarters. If you had asked *him*, he would probably have answered,

'Well, I jest thinks of 'er fice, see? I thinks of 'er lyin' there orl pale and quiet, like, and, well, wantin' a cup o' tea. Well, there you are, see?'

145

By such incoherent logic are most heroic acts performed! . . .

And while Molly drank the tea, sitting up on the bed and patting odd bits of Ben with her disengaged hand as the odd bits hovered around her, he felt as though heaven had heard of him at last, and was giving him a little fore-taste of what it was going to be like.

'Owjer feel, miss?' he asked, when she laid the cup down.

'You just *can't* stick to "Molly," can you?' she smiled.

'I fergit, like,' he murmured. 'Well, 'ow are yer, Molly?'

'Getting O.K.'

'O.K. enuff fer the chimbley?'

'I don't know. But—what's happened, Ben?'

'Tell yer later, miss. Molly. Fust job's ter git clear o' this blinkin' plice, ain't it?'

'And to fetch the police?'

'Eh? Police?' Ben considered. 'Well, we'll talk about *that*, later, too.'

'I'm afraid we've got to talk about that *now*,' she answered, gravely. 'You see, Ben—I've seen Mr Lovelace commit a murder.'

18

Molly's Story

Then Ben and Molly told their stories. It took several moments to convince Ben that this was the time and place for the narrations, but Molly supplied an argument that was irrefutable. In spite of her pluck and her optimism, she had not yet recovered sufficiently to face a voyage down a chimney.

'Still a bit wonky, Ben,' she said, while she regarded a bruised foot, 'but I'll be as right as rain presently. It's not been exactly a picnic, you know. Or for you, either. Well— fire away!'

Ben's story we know. How far Molly knew it when he had finished narrating it is not certain. Ben could invent remarkable yarns, but he found difficulty in remembering actual ones. As instance the trouble he had had, until he had been assisted by Mr Lovelace, in recalling where he had left his cap.

'So it's your cap they're all after!' exclaimed Molly, when he was dealing with this point. 'Lovelace and Diablo and the lot!'

'Yus, but why?' demanded Ben.

Molly shook her head.

'Don't know,' she answered. 'There's a lot we don't know, Ben.'

'That's right,' he nodded, glancing towards the door. 'We don't know why 'e killed a dawg.'

'And—a man!'

'Yus. Or where the man is! Funny 'ow nasty they feel when yer touches 'em with yer foot. And 'ere's another thing we don't know—why that there gal wot I meets at the pillar-box comes along 'ere, puts up a bluff abart bein' orl in, and then goes pokin' arahnd the room jest below where we're now torkin' lookin' fer somethink!'

'Was *she* looking for your cap?'

'Well, she didn't find it!'

'No. But you say you thought she found something?'

'Yus. When she hopens one drawer I 'ears 'er give a sort of hexclamashun as if she was thinkin' "'Allo, 'ere it is, I got it, wot a bit o' luck!" That sort of hexclamashun. And then I 'ears a sort of paper sahnd—'

'What's that?' she interrupted.

'Eh?' he jerked.

'What did you say?'

'Oh! Sahnd! That's a noise. I thought you meant *you'd* 'eard a sahnd! 'Allo! Ain't it?'

He jumped up and stared towards the door. She stared after him.

'I don't hear anything!' she muttered.

'Not like—dawg's feet?'

She shook her head. Then Ben gave a sigh of relief.

'It's that there clock on the stairs,' he said. 'It ticks with a limp, like.'

'Well, if you don't stop hearing things, like,' she retorted, 'you'll hear me scream, like! Are you quite *sure*, Ben, that you heard the girl's exclamation, like?'

'Yus. P'r'aps she was lookin' fer a will, like?'

'Oh, Ben!' exclaimed Molly, in muffled tones. 'One moment you make me want to shriek and the next you make me want to laugh. Do let me know which is coming!' She sank back on the bed, and buried her face suddenly in the pillow.

He looked at her concernedly, trying to interpret the noises that issued from the pillow. She seemed to be both laughing and shrieking. Then the fit of hysterics passed, and was followed by a reaction of increased solemnity. Molly now seemed to be ashamed of her laughter and of her momentary yielding to it.

'Little fool I am!' she muttered, as she raised her head from the pillow. 'Going off like that!'

'You couldn't 'elp it,' Ben tried to console her, feeling it was his fault but not knowing why. 'Shall I pop dahn and git yer another cup o' tea?'

The remark was intended to soothe her, but it had the effect of making her lips tremble ominously again. Perhaps the mental picture of a blackened parlourmaid popping down a chimney for a cup of tea had something to do with it.

'No, Ben,' she answered. 'We've got to get busy. Now I'll tell you *my* story, and then we'll decide what's best to do.'

And this, though she told it more shortly, was Molly Smith's story.

When she had dived up the side lane on the previous evening and had hopped over the stile, she had had no

149

notion that Ben was not still at her heels. So vivid can imagination be after a robust push-off by reality that she even thought she heard Ben swear while stumbling over the stile, and she called back a quick encouraging word. But after she had crossed a couple of fields and negotiated a dense wood she became conscious of empty space behind her, and, stopping suddenly, she turned.

Then she got a shock. There was no Ben. What had happened to him?

She began to retrace her way. In daylight she could have found it easily, but now the task was impossible. The wood was full of paths and twists and tangles, and when at last she emerged into a field, it was not the field from which she had entered the wood. It was an entirely new field.

She returned to the wood and tried another route. It ended in the same field. She took a chance and crossed the field, in the hope that this would lead her to some familiar spot. She became utterly lost.

Once, in the distance, she thought she saw Ben, and dived towards him. It turned out to be the Spaniard! She wheeled away, and ran for her life . . .

'Did 'e see yer?' asked Ben.

'I didn't think so, then,' answered Molly, 'but now—I'm not sure!'

'Eh? Why ain't you sure?' exclaimed Ben, glancing for the ninety-ninth time towards the door.

'You'll hear in a minute,' she replied.

And she, also, glanced towards the door. But *she* had only done so about eighty-eight times.

At last she had stopped running. She had come to a lane.

A man was sitting in the lane. It was the bibulous gentleman who had disturbed them outside the barn.

Despite his condition, he had managed to change his pitch.

'Hic! Who goes there?' he called. 'Frien' or hiccopotomus?'

Molly, anxious of the time, did not relate the complete conversation to Ben, but we may hear it.

'How did you get here?' asked Molly.

She had no special reason for asking the question. It just filled the moment while she decided whether to stay and converse or not.

'On my legs,' replied the tipsy man. 'On all three of them.'

He seemed harmless. He might know something. Molly decided to risk it.

'Tell me—have you seen anybody?' she inquired.

'Hundreds,' nodded the idiot. 'Includin' Walter Raleigh.'

'Oh, dear! Can't you talk sense?' she begged.

'Much too dull!' he protested.

'Well, try! Have you seen my friend?'

'Frien'?'

'Yes!'

'*I'm* your friend!'

'Don't be ridiculous!'

'Ridicklus?' beamed the tipsy man. 'Tha's long word for the time o' night. Hic! Nine syllilibles!'

'Listen, please! I'm serious!' exclaimed Molly, and gave the man's coat a vicious pull to incite his proper attention.

'Come in,' he murmured.

'Have—you—seen—the—man—who—was—with—me!'

Now he discarded his smile, and bent forward as though his waist were hinged.

'You want to *know* something,' he informed her, earnestly.

'Yes! Where is my friend?'

'*I've* not got him.'

'But have you *see* him?'

'Let me think,' said the tipsy man.

The hinge gave way, and his head fell forward, face downwards, in his lap.

Molly was about to leave him when the head suddenly popped up again.

'Is your frien' Kruger?' its owner asked.

'Do you mean, has he got a beard?' she replied.

'Oh, no! Bird's-nest,' he corrected. 'Yes, I've seen a man with a bird's nest.'

'Where?' cried Molly.

The tipsy man raised his left hand flabbily, held it firm with his right, and twisted the fingers round till they made a sign-post.

'There,' he said. 'Where all my fingers but nine are pointin'!'

'You saw him go along there?' inquired Molly, looking along the road that seemed to be indicated.

'Tha' right! Call me a liar!' he frowned.

'When did you see him?'

'When I sat down. "Help me up!" I said. "Be a Good Companion!" But, no! On he goes with his bird's-nest!'

Sticking determinedly to the point, Molly pressed.

'What time was it?'

'Time—?'

'Yes! How long ago?'

'Ah, how long ago. Tha's hard to say. Things happen before you can catch them. This year.'

'Five minutes ago? Ten minutes ago?' She prompted, to bring him out of calendars into clocks.

'Yes. This year five minutes ago. *And* ten minutes ago. All the lot.'

There was nothing more to be gained from him, and what she had gained, as matters turned out, was negligible. Ben had not passed the tipsy man along the road. Probably it had merely been Sir Walter Raleigh.

But the road led back to Southampton, and, in the absence of Ben, Southampton was as near as Molly could get to him. For Ben had read her mind correctly when he had deduced that she would remember the letter waiting for her at the Post Office.

In this letter would be the address of the house to which Ben had been going; and although Molly believed he had lost the address, she also believed—again in accordance with Ben's theory—that he might remember it again, and that in any case it formed the only possible link between them.

Even if Ben had been caught by the Spaniard, Molly would still have to go to the address . . .

'Why?' asked Ben, at this point.

'Because of Don Diablo,' explained Molly.

'Yer mean—'e'd be goin', like?'

'Yes.'

'Well, that'd be a reason for you *not* ter go,' said Ben.

'But—have you forgotten—we were coming here to warn Mr Lovelace,' Molly pointed out.

'It's hother people want warnin' agin' 'im—not 'im agin' hother people!'

'That's right, Ben. But you and I didn't know that till we got here, did we?'

'No more we did, Molly!'

'And then—there was another reason why I had to come here—even if you *were* caught by Don Diablo.'

'Wot?'

'Why—to see Don Diablo—and to get you back again.'

Ben swallowed.

''Ere, miss, wot's orl this abart?' he demanded, rather huskily. 'Are you savin' me, or am I savin' *you*?'

'P'r'aps we're both saving each other?' she responded. 'Let it go at that, shall we?'

And so, very late, Molly had reached Southampton again, and had retraced her way to the little inn where she had hidden during the last few nights, and which she thought she had left for ever.

'Oh, so you're back!' the woman who ran the place greeted her doubtfully.

'I know a comfortable bed when I meet one,' smiled Molly.

The compliment, plus payment in advance, had warded off questions. She was too tired even to eat, though the proprietress insisted, rather unexpectedly, on making a cup of tea. Then she climbed up to her little room. And, just as she reached it, the door of the adjoining room closed softly . . .

'Lummy!' cried Ben, with a gulp.

'What's the matter?' asked Molly, jerked out of her story again by the interruption.

'That—closin' door!'

'What about it?'

'Well—jest while you was menshunin' it—I thort I 'eard another door closin'. '*Ere!*'

They listened, with ears strained.

'Oi! Wot's 'appenin'?' chattered Ben, suddenly. 'The clock's stopped tickin'!'

19

Don Pasquali

The ceasing of the clock's ticking formed an uncanny
interlude in Molly's story, for silence can be as disconcerting
as sound.

There is an underground stream in a Derbyshire cavern
that sends an eerie gurgle through the darkness but when
the gurgle ceases the water has risen to block the only
exit from an inner cave; then, if you are occupying the
inner cave, the atmosphere is far more eerie. Did the
ceasing of the ticking portend, in some as yet unrevealed
way, that the only exit from the room Molly and Ben
were occupying was going to be blocked? The exit down
the chimney?

Responding impulsively to this thought, Ben crept to the
gap by the fireplace and stared gingerly down.

Through the black sooty tunnel a vague, dying white light
loomed up at him. Ben half-expected to hear the ticking
from this new place, for the grandfather clock he concluded,
must either have shifted its position or died; but no sound
rose through the tunnel, and no movement disturbed the

white light. The chimney seemed to be in a state of expectant suspension.

Somebody bent over him. It gave him a shock, though it was only Molly.

'So that's our way out, is it?' she murmured

'Yus,' answered Ben. 'Can you manage it?'

She peered down and shuddered. That wasn't like her. Ben looked surprised.

'Afraid I'm still a bit dizzy,' she explained, apologetically. 'Wonder if that brute's been using any of his damned dope on *me*!'

'I could go fust, and you could tread on me, like,' suggested Ben.

But she shook her head and made her way back to the bed. 'Ben,' she said, gravely, 'I'm no good for a bit. Rotten, isn't it? You think you can stick anything—and then you find you can't!'

'Go on! No one can stick wot they can't,' consoled Ben.

'*You* seem able to.'

'Wot? Me?' He turned from the fireplace and stared at the bed.

'Yes, you! Right to the end!'

'Shurrup!' murmured Ben, fighting bashfulness. 'Corse, yer've never seen me run, 'ave yer!'

'Yes—and I've run with you! But you always go back again, if you can help anyone—'

''Ere, wot's orl this?' exclaimed Ben, indignantly. 'The on'y time I don't run away is when I can't, see?'

'That's not true,' she smiled, 'and if you like, I'll prove it.'

''Ow?'

'That chimney. *I* can't go down it—but *you* could.'

157

'Wot, and leave you 'ere?' He reddened as Molly laughed. 'That's just silly, that is,' he growled. 'Let's 'ear the rest of yer story. Wot 'appened last night when yer went up ter bed?'

He moved back to the fireplace as he spoke and sat down on the little unhinged door. Just as well to keep an eye cocked on that chimney hole!

And Molly continued with her interrupted story:

The door of the adjoining bedroom had closed softly, just as she had reached the landing. It had also closed deliberately. As though it had planned to close at this particular moment.

Before entering her room Molly paused for a moment to stare at the door. She was holding a candle—apparently there was no gas on the top floor, or it had been turned off—and the flame of the candle flickered on the number of the door that had just closed. It was No. 10. Her room was No. 12. She wished devoutly that there had been a Number 11 in between!

Well, no good staring! No. 10 might open again. She slipped quickly into her own room, laid the candle down on a chair—the only available surfaces were the bed and this chair and a mantelpiece—and turned to lock the door. There was no key.

This gave her a nasty jolt. Previously there had been a key. She knew, because she had used it.

She stood, hesitating. The softly closing door of No. 10 and the absence of her key were too disturbing to be ignored. She decided to descend and interview the proprietress.

But when she opened her door to leave the room, the door of No. 10 also opened. She heard the little dry crackle proclaiming it. The passage promptly became an impossible No Man's Land, and she closed her own door again hastily.

She took the candlestick from the chair and placed it on the mantelpiece. The edge of the candlestick protruded too far over, however, so she had to put it on the bed. Then she moved the chair to the door—it wasn't a long move— and fixed it under the knob.

Of course, the candle couldn't remain on the bed. The only place left was the floor. This cast horrible shadows upwards, but she wasn't going to put it back on the chair. If the door were tried the chair might shake, and if the chair shook the candle might topple, and if the candle toppled it would go out! She wasn't going to risk *that*!

Nor was she going to risk taking off her clothes . . .

'Wot, 'ave yer 'ad 'em on orl night?' ejaculated Ben.

'All night,' she nodded. 'But so have you.'

'Yus, but you're a gal,' replied Ben. 'That's dif'ren, ain't it?' . . .

Different or not, she lay on her bed fully clothed, with the exception of her shoes, and tried to shut out the big black shadows that rose from the floor to disfigure the walls and the ceiling. Molly had pluck, but, like Ben, she had passed through some dislocating hours, and things were beginning to get on top of her. As a rule, she laughed at shadows. These refused to be laughed at.

At last, however, she fell asleep. She did not know it until she found herself waking up. The shadows were no longer separate; they had joined up and they enveloped her. The room was in darkness. The candle had either burnt out or been put out.

'Who's there?' she tried to gasp.

But no words came. Only the thought. And the thought

was answered when, beginning to sit up, she felt an unusual tightness of the bed-clothes at her feet—the tightness of a weight.

Then, for the first time, she noticed that the room was not absolutely dark. There was a little glow in it, a ruby speck that became bright and dull by turns. It was about two feet above the weight that was holding her legs down. Somebody was sitting on the end of the bed, smoking.

She did not need the light to guess who the somebody was. His name was Don Pasquali—more pictorially described by Ben as Don Diablo—and once before he had sat on the end of Molly's bed. The other time had been on board a ship, and she had nearly scratched his eyes out. And he had laughed and sworn that a Don Pasquali was not to be diverted by a little thing like that. A Don Pasquali could wait. A Don Pasquali was in no hurry. For, in the end, a Don Pasquali always got what he wanted.

There were two things Don Pasquali wanted. Molly was only one of them.

Now, for the second time, the Spaniard sat on her bed. And, though it was dark, she seemed to see him smiling.

'Awake?' he said, softly.

'Go away!' she managed to murmur.

'After you talk, yes,' he answered. 'But, if no, I stay.'

'Beast! What am I to talk about?' she gasped.

The cigarette glowed, then came a little closer as the Spaniard said,

'The fool you help! Say where he is?'

'I don't know where he is!' she retorted.

'Oh, yes!'

'I tell you I don't!'

'I see you with him—'

160

'Well, you don't see me with him now!'

'So? Then Don Pasquali make you talk!' The voice, despite its threat, was soft like a regretful sigh. 'But not with pain. No! With—what is your word?—the heart?'

A puff of smoke played over her face. The glow came nearer still. Pasquali's hot breath mingled with the smoke, poisoning it.

She struck at the glow, but it slipped aside, and her hand was caught in mid-air.

'Beast! Beast!' she choked. 'I tell you I *don't* know where he is! I don't! I don't! I've lost him. And if you come any nearer, I'll show you what my teeth are like!'

The invisible figure hesitated. Perhaps Pasquali was impressed by her sincerity. Drawing no closer, but still holding the determined little wrist in his no less determined fingers, he said,

'Listen! If the beast give you money? Bracelet for the little hand. Pearls for the little neck! Eh? Soon—very soon! Then you not call Don Pasquali beast? Eh? Eh?'

And now, suddenly, Don Pasquali's head loomed over Molly, while the imprisoned wrist was forced down to her side. But her other arm was free, and with a frantic twist she brought it from under her and struck. This time she struck more than air, screaming while she did so. So loud was her scream that Pasquali's roar was drowned in it. Then the blackness increased, and when she came out of it the proprietress was standing in the door-way, with a candle in her hand and disapproval on her face.

'Havin' a nightmare?' she demanded, as Molly sat up galvanically.

There was no one in the room beyond themselves.

'The man in the next room!' panted Molly.

161

'The man in the next room!' retorted the landlady. 'There's no one in the next room!'

The retort was so idiotically erroneous that it whipped Molly into anger.

'Do you think I'm an idiot?' she blazed. 'A Spaniard—he's just been here!'

'Spaniard?' frowned the proprietress. 'Ain't one of the two men they're after for this murder a Spaniard?' She departed into the adjoining room, and returned a moment later, grumbling. 'A nice thing, waking me up like this! You'll be dreamin' of the drunken sailor next.'

'Wot, did she say "drunken"?' interrupted Ben.

'I'm afraid so,' answered Molly. 'She was an old frump, anyway.'

''Ear, 'ear! But—you *adn't* been dreamin', 'ad yer?'

'No, Ben, though for a moment I thought I must have been! But—the key. He'd removed *that*! And after the old frump had gone I found some cigarette ash on the bed. I expect he must have slipped in and out of the place somehow or other.'

'That's right,' nodded Ben, gloomily. 'They ain't solid, these Spanish blokes—they're shadders. Well, and wot 'appened then? Arter that?'

'I sat up for the rest of the night, you bet! And next morning—*this* morning—my goodness, it seems a year ago!—I called at the Post Office and got your letter.'

'Givin' yer the address—'

'Yes, and I didn't waste any time about coming here, *you* can wager! I took the first train I could catch to Waterloo, jumped in another train from Waterloo to Wimbledon, and—raced you, didn't I?'

'Wot! Get 'ere d'reck from Waterloo?'

162

'Of course! That's the best way.'

'Lummy, you was quick!'

'A bit too quick!' She shuddered. 'If I'd paused at the gate, instead of slipping through like a fool, I—I wouldn't have seen Lovelace—'

She stopped and gulped.

'Wot?' whispered Ben.

'Strangling a little fellow with his fingers!' She took a deep breath, and set her lips. 'I reckon that finished me, Ben. Knocked my brain out! I don't know what I did. All I remember is suddenly finding myself struggling in that damned old devil's arms and trying to shout. And then—blank—till I was in this room, bound and gagged, and—and *you* came along. Don't ask me how long I've been in this room? I've no idea. Most of the time I've been in Kingdom Come! But when I could manage it I choked up a sound, in case there was anybody around to hear it, and—well, that's *my* story, and so now let's get on with it!'

But Ben had suddenly risen from the ground and darted to her side.

'Oi!' he whispered, catching hold of her arm. 'Some'un *is* dahn there—and 'e's comin' hup!'

20

The Contents of a Chimney

You cannot decide on your tactics until you know your weapon. For instance, if the weapon is a poker you must stand close to your opponent, but if it is a china ornament you can then use the advantage of distance. Unfortunately for Ben the only weapon he could find in this ill-furnished room, apart from really heavy artillery, was the chair in which Molly had been bound, and as the ominous noise below—the noise that had diverted him from the final words of Molly's story and had brought him scurrying away from the fireplace—began to scrape upwards from the drawing-room chimney, he dashed to the chair, seized it, and holding it aloft, staggered with unwilling courage back to the ominous aperture.

He was handicapped by another disadvantage. He did not know who the enemy was. This, however, was not a very serious matter. Whoever the enemy was, he had to be hit.

He felt something touch his side.

'Git back!' he muttered. 'You ain't in this!'

But Molly, who had slipped off the bed and had followed him, refused to get back. She had a weapon of her own—a small clenched fist, the knuckles of which were already white with preparedness and determination—and she was not going to be out of it. The ascending enemy seemed in for a hot time.

Was he aware of it? He did not hurry. Slowly, laboriously—now rising a few inches, now pausing, now rising again, now pausing again, now scraping around for a new position—he signalled his gradual approach by a series of unpleasant noises; noises which seemed no less ominous because of their vagueness and indecisiveness.

Swish—swish—halt. Swish—swish—halt. Swish—swish—plop. Swish—swish—would his head never appear?

Molly glanced at Ben with puckered brow. Something new was worrying them both, and they didn't know what it was.

'Jest 'is tictacs,' muttered Ben. 'That's orl. Tictacs!'

'Be careful!' whispered Molly, as Ben took a step forward.

'It's '*im* wot's bein' careful!' whispered Ben, giving his raised chair a little shake. ''E knows *I* got a tictac, too!'

Nevertheless, he did not reduce his own caution, and easily resisted an impulse to look down.

'Yer see,' he told himself, in extenuation, 'by not showin' meself I'm givin' 'im a surprise, like.'

But the enemy took so long to rise to the surprise that once again Molly and Ben turned and glanced at each other perplexedly.

'What *is* he doing?' faltered Molly.

'P'r'aps 'e's stuck,' answered Ben.

This theory was not unwelcome. It would save a nasty mess on the chair. But it received a set-back when the sounds recommenced, after a silence of several seconds, and became more violent.

Swish—swish—clatter. Clatter—clatter—scrape. Scrape—scrape . . .

Silence again. This time, a much longer one.

'Lummy, now 'e *as* stuck!' whispered Ben.

'Do you think so?' she whispered back.

'Corse 'e 'as,' answered Ben. 'Carn't you ear 'im not movin'? Yus, but why ain't 'e swearin'?'

You always swear when you get stuck. It's dull and monstrous otherwise. Of course, if you find yourself stuck in such a way that your head gets fixed and your jaws won't move—like Ben had found himself once in that narrowing part—then you can't swear. Barring in your thoughts.

'What are you going to do?' demanded Molly suddenly, as Ben lowered the chair.

''Ave a look,' answered Ben. 'If 'e's stuck, see, we can drop on 'im.'

'Why not leave him?' she gasped.

'Cos we can't git through 'im,' replied Ben, 'and 'e's blockin' the way to Hempire Free Trade. Doncher worry, miss. Molly, that is. If I drop somethink 'eavy 'e'll go dahn plonk, and brike 'is skull, and we can git aht over the pieces.'

'Don't!'

'Wot? The pieces? Lummy, miss, a bit o' picktorial langwidge like don't 'urt us arter all we bin through! Afore long I'll be eatin' supper orf corpses and not turnin' a 'air. Usin' 'em fer tibles, I mean,' he explained quickly, lest there should be any misunderstanding on the point.

He was speaking mainly through bravado, to reinforce

himself for the ordeal of looking down at the thing that had got stuck, but his last suggestion nearly undid all his good work. If one could really get numb to corpses, Ben would have been corpse-proof years ago!

Now he tiptoed to the aperture, nearly tripping over the unhinged door as he did so. He heard a gasp while he bent forward and peered down the hole. It was his gasp. The gasp was repeated a moment later. He had not really expected to see what he found there. The reality momentarily overpowered him.

The faint whitish light that, in previous views, had marked the bottom of the chimney—the light from the drawing-room window falling on a small space of dusty hearth—was no longer visible. It was blocked by a wedged, undeniably human shape.

Ben had been down there, in that exact spot! Might this have happened to *him?*

But even at such poignant moments one must be practical. So he swallowed, to render his dry throat vocal again, and after the third swallow he managed to emit a very faint 'Oi!'

The thing that blocked the chimney did not respond.

'Oi!' called Ben again, after three more swallows.

The 'Oi' went down the shaft, blundered against the obstruction there, then bounced up again, unaccompanied. Ben was preparing a third 'Oi' when it froze in his throat. For now, at last, a sound ascended to him. And it did not come from the obstruction in the chimney. It came from the floor below.

Someone was moving in the drawing-room.

Ben discovered himself hugging Molly. He did not know whether he or she had started the hug; but, whichever it was, the other held on. Affection may have been in that embrace, but terror was uppermost. Their mutual need was something comforting—something warm amid this dying coldness!

Meanwhile the movement below continued. They heard it in its stealthy course across the room. It had begun at the fireplace. It ended at the drawing-room door. Then there was a silence. Then, a soft bang. The bang of the front-door.

'Gorn!' chattered Ben, hysterically.

He felt Molly trembling against him. Her need steadied him.

'She's bad!' he thought. 'I must do somethink!'

He carried her back to the bed. He turned back towards the fireplace. His eyes nearly started out of his head. The little door was no longer lying on the ground. It had been propped up against the aperture.

''Oo did that?' he gasped.

He had done it himself. There are moments one does not remember. In the supreme of bliss or of agony we are oblivious!

Then he got another shock. He was surprised with anything less than ten shocks a minute. Molly was not lying on the bed, as she ought to have been. She was on her feet, quivering.

'Lie down agine,' he ordered.

But she shook her head angrily. Indignation as well as fear was now moving her, and giving a new light to her eyes. Or, rather, restoring a light that had been temporarily extinguished.

'What's the matter with me?' she cried. 'Talk about cotton-wool!'

She brushed by him and ran to the window. The mist was considerably less thick than it had been, but evening darkness was now replacing the fog and not much could be seen in the garden. As she stared out, Ben stared at her. He expected her to topple over any moment. How had she crossed the floor so quickly? Mind over matter?

'Ben!' she exclaimed, turning abruptly. 'We've got to get out of here!'

'Ow?' replied Ben.

It was the obvious reply. The door was locked and the chimney was choked. But the third alternative remained. The window.

'Yes, and break our necks,' said Ben, when she indicated it.

'Not if we make a rope out of the bed-clothes,' retorted Molly, and was back at the bed as she spoke. 'Come along! Help me rip these things off.'

'Yus, but wot are we goin' ter do when we git aht?' asked Ben apprehensively, as he obeyed.

'Two things,' answered Molly. 'One for each of us. Here, twist this sheet!'

Her sudden access of energy was somewhat breathless.

'Wot are they?' inquired Ben, twisting.

'The police and your cap. See you get it tight. Yes, Ben, we've got to get busy, you and I. Got to prove ourselves now as a team, haven't we?'

'That's right.' He liked the word 'team.' 'But—wot are we goin' ter tell the pleece? Yer ain't forgot, 'ave yer, that I'm on the placards?'

'No, I've not! That's why *I'm* going for the police, while you go for the cap.'

'Don't be silly!' retorted Ben.

'I'm not silly, I'm sensible,' she answered. 'Now, then. The pillow-case. Oh, and these cords I was bound with. Don't you see, both the jobs are urgent, and we mustn't waste time with either of them. That's why we must split.'

'Yus, but why shouldn't *you* go for the cap—'

'Because you know where the shop is, and I don't, and because I can't claim a cap that isn't mine, and because a hundred other things. Don't argue, Ben! Can't you see, it's only waste of time? If you're worrying about me and the police, you needn't. *I'm* not on the placards!'

Ben was silenced. Nevertheless, he was not happy. He knew that Molly was wise, and that this was the best way to divide the duties, but St George is not the friend of wisdom when wisdom provides the easier task.

But was his task going to be so easy, after all? To overtake Mr Lovelace, who had had an exceedingly long start, and who might have got the cap already . . .

'Bed!' cried Molly. 'Help me shove it near the window!'

'Wot for?' asked Ben. 'Are we goin' ter slide out in it?'

'No, idiot! But we want something to tie one end of our rope to, don't we?'

'Corse,' observed Ben, 'you got a brine!'

They moved the bed to the window. The noise it made sounded in their ears like thunder. Then they tied the improvised rope to the bed-rail, and, opening the window, dropped the other end out. There was an anxious moment as the rope descended. Would it touch bottom? Molly leaned so far out that Ben caught hold of her legs to prevent her from toppling.

'O.K.!' she reported, and he pulled her in. 'Only a foot or two off.'

Now came the final instructions. Molly delivered them in a rapid gabble, and they ran something like this:

'Listen, Ben! You're going down first, and the moment you get down you scoot. The very moment, mind. Don't interrupt! I'll give you five minutes' start, because I want you clear before I start searching for my bobby. You've got money—we'll thank Lovelace for *that!*—so you'll be able to get to Waterloo the quickest way, but you'll probably find the best way by train, like I did. If you're lucky and get the cap, come back and meet me at—I know, Southfields station. That's not too near here. I'll be waiting there for you—'

'Yus, but s'pose Mr Lovelace beats me to it—and s'pose I don't catch 'im arterwards?'

'You'll come back and meet me at Southfields just the same. Maybe, in that case, *I'll* have the cap! If that devil returns with it, I shan't be far off! Now, then! Quick!'

Ben put one leg over the window. Astride the ledge, he offered a final protest.

'Look 'ere, Molly!' he urged. 'Wot abart lettin' the cap go?'

'Not on your life, Ben,' she retorted. 'I'd feel like a quitter. Wouldn't you? That cap's worth something to somebody, and you and I are going to find out all about it! Over you go—partner!'

So over he went, and slid down with whirling mind as well as body to the ground.

'Don't wait! Run!' came the injunction from the window.

He obeyed. Without looking back, he ran along the gravel path till he reached the gate. He was in a sort of mental panic. But, just as he reached the gate, he stopped suddenly. A small object lay on the ground.

He stopped and picked it up. It was a tiny card-case. Very elegant. And obtruding from it was a visiting card. He looked at the card and read the name:

'Miss Violet Medway.'

Medway? Who was Medway? Hadn't he heard that name before, and wasn't it, in some odd way, mixed up with his own? Then, in a flash, he remembered. He and Medway were 'in the news' together! Half the day's posters were saying,

'Where's the Sailor?'

And the other half,

'Medway Bill This Week.'

And, now, here was Miss Medway's visiting card . . . Queer!

21

Back to Waterloo

But there was no time just then to pause over Violet Medway and to wonder whether she were daughter, sister, aunt or niece of Joseph Medway, M.P., whose proposed legislation was sharing the nation's attention with a murder mystery. Later on the visiting-card could be re-examined, but at the moment it had to be slipped back into the tiny case, and the case into Ben's left boot—the one without the hole in the toe—while more urgent matters were attended to.

Waterloo—in the quickest possible time! That came first on Ben's list.

He passed through the gate, and wondered why a sense of relief did not immediately assail him. The reason was that Molly was still on the other side of the gate. Not until he knew that she as well as he had the gate of Greystones behind her would he feel like bursting thankfully into 'There were three sailors of Bristol City,' and he longed to linger by the gate until he saw her trim, tired little figure running towards him up the gravel path. But that would

173

be disobeying orders, and for the moment Molly was captain of the ship. You can't have two captains.

So, dutifully, Ben turned away from the gate and glanced along the lane. And Fate, with a sudden whim for a surprise gift, sent him a taxi-cab!

'Oi!' called Ben.

The taxi-cab stopped. If there had been more light to see Ben by, the driver would not have paid him this compliment. The driver merely heard the summons, however, and the word 'Oi' is used by Oxford undergraduates, and even by Wireless Announcers in private life. Taking advantage of the gloaming, Ben nipped like his own shadow into the cab. Then he huddled himself into a corner.

The driver waited, frowned and descended, feeling vaguely disturbed. Ben saw his head coming, cleared his throat quickly, and cried, in his lordliest tone:

'Sarthfield.'

'Where?' demanded the driver.

'Sarthfield, wot?' repeated Ben, endeavouring to increase the lordliness. 'Stishun.'

And he spat out of the window to clinch the matter.

The driver, however, still hesitated. None of the lords he knew spat.

'Let's see your fare?' he demanded, suspiciously.

Ben took out a ten-shilling note—one of the four he had received from Mr Lovelace—impressed it with his thumb-mark, and held it up.

'That good enuff fer yer?' he asked, sarcastically.

'Let's see closer,' retorted the driver, and snatched the note.

Just in time Ben saved himself from snatching it back.

He remembered that people in the Upper Class can watch a note leave them without wincing.

'Looks all right,' admitted the taximan. 'I'll give you the change at Southfields.'

Then he returned to his seat, and the car moved.

Indignation stirred the passenger. He felt certain that this was not the usual treatment meted out to nobility. But a row had to be avoided at all costs, so he swallowed his pride and contented himself by visualising the driver being cut up into very small pieces, and spread on bread-and-butter, and eaten by Chinese brigands in Maninchooria.

The taxi wound out of the lane. Staring out, Ben recognised the pillar-box as they went by it, but when they passed a policeman Ben quickly ducked back to his corner. Fortunately the cab was not one of those taxis with windows all the way round.

He remained in his corner for the rest of the journey, saving for one moment when he was dissatisfied with the pace of the cab.

'Is this a taxi or a 'earse?' he called.

'Well, it was a taxi when we started,' the driver called back, angrily, 'but by the time we finish—'

'Yus, yer needn't end it,' interrupted Ben. 'That's your trick, cocky.'

The generous admission produced what the complaint had not. The driver celebrated the occasion with more juice.

'Where's this?' asked Ben, when at last the taxi stopped.

'Southfields,' answered the driver. 'Isn't that where you said?'

'Oh! We're 'ere, are we?' muttered Ben.

He left the cab abruptly. The driver began looking at him rather hard. He dived into the station.

'In a hurry, aren't you,' the driver called.

'Trine,' Ben called back. 'Jest goin'.'

'Don't you want your change, then?'

Taximen may be suspicious, but they are honest. Ben hesitated. *Did* he want his change?

Arguments against: a train *was* just coming in, and it might be his, and if he missed it he might have to wait an hour. Also, he didn't want to impress his visage on the taximan's mind by showing him too much of it.

Argument for: 7/3.

The 7/3 won. He dived back and got it. Then he dived for the train. Then he dived for the ticket-office. Then he dived for the train again. Then he dived into the train, and sat down breathlessly on an old woman.

'Who do you think you're sitting on?' cried the old woman, as she bounced him off.

'Beg pardon, mum,' muttered Ben. 'I didn't know it was you.'

It was a nuisance. He didn't want to attract attention, and now everybody began staring at him. He closed his eyes, to shut them out.

Behind him, two men were talking.

'Yes, it'll be a damn good thing, if it's pushed through,' said one. 'The country's simply marking time.'

'But *will* it be pushed through?' replied the other. 'Medway's not too popular.'

Medway again! Wasn't there any getting away from the name?

'What's that to do with it?' demanded the first speaker.

'A lot, I should have thought,' answered the second.

'Nonsense, nonsense! If an Act's good, it's good! Who cares a damn about the man behind it?'

'We care a damn lot about the man behind it! What, never heard of a politician losing his influence through a private scandal? I could give you half-a-dozen cases—'

'Oh, well, let's drop politics! What's the latest about that sailor? I see they're on the track of him.'

Ben's heart leapt. So did his frame. The old lady got another bump.

'Any more of your freshness, young man,' she cried, shoving him away a second time, 'and I'll have you put out.'

'There's a girl, too, isn't there?' went on one of the voices behind him. 'The trouble is they're making the prisons too comfortable, nowadays! People go wrong for a rest cure! Did you hear Edgar Wallace broadcasting on the subject the other day? According to him—'

The train stopped. Ben got out, and waited for the next.

The service between Southfields and London is, happily, a frequent one, and if Mr Lovelace had chosen this route there would have been no possibility of catching him up. Fate, however, does not confine its enthusiasm to surprising gifts. It also likes a close race, which may explain why Mr Lovelace chose a taxi-cab instead of a train and said 'Waterloo Station' to the driver. 'Wot, all the way in this fog?' the driver had replied, for the mist had not then begun to abate. 'Yes, all the way in this fog,' Mr Lovelace had retorted.

And the driver had got lost in the fog. He had also driven into a lorry and a lamp-post in the fog. The betting, thus, was level.

Ben, however, did not know this; and when he had caught his second train, arrived somewhat surprisingly at The Mansion House instead of Waterloo, and had exchanged E.C.4 for S.E.1, he imagined that he was about to prove himself a hopeless 'also ran.' Still, he told himself, as he fought an uneasy sensation aroused by his memories of the Waterloo district, he'd have to finish the race, no matter where he came in, and he'd have to prove that the cap was no longer at the winning-post, or hang his head in shameful humility when he next met Molly at Southfields station.

'Arter all, it'll soon be over,' he muttered, while he drew near the first of the two restaurants he and Mr Lovelace had selected as the likely ones.

At the identical moment, Mr Lovelace was approaching the other restaurant.

Ben recognised immediately that he had made the right choice. Little though he had seen of the restaurant's exterior through the morning's fog, there was no mistaking the portly proprietor who had served him and who now stood outside talking to a little man with side-whiskers. Moreover, the subject of their conversation, as Ben noted when he slithered near enough to hear, would have provided ample proof had there been no other.

The subject was Ben himself!

'Yus, 'e comes into 'ere this mornin', and orders breakfast like you'd think 'e was the King!' the proprietor was saying. 'And says 'e wants a 'ole loaf!'

'Well, I never!' replied the whiskered one.

'"Sure you don't want the 'ole shop?" I told 'im. "If you do, you won't mind mentioning it, will you? Or Windsor Castle, or any other little thing like that."'

'Ah! Wag!' smiled the whiskered one.

'Ay, and you *need* it, to tell some of these fellers off! Yes, and then 'e starts shedding money from his clothes—like a slot-machine, as I told 'im.'

'Well, I never!'

'Shillin's and 'arf-crowns—'e'd picked up a bit some-where, you could see—ay, and pushed it down 'is trousers 'stead of 'is pockets in 'is 'urry. But I don't think anything of it—we get all sorts round 'ere—till I start talking about this murder, see? And when I says there's fifty pounds reward for catchin' the sailor—'

'What, is there?' exclaimed the whiskered one.

'Well, so I've *'eard*,' replied the proprietor, 'though it ain't out yet, in fact I was just goin' out to get a paper and see when up 'e jumps and off 'e goes, like a stone from a sling!'

'Well, I never!' muttered the whiskered one. 'But what about the cap you were mentioning? That's what I want to hear about! What about the cap?'

'Stay there—and I'll *show* you the cap!' cried the proprietor, and dived back into the shop.

He was only gone for twenty seconds, but during those twenty seconds Ben slipped suddenly into a doorway and transformed himself into a pancake. For, from the opposite direction, came an old man who imagined that Ben was sleeping peacefully over a kitchen table in a house on Wimbledon Common.

22

Re-enter the Cap

If the imminence of the cap had thrown Ben into a flutter, the imminence of Mr Lovelace threw him into a panic. A situation was developing that required the brain of a Sherlock Holmes, the courage of a Bulldog Drummond and the luck of a man who could fall over Beachy Head without hurting himself, and Ben was weak in all three necessities. 'It ain't fair,' he told the door against which he was struggling to flatten himself, 'ter do orl these things ter me! I'd chinge with Aunt Sally any time!'

The door remained unsympathetic. It did not open and receive him.

And that being so, he had to endure out of the corner of his eye the spectacle of Mr Lovelace growing larger and larger, while the little man with the side-whiskers waited for the restaurant proprietor's return with the cap.

And now here came the proprietor, bustling with importance and significance.

''Ere it is!' he exclaimed. 'Large as life! Left it on the seat aside of 'im.'

He held up the headgear as he spoke. A few yards away, Mr Lovelace paused. A triumphant light shot into his eyes, to be extinguished the next instant. For the moment he was not betraying his interest.

'Well, I never!' said the whiskered man, making use of his stock phrase while he stared at the cap as though it had been a royal crown. 'So that's it, is it?'

'This is it,' nodded the proprietor, as though he had made the royal crown.

'Looks new,' commented the whiskered man.

'Newish, any'ow,' conceded the proprietor, 'and better-lookin' than the 'ead that was under it! Talk about a scarecrow! But there, it takes all sorts to make a world, don't it?'

The whiskers wagged up and down. Mr Lovelace advanced a step or two closer. The proprietor held the cap up so that they could have a better stare at it.

'Well, what are you going to do?' inquired the whiskered man.

'There you are!' answered the proprietor. 'What'd *you* do?'

'That's easy!'

'Let's 'ear it, then?'

'Earn that fifty pounds!'

'Ah!'

'What's keeping you?'

The proprietor hesitated, then said,

'Well, of course—it mightn't be the man, might it? As I say, it never come over me at the time. "There's a mug," I thought, "poppin' off like that!" But 'e might 'ave seen a friend or anything. As I say, it never come over me.'

'No, but it's come over you now!'

'That's right.'

181

'Well, then!'

The proprietor smiled.

'As you say,' he observed, 'well, then!'

'I can't make you out,' frowned the whiskered man. 'What are you waitin' for?'

'Ah, now you've struck it, lad!' grinned the proprietor, with a wink. 'What *am* I waitin' for?'

'I'm askin'!'

'Yes, and I'm tellin'!' said the proprietor, dropping his voice. 'That fifty pound ain't ackerchelly offered yet, but I 'ear it's goin' to be, and so that's why I'm waitin', laddy! See?'

'Well, I never!' exclaimed the laddy.

Then for a moment there was silence. Ben's ill-equipped mind struggled for a brain-wave. The only brain-wave was so obvious that it scarcely deserved the title. It was to dive out of his doorway, snatch the cap, and run. Probably no mortal in the country was better fitted to attempt this policy, for Ben was so swift that, when in form, he could sometimes be running away before he started. At this instant, however, he felt sadly out of form, and he was convinced that as soon as he grabbed the cap Mr Lovelace would grab him!

And while this distressingly inadequate thinking was holding Ben static, Mr Lovelace suddenly became mobile, and advanced to the restaurant door with a brisk smile.

'You'll forgive me for intruding,' he said, 'but I'm afraid you'll have to give up that cap!'

The proprietor wheeled round and stared at him, while the whiskered man drew away sharply as though he had been shot at.

'I am afraid I overheard your conversation,' Mr Lovelace went on, 'so, you see, I know all about it.'

Then the proprietor found his voice.

'Well, s'pose you do?' he retorted. 'Does that make the cap out yours?'

'No, but it makes it common property.'

'Eh?'

'Come, come, you must understand me!' retorted the old man, sharply. 'A murder has been committed, and any evidence that will help to bring the murderer to justice must be produced—in the public interest! That's obvious to anyone, isn't it?'

The proprietor scowled, and the man with whiskers nodded anxiously.

'That's right, it's just what I was going to tell him,' he exclaimed. 'I was just saying, when you came along, that he ought to take it to the police.'

'Well, who says I ain't goin' to take it to the police?' snapped the proprietor. 'Yes, and who says they won't call me a mug for doing it? After all—'

'After all, your suspicions may be quite unfounded,' interposed Mr Lovelace, soothingly. 'Probably they are unfounded. Let me have a look at the cap.'

He advanced a step closer and held out his hand. Ben prepared to hurl himself forward without the slightest idea as to whether this would do any good or not. But the proprietor postponed the crisis by moving back a little and holding the cap behind him.

'Yes, but wait a minute!' he exclaimed, with sudden doubt in his eye. 'The cap won't tell you anything about whose face was under it, will it?'

Now Mr Lovelace frowned, while Ben wondered whether it would be possible to nip in and snatch the cap while it was behind the proprietor's back. The proprietor had his back towards Ben, but unfortunately the whiskered man was standing between.

'I'm only trying to help,' snapped Mr Lovelace.

'Well, p'r'aps I don't want any help,' answered the proprietor, and suddenly added, 'Yes, and if you got hold of the cap, you mightn't give it back again.'

'Well, I never!' muttered the whiskered man, shocked at the notion, and also at the proprietor for mentioning it.

'Why shouldn't I give it back to you?' demanded Mr Lovelace, indignantly.

'Maybe you've heard of that little reward, too!' grinned the proprietor. 'Anyhow, we'll soon settle the matter. I'll go off to the police this minute. There's a bobby round the corner.'

'No need to go as far as the corner, my man,' said Mr Lovelace, quickly.

'Why not?' blinked the proprietor.

'Because there happens to be a police official nearer than that.'

'Where?'

And the proprietor looked along the road. So did the man with the side-whiskers.

'Here,' said Mr Lovelace, quietly.

'Eh?' jerked the proprietor, bringing his focus back sharply. 'What—are—you—?'

'I am,' nodded the old man, now introducing a new note of authority into his voice. 'And, that being so, let me tell you that you will get into serious trouble if you don't hand that cap over at once. You ought to have done it before,' he went on severely, while the proprietor began to look worried, 'but I'll overlook that if you'll behave sensibly now and do exactly what I tell you.'

'And what *I've* been telling him all along,' interposed the whiskered man, endeavouring, apparently, to win official favour. 'Hand it over, Tom. Or shall I?'

'Shurrup!' growled the proprietor, snatching his hand away as the whiskered man advanced his. 'You speak when you're spoken to!' He turned to Mr Lovelace, suspicion not yet quelled. 'So I'm to 'and the cap over to you, eh?'

'Unless you prefer to do so under pressure?'

'Pressure be blowed! And what 'appens then?'

'You can leave that to me.'

'But won't you want my evidence?'

'Oh, certainly.'

'Then I'll come along with you to the station!'

'You seem exceedingly anxious to, all of a sudden!' observed Mr Lovelace, dryly.

'That's right, I am,' retorted the proprietor. 'I'm thinking of that reward, and I don't mind admitting it.'

'If there is any reward, you shall have it.'

'I'll see to that! Wait while I get my own cap, and we'll go along together.'

'Come, come, my man!' exclaimed Mr Lovelace, testily, 'are you running matters, or am I? We want this cap first, and we'll have your evidence afterwards. A detective will call on you—'

'Yes, and meanwhile you go off with the cap!' interrupted the proprietor warmly. 'I don't think. Let's see your ticket? Ain't you got a badge or something?' 'Ow do I know you're what you say you are? There's been tricks of that sort before, and I wasn't born last Sunday!'

The man with whiskers looked scandalised. Mr Lovelace looked black. Then, all at once, Mr Lovelace's expression changed, and it was impossible to describe it by any colour. It became variegated.

There was an electrical moment. The human kaleidoscope was in the process of violent, instantaneous transition. The whiskered man cried, 'What's up?' and ducked, though no blow threatened him. The proprietor stared at the old man with his mouth open, and then, as though somebody had clapped him on the side of his head, swung round. Ben held his breath, and felt as though he were standing naked in a lime-light.

'There he *is*,' said Mr Lovelace. His voice, to Ben, sounded a mile away. 'Seize him!'

The whiskered man sprayed forward, with arms wide. The proprietor leapt. As he did so, the cap dropped from his hand, and Mr Lovelace also leapt.

But so did Ben. Events were taken out of his hand, and the world had suddenly become simple again. There was nothing to decide. The problem was set. He simply had to see whether he could plough through it.

Before anyone knew he was moving he had hit the proprietor five times and the whiskered man twenty-two. Then he dived through the pieces and grabbed the cap. A strong, bony hand had already seized the other end of it.

The bony hand was stronger than his, and the mind that controlled it was keener, but when brain and brawn failed Ben summoned emotion to his aid, and he summoned it now. In a terrible red flash he visualised the bony hand throttling the life out of a fellow-creature, stuffing a rag in a girl's pretty mouth, and pouring drugs into a tea-pot. The hand looked white to others, but, to Ben, it was crimson. And, with his own free hand, he struck for all he was worth.

The blow went wide, for Mr Lovelace was no novice and ducked; but it shot Ben forward off his feet, and since he still held grimly on to his side of the cap it also jerked his antagonist off his feet, for his antagonist was holding on to his side of the cap with equal grimness.

Ben was the first to rise. He saw, through a mist, two figures leaping towards him, one big, the other small. He received eight blows and gave eighteen. Then, after a spell of confusion which was rendered wholly unintelligible by bright lights and dark dots and whirling limbs and millions of shouts, Ben discovered himself erect, with his own limbs moving very rapidly—when he counted he found he had all four of them—and the streets of London flying past him backwards at a pace they had never known before.

'I b'leeve I'm runnin',' he told himself.

23

Ben versus London

By all the rules of logic Ben should have been caught. A crowd had begun to collect outside the restaurant before he shot away from it and some of the new arrivals loomed up as obstacles. One man indeed succeeded in tripping him up and making a grab at him, 'but before I could lay hold of the fellow,' this would-be captor explained subsequently to a policeman, 'he'd rolled through my legs like a barrel! Talk about quick! This wasn't a man at all, it was a bullet!'

Three blocks away, a motorist was arriving at the same conclusion. The bullet leapt into the back seat, was carried thirty yards, and then leapt out again.

'Catch him!' shouted someone.

'Who? Where?' cried the motorist.

Nobody knew who and nobody knew where. Ben only had the foggiest notion himself.

And so, by dizzy ducking and impossible twisting and outrageous behaviour generally, Ben confounded logic and knocked the bottom out of the Einstein Theory, pulling up at last as he emerged from a by-street into a crowded, congested thoroughfare.

The crowd, with a blessedness unusual in his experience, swallowed him up. Unconsciously it directed his course and afforded him protection. It bore him to a bridge under which the Thames ran darkly. Ben found himself elbowed near the parapet. He squinted over.

Mist, wraith-like, curled over the surface. It had a queer fascination. A quick little jump, and there would be no more chasing of Ben in this world! Yes, but what about the next world? Ben jerked his head back again. If one had to be chased, it was better to be chased by solid matter. Even Mr Lovelace was preferable to a horned individual with a tail!

As he jerked his head back something fell from it and began to descend over the bridge. He caught it in mid-air. It was his cap.

He made his way from the parapet to the curb, striking a forward diagonal course and advancing like a bishop on a chess-board. When he reached the curb he jumped on to a bus. The conductor stared at him and he jumped off again.

Above him towered the Houses of Parliament. In spite of his need to keep moving he paused for a few moments to gaze up at the impressive building. He didn't know why he paused, yet he felt there was some reason. What had he to do with the edifice from which came the nation's laws—those laws he always seemed unwittingly to be breaking? Then, all at once, the reason came to him, and he knew why he had paused. It was a sort of salutation from one poster to another!

'That's it!' he murmured. 'Me and Medway!'

The sailor and the statesman, bound together by an

invisible thread, and unconsciously drawing closer and closer each moment!

And then another thought flashed into the humbler man's head, emphasising the association in a more whimsical way.

'Big Ben and Little Ben! Well, I'll be blowed!'

A policeman eyed him. Ben was born to be eyed. He could never stand long in a London street without becoming what he'd heard was called a cynosher. He jumped on another bus with 'Mansion House' written upon it.

As he sank into his seat, two passengers in front of him were conversing eagerly. The backs of their heads bobbed and wagged as though they were on wires.

'Somewhere near Waterloo, so I've heard,' said one.

'That's right,' nodded the other. 'I saw the crowd as I went by.'

'Tork abart famous!' groaned Ben. 'I'm orl hover Lunnon!'

Which being the case, what was the use of getting out of the bus again? He'd only bump into himself somewhere else! Nevertheless he kept a sharp eye on the backs of the two heads, and was ready for a fresh bunk the moment they ceased to be backs and became fronts.

'What, were *you* there?' exclaimed the first head. And added, when the second head nodded, 'Did you see him?'

'Only a glimpse,' replied the second.

'Fare, please,' said the conductor.

'What was he like?'

'Smallish chap—'

'Fare, *please!*' repeated the conductor.

'Eh?' muttered Ben. It was his fare the conductor was requesting. 'Oh! I'm jest gettin' out.'

'Just getting out?' frowned the conductor. 'Why, you've only just got in!'

'So I 'ave,' murmured Ben. 'I was thinkin' o' the last bus.'

The second head was saying,

'No, I don't *think* he had a moustache.'

'Beard, then?' exclaimed the first head. 'I'd like his description. What about a beard?'

The conductor began to grow impatient.

'Where *to*?' he demanded.

While Ben had trouble with his throat, the second head went on,

'Well, he was a bit grubby about the lower portion of his face. Yes, he could certainly have done with a shave.'

The conductor regarded Ben's chin.

'How about his eyes?'

Now the conductor regarded Ben's eyes. Ben closed them and said,

''Ammersmith.'

'Hammersmith? We don't go to Hammersmith!' retorted the conductor, sharply.

And before he could say any more, Ben replied, 'Oh, doncher?' rose rapidly, and jumped out.

He walked to the Mansion House. Waterloo would have been quicker, but he was giving Waterloo a wide, wide berth.

He preferred streets to conveyances. In conveyances you were packed too close, like. At the Mansion House station, however, he had to risk another conveyance, and he took his seat in the Southfields train wondering which of his fellow-passengers would start talking about him this time. For a change, none of them did. Of the four in his immediate vicinity, one was asleep, another was doing a crossword puzzle, while the third and the fourth were discussing the best way to make an omelette. He reached Southfields without any further shocks.

But at Southfields, after alighting, he received a bad one. Just as the train was beginning to move on again the man who was doing crosswords looked up from his paper, having caught sight of something out of the corner of his eye.

'Hey, don't you want this?' he cried.

'Lummy!' gasped Ben.

And watched, with a sick feeling, his cap come sailing out of the window. Another second and it would have been lost for ever!

He made a grab at it, but a young porter was before him.

'Now that'll just suit me nice!' grinned the porter, and removing his own cap he stuck Ben's on his head.

''Ere! Give it hover!' muttered Ben, not in a mood for play.

'Let's see your name inside it first!' replied the porter, irritatingly. 'I want to know if it's Rockefeller or Ivor Novello!'

He took the cap off and, turning it over, began examining the lining.

'Oi!' protested Ben.

'Hallo! Shop in Southampton—' began the porter.

But the next moment the cap was snatched from him, and the owner was beating a rapid and indignant retreat.

'Well, I'm blowed!' exclaimed the porter. And, all at once, repeated 'Southampton' and whistled.

Before the porter whistled, however, Ben was outside the station, eagerly scanning faces.

He scanned in vain. The face he desired to see was not there. Depression seized him. He had expected this moment to mark the end of his troubles, but now responsibility descended upon him with all its arduous demands upon his brain. Something had gone wrong somewhere, and it was up to him to find out what it was.

Impossible to make inquiries. Inquiries would invite publicity, and publicity was a thing to be avoided. Yonder paper man could probably tell him whether a small, attractive girl had been hanging around here during the past hour or two, but it would be folly to ask him. It was folly to hang around oneself! That fresh young porter had been mighty curious. He'd seen 'Southampton' inside the cap. S'pose he popped out, and brought the station-master with him?

Ben crossed the road, and continued his miserable thoughts a little farther away from the station. Now, then! Get your mind on to it! The position was—Molly wasn't here. The question was—where was she?

He tried to visualise her actions after he had left her, but all he visualised was a fog. He supposed she had got out of the window and had found a policeman—probably the policeman he had passed in the taxi just beyond the pillar-box—but what after that? What had she told the policeman? Yes, lummy, what *had* she told him? That an old man had killed somebody at his house, and that the old man had then bound her up in a chair, and that the old man had then gone to Waterloo to try and get a cap, and that while he was still gone he had come back again and stuck the person he had killed up the chimney?

And then the policeman would ask:

'Who is this dead man?'

And she would reply:

'I don't know.'

And he would ask:

'Who stuck him up the chimney?'

And she would reply:

'I don't know.'

And he would ask:

'What did the old man want the cap for?'

And she would reply:

'I don't know.'

And he would ask:

'Why did you go to the old man's house?'

And she would reply:

'I don't know.'

And he would ask, and this would be a particularly nasty one:

'If the old man was at Waterloo and you can't say who else was in the house, or if anybody was in the house, who untied you?'

And she would reply:

'I don't know!'

It was a lot not to know! Yet how, if she gave any other answers, was she going to keep Ben out of it? In fact, *could* she keep Ben out of it? And *had* she?

For the first time Ben wondered whether, after all, Molly's plan had been a good one, and whether he himself had not been remiss in trusting to a tired brain. But she had been so dominating, all of a sudden, and *his* brain was tired, too. P'r'aps her idea was just to shout at the policeman, 'Hi! Go to Greystones, there's a deader up the chimney!' and then run. The policeman couldn't run two ways at once, so he'd run to the deader while she ran to Southfields . . .

'Yus, but she *ain't* at Sarthfields!' thought Ben, desperately. 'If that's wot she meant ter do, she ain't done it! So wot's she done?'

The answer shot out of a shadow.

'Is your name Ben?' piped a small boy.

Ben eyed the urchin with disfavour as he retorted, 'S'pose it was?'

'Well, if it was,' said the urchin, 'the lidy sed you was ter go back again to the 'ouse at once. She wants yer.'

24

Back to Horror House

Back to the house again! At once! Lummy!

Back to the house where every second was a shriek and every moment a murder! Back to the house which, bad enough in a white mist, would now be enshrouded by black night, with the ghosts of a dead dog in a corner and a dead man in a chimney creeping from their corporeal sources and making the stairs creak with invisible feet, while a clock that had lost its rhythm ticked jerkily . . . no, the clock had stopped . . .

'Oi!' called Ben.

He shot out his hand several seconds late. The urchin, having delivered his message and earned, presumably, his ounce of sweets, had disappeared. The urchin was not working overtime.

So that was it, was it? Molly was still at Greystones, in the middle of Wimbledon Common! She'd gone away from it and gone back to it, or she'd never gone away from it at all. But whichever it was, she was there now, at this moment, and had summoned Ben to join her.

And, however ominous the summons, it was not one that could be evaded.

Yus, thought Saint George in rags, but what had kept her there, or taken her back there? He had the cap. There was nothing left to do now but to run away with it to Sahara, bury it, and see what came up!

Someone emerged from Southfields Station, and began glancing about. Ben recognised him, even at this distance. It was the fool of a young porter. He also recognised the manner in which the porter's head was twisting from right to left and then from left to right. It was what he called the looking-for-me twist, and half the world suffered from the complaint. As a second figure emerged from the station, a larger, stouter figure, and caught the disease, Ben decided that Southfields was not the place to live in, and he vanished from the team of head-twisters as suddenly and as rapidly as, a few moments earlier, the urchin had vanished from him.

Having eliminated himself from Southfields Station, his next job was to impress himself upon Wimbledon Common. Should he walk? He did not know the way. Should he inquire the way? That, again, presented difficulties. His enemies were increasing so alarmingly that, ten to one, the person of whom he inquired the way would already be inquiring for him!

'And then 'ow long 'll it tike ter walk?' was another argument against Shanks's pony. 'She's waitin' fer me, ain't she? Countin' the minits, p'r'aps! 'Ere 'e is—no, 'e ain't—yus, 'ere 'e is—yus, no, e' ain't!' Ben knew the sort of thing. It knocked the bottom out of a hippopotamus.

Taxi, then? Like he'd done before? That was an idea. But where was a taxi? And by this time wouldn't all the taximen have been warned?

'Corse, wot I really want,' decided Ben, hopelessly, 'is a hinvisible hairyplane!'

Then the next best thing came along. A hooded van, with Wimbledon Common written big on the hood, and the back open. And a rope, too, which hung from the top of the hood at the back. That rope was asking for it!

Like the monkey that he almost was, Ben seized the rope and swung up. Darkness happily concealed the manœuvre. In a couple of seconds he was lying in the rear of the van, beginning a free ride towards his goal.

Here was a bit of luck! The first he had struck since about the reign of Richard III. It was unlikely that the van would take him right to the gate of Greystones, but it would deposit him somewhere on the Common, and he could conclude the journey on foot when he felt the Common around him. There was no difficulty in recognising the feel of Wimbledon Common. It clawed at you.

An unpleasant thought marred the start of the journey. The van might be on an outward trip! But this was the time for homeward journeys, and as buildings grew less and open spaces grew more, he felt convinced that he was going the right way. The district was becoming distinctly commonish.

He raised his chin and took a squint at the unconscious driver's back. It was a large back. It would be. And beside it, he suddenly noticed, was a second back. A larger back. It would be. He hoped they wouldn't talk. If they talked, he knew what they would talk about!

Lummy! They were starting!

'What's the latest, Ted?' asked the driver.

Now they were off! But evidently Ted didn't read his paper, for he replied,

'What about?'

'Waterloo Road,' said the driver.

'Oh!' exclaimed Ted, waking up. 'Twins!'

And they all three laughed.

Then one of the three stopped laughing.

'Did you fix things up at the back?' inquired the driver.

'Not yet, I 'aven't,' answered Ted.

'Well, what are you going to do about it?'

'Tell 'im that if 'e don't stop practising 'is cornet, I'll take up the violin!'

Then they all three laughed again. But the full beauty of the joke did not descend upon the third until the other two had almost stopped, and the hysterical cackle he emitted echoed through the hood.

''Allo! Chicken got in or something?' exclaimed Ted, and looked back over his shoulder.

There was no time to retreat. Ben was discovered. Even while he was realising it, Ted demanded, with ominous sarcasm,

''Aving a ride at the Company's expense?'

'That's right,' murmured Ben. 'Got a fag?'

The ghost of a French aristocrat who had joked on the scaffold smiled approvingly. Even the more solid substance of Ted was momentarily softened. He turned to the driver and cried,

''Ere, stop and look at this!'

The van stopped. Ben prepared to jump out. To his surprise, however, the driver did not shout at him when he turned round. He stared, and then suddenly smiled.

'Where've you taken your ticket to?' inquired the driver.

'Nowhere pertickler,' answered Ben, warily.

'I see. Anywhere will do?'

'That's right—s'long as the scenery's pretty.'

'Oh! Well, how will Wimbledon Common suit you?'

'Wimbledon Common? That's my idea of 'Eaven!'

'Good! Then sit tight, mate, and we'll take you there! Always willin' to oblige!'

After which surprising conversation, the driver turned round again, glanced at his companion, and let in the clutch.

The friendly interchange and the absence of anger ought to have cheered Ben, but it did not. It had been too friendly, and the anger had been too notably absent. Had he just happened to strike the world's prize Christians, or was there any more to it?

It very soon dawned upon him that there was more to it. The driver and Ted exchanged a number of glances—Ben was watching their heads earnestly for signs—and once Ted was about to say something, but the driver shook his head as though to silence him. Then Ted glanced back, and the driver again shook his head. He seemed to be annoyed with Ted. Why shouldn't Ted have looked back?

Another thing. They weren't talking any more. Another thing, they were going very fast—much faster than they had been going before. Another thing, Ted took an evening paper from his pocket and began to study it under a light, till the driver knocked it out of his hand. Another thing, there was a bit of Wimbledon Common on their left, and they were turning to the right.

Ben's uneasiness grew. 'They're on ter me!' he thought. 'Yus, and they're tryin' ter keep me quiet, like—till they gits ter the police stashun!'

Could he leap out at this speed? Not a chance! But ahead

was another van, and it was going slowly, and it was sticking to the middle of the road.

'Gawd's above if it don't budge!' prayed Ben.

It didn't budge. Despite hoots and toots, it kept to the middle of the road, and Ben's driver had to slow up with a sudden application of brakes. Ben leapt.

He aimed for a bush and hit it. As it closed over him he felt as though he were in the middle of a porcupine's stomach, but he didn't move, although every separate portion of him was screaming to.

He heard the van stop. He heard cries of 'Where's he gone?' and 'Well, I'm blowed!' He heard feet tramping around. He heard others cursing the darkness that he blessed.

The darkness helped to save him, but he owed his escape to two other factors, as well. The first was that the driver had underestimated Ben's leaping power—who but the original fool would have leapt from a car like that?—and the second was that nobody but Ben could have remained both alive and silent inside a porcupine's stomach.

At last they gave up. Ben heard one saying, as they climbed back into the van,

'You know, I believe you were wrong—I don't believe it was the fellow at all!'

'Then why did 'e jump out, eh?' retorted the other. 'If on'y you'd stayed still and not kep' looking back, we'd have got 'im.'

'Well, 'e's gone, anyway.'

'Jest the same, I'll report 'im!'

Then the van moved away, and the voices were heard no more.

Forgetting himself, Ben took a deep breath of relief. Previously he had been taking little breaths, because breathing pricked, and his relief produced several serious punctures. They were so serious that he bounded out of the bush as startlingly as he had bounded in, and if an old woman with a weak heart had been passing at that moment she would have died on the spot.

Ben lay limply for a minute or two. He wasn't feeling very well. Then three words whipped him to his feet. '*She wants yer!*' Lummy, and here he was, lying down like a mug, and wasting time!

He turned back along the road, wandered vaguely for a few minutes, and leaned against a pillar-box to rest. It's all very well, but you can't get your breath back all at once without a little help. He stared dully ahead of him. A light glimmered down from somewhere. Lamppost, eh? It glimmered on two words a few feet off . . .

'*North Lane.*'

'Strewth! Here he was!

He left the pillar-box, and staggered along the road he had last traversed in a mist. Thin wisps of white still hung about, making queer shapes in the blackness. They looked like lost souls in a world of giant trees. 'P'r'aps I'll be one of 'em one day,' thought Ben.

The lane twisted and turned. Ben didn't meet many lanes that went nice and straight. He wandered along in a sort of dream, till all at once Reality gripped him and he came to the gate.

He stopped dead and gulped. If Molly had not been somewhere on the other side of the gate he could never have brought himself to pass through it. His one consolation was that in all probability Mr Lovelace would still be away, looking for him in London. But, of course, Mr Lovelace would return . . .

He opened the gate cautiously, and entered the horrible garden. 'Corse,' he consoled himself, 'it 'elps ter know wot 'Ell's like afore'and.' His boot made a deafening crunch on the gravel. He leapt on to the grass. Then he took another leap off the grass, recalling what he had encountered there last time.

'I wunner why I 'ave ter do this sort o' thing?' he queried within himself. 'I ain't really good at it.'

Feeling now for the edge of the grass, he regained its soft protection. Slowly he crept forward, following the edge's contours. Soon he came round a bend and saw the dark, gloomy building where he was to meet fresh adventures not encountered in polite society. The grass ran away from him. Now he would have to cross gravel again, to reach the building.

No light showed anywhere. Was it, after all, empty? He tiptoed forward. His toes were ready to kick, his knuckles to hit, his fingers to scratch, and his teeth to bite. Every bit of his anatomy was ready to do all it could in defence of every other bit . . .

He reached the building. There, ahead of him, loomed the door. What secret lurked behind? While he stared, something creaked above him. A window was opening.

25

Played in the Darkness

Wrenching his eyes from the door to the window, Ben looked up. Then followed five seconds of such breathless happenings that he did not know they had begun before they were over.

A dim face appeared at the window. Since there was light neither inside nor outside it was impossible, at the first rapid glance, to distinguish anything about the face beyond the fact that it was a face; but when a voice called softly, identity was established. The dim face at the open window was Molly's.

There was no time for expression of gratitude at this revelation, however. The voice was pregnant with acute urgency. For a moment only the urgency descended to him, accompanied by the swift knowledge that he had to do something mighty quickly, yet without any idea of what it was. He stared up with his mouth open, whereupon the voice descended to him again, this time reaching his brain— via, assumedly, the open mouth, which was the only portion of him actively receptive.

'Cap!' called the voice. One point above a whisper.

'Yus!' Ben whispered back.

'Cap!' repeated the voice.

'On me 'ead!' replied Ben.

'Throw it! Quick! Quick! Oh, my God!'

He seized it and threw it. He didn't understand. It sailed upwards, a hand shot out, the cap vanished, the window closed. And then something began to happen lower down. He saw it out of the bottom corner of his eye. The front-door was beginning to open.

He ceased to look at the window. He looked now at the front-door. A blackness blacker than black widened before him. At first a narrow, vertical slit, it grew into a tall, broad space, and he knew he was expected to walk through the space.

There are times when stronger men than Ben cease to function on their own initiative. A tide catches them, and they go where the tide wills. Ben now functioned in complete obedience to the black space that beckoned him when the door, half-open, paused.

'Come in,' said the space.

'I don't want ter,' replied the space in Ben.

'Come in,' said the space.

'Ain't you a darlin'?' replied the space in Ben.

He felt himself moving forward. He pretended he was standing still. 'You know—like a trine in a stashun, when it's the hother trine wot's movin',' he explained to himself. (It was probable that, on his death-bed, he would quietly argue about it.) Now he was off the gravel and on to the low stone step. Bushes on either side of the porch advanced, seeming to curve round him and cut off the garden behind. 'Well, I don't like the garden, do I?' he thought. 'So that's orl right!' Now he had reached the door, and was beginning to pass into the tall, wide space that was blacker than black.

'Funny!' he reflected. 'I don't seem ter be doin' anythink. I wunner wot's mikin' me go?'

The position was so atrocious that one simply had to pretend it wasn't there.

'That was a nice day,' thought Ben, 'when I was a little boy and went fishin' in the Welsh 'arp with a bent pin.'

Now he was in the middle of the gap.

'Corse, I didn't catch nothink.'

Now he was right in.

'Barrin' weeds.'

Now the front door was closing behind him.

'I know wot it is,' he thought. 'I'm bein' mesmeridged.'

Yes, that must be it. A hand was descending on the top of his head.

Then, all at once, the fingers of the hand spread out in a sort of a spasm, and under the indignation of the fingers Ben woke up. He gave a jump, but the fingers flashed from his head to his arm, and held him in a fierce grip.

'The cap!' hissed a voice. 'Say where it is!'

It was Don Diablo's voice.

Even in the confusion of the moment and the pressing darkness, Ben began to understand. These fingers had been waiting to seize his cap. It was for his cap that the door had opened! But, above, a mind even cleverer had secured the cap, and had seen that Ben entered the house without it.

'Where? Where?' repeated the Spaniard's voice, while the fingers dug into Ben's arm like claws.

206

'Wot cap?' muttered Ben, thinking hard. Or trying to think hard. He didn't know which.

'You went for it—'

'Go on!'

A hand struck Ben's mouth savagely.

'I know! I hear! You think me fool? Say where, or—' The hand struck Ben's mouth again.

He knew and he'd *heard*, eh? Then it was this Spaniard who'd been in the house after Lovelace had left it? This darned skunk who'd been creeping about the place, and listening outside doors, and—and—cutting off retreats by shoving corpses up chimneys? And who'd waited for Ben to return, expecting to pounce on him the moment he got back and seize the cap from his head!

'Well, I ain't got it, see?' cried Ben, trying unsuccessfully to free his arm.

'That is a lie!' retorted the Spaniard.

'Orl right! Search me! Yus, and wot's wrong with a light while yer doin' it?'

The search materialised, though the light did not. Ben learned the reason later. He felt fingers prodding all over him like large electric needles.

'Easy in the sarth-west!' he muttered. 'That's where I'm ticklish.'

A blow in the north-east silenced him.

The search was fruitless. It may be noted that it omitted Ben's left boot. Through the depressing darkness the Spaniard spoke again.

'Then where is it?' he demanded, standing very close. Ben felt his breath on the top of his head, and wished the cap had been there to protect it.

'On Moosolini!' he growled.

'Say!'

''Ow can I?'

He could, but he wasn't going to!

'Dios! But you went for it!'

'Yus, you 'eard that, didn't yer, yer heaves-droppin' Nosey Parker!' Then the solution dawned upon him. 'Well, if you 'eard that, yer must 'ave 'eard somethink helse! Yer must 'ave 'eard as 'ow that hother bloke, Lovelice 'is nime is, gone arter the cap, too. Orl right, then. We both goes arter it, but we can't both git it, can we? Orl right, then. He starts fust, and 'e got there fust, and 'e got the cap fust. Orl right, then. *Now* are yer satisfied?'

There was a silence, while the Spaniard considered the story. In the silence Ben heard the clock. It was ticking again . . .

'So! He got it?' murmured the Spaniard, softly.

'Yus!'

'And—he will return here?'

'Yus! Well, 'ow do I know?'

'But *I* know!'

'You know a lot!'

'Oh, yes!' In the blackness Ben felt Don Diablo smiling. 'I know that *you* return!'

'Didjer?'

'Oh, yes.'

''Ow didjer know?' inquired Ben, with sudden curiosity.

'Because I send for you,' answered the Spaniard, and Ben felt the Spaniard's smile expanding. 'A little boy, eh? Who go to Southfield—I hear that, too—and say the lady sent him. But *I* sent him. And then I know you will come! The so brave Inglis!'

The information rendered Ben speechless. He gulped. Speech may come and speech may go, but gulps go on for ever. Meanwhile the Spaniard went on.

'Yes, you come. And you stay. You stay till Signor Lovelace come. He will have the cap, eh? Perhaps! But if he have not the cap—then, again, I search you! Compreno?'

Ben comprenoed. He comprenoed that Molly might then be searched, too. Lummy, he must put this Spanish devil off the track of Molly . . . 'Yus, and I know 'ow ter do it!' he suddenly thought.

'Look 'ere, yer dirty bit o' Europe, you!' he muttered. 'Yer bit o' the map that ain't wanted! If Molly—if the gal didn't send me that there messidge, wot 'ave yer done with 'er? She ain't still 'ere, is she?'

Not bad, that, for a simple sailor!

'You do not know where she is?' queried the Spaniard.

'Yus, I'll tell yer where she is,' retorted Ben, continuing with his subtlety. 'She's at a pleece stishun—yer don't seem ter 'ave 'eard *that*—and in a cupple o' ticks she'll be 'ere with the 'ole of Scotland Yard!'

It was a good move. If Don Diablo believed that Ben imagined Molly out of the house, the idea that Ben had seen her at the window and had passed his cap on to her could not occur to him. Anxiously Ben waited for confirmation that his ruse had been successful. He had to wait for several seconds. At the end of them the Spaniard said:

'Well, well, I must risk your Scotland Yard. Perhaps—who knows?—Scotland Yard is too busy. Or—perhaps—she is not there, eh? Now, please, come!'

'Come?' exclaimed Ben. 'Where?'

'You see, when I show you.'

'If yer don't switch on a light I shan't see nothink.'

'Light? But there is no light! Watch!'

With his free hand—the other was still holding Ben—the Spaniard stretched towards the hall switch. Ben heard the click that should have preceded a flood of illumination. There was no illumination. The click was repeated several times. The hall remained in darkness.

'Signor Lovelace, he very careful of his lights,' said the Spaniard. 'He turn all off somewhere, before he go. Well, what matters? I receive him in the dark just as well—like I receive you, eh? And, now—come, Signor Ben! It is time to—how is it said—put you away.'

'Yus, but I got a few questions ter ask afore yer put me away!' cried Ben. 'Wotcher *want* the blinkin' cap for, any'ow?'

Don Diablo did not reply. Instead, he propelled Ben towards the back of the hall. Ben knew it was towards the back of the hall because he heard the clock ticking louder as they advanced.

'Is the cap wotcher left yer 'appy 'ome for?'

They reached the stairs.

'Is it wot yer follered that chap White for?'

They were mounting the stairs. The clock was ticking very loudly now.

'Is it wot yer *killed* White for?'

They paused. They were on the wide half-landing, and the clock was ticking more loudly still. He'd never heard it so loud before! Lummy—the case was open!

'So! I killed White?' murmured the Spaniard. 'You think that, eh? You think too much, Signor Ben! It is quite time—yes—that you were put away!'

Then a comet bounded out of the sky and struck Ben. And, a moment later, the clock was closed again and the pendulum had ceased to tick.

But Ben did not know this, for the simple reason that he did not know anything.

26

The Cap's Secret

During the rare and peaceful moments of his life Ben sometimes amused himself, to dissipate the dullness of comfort, by thinking of all the unusual places he had been in. These included a well, a coal-bunker, a coffin, seventeen cupboards (but they were nothing), a couple of dozen cellars, a Spanish garret, a precipice (hanging over, head downwards), a ship's side (hanging over, head downwards), the world's prickliest bush, and two or three thousand other specially selected locations.

'But 'ave I hever bin dahn a drine-pipe?' he asked himself during his last inventory. He thought hard. 'That's funny! I've never bin dahn a drine-pipe!' For such a far-travelled man, it was almost humiliating.

Doubtless the drain-pipe would come, and a waterfall, and an oven. Meanwhile, though for a considerable time he was quite unconscious of the fact, he was now adding the inside of a grandfather clock to the catalogue.

Tucked away inside the clock, he presented a double anomaly. It was anomalous that he should be in the clock at all, and it was anomalous that he should be both so close to time and yet so far away from it. But time had stopped in the clock as well as in Ben, and both stayed stationary as the seconds and the minutes flowed heedlessly by outside them.

The blow that had knocked Ben senseless had been a particularly vicious one. 'I almost felt it,' Ben said, later. "'E'd mike 'is forchune at hox-killin'.' He slid down limply beside the harassed pendulum, and was not even conscious that, after a fit of indignant trembling, the pendulum came to roost in his open mouth and acted as a stopper.

It is possible that this pendulum saved Ben's life. Your own years of joy or of sorrow may be due to some tiny inanimate cause. A button has won a war by stopping a bullet, and now the pendulum may have preserved Ben for his war, as yet unwon, by stopping his mouth. For when your mouth is stopped, what happens?

Nothing, if you are utterly, utterly unconscious, and still possess your nose. Nothing, if you gradually return to consciousness, and your nose still functions. But a nose in a clock collects the dust of ages, and becomes, at last, oppressed. Then it protests—quietly at first, loudly subsequently—and calls upon the stopped mouth to help it.

That is exactly what happened to Ben. For a while he lay uncomplainingly where Don Pasquali had put him. During this period he raced five two-headed lions, spanked a star for getting in his way, and exploded on to the throne of England, from which he immediately gave an order for a large plate of gooseberry tart. Then everything faded into the Great Blackness out of which it had sprung, and the Great Blackness was replaced by a Great Greyness—the greyness that faintly colours the borders of consciousness.

Into this greyness grew a ticking. Time coming back, eh?

Ben was not in a condition to explore the theory, but we, who are, can prove its fallacy. The pendulum was not ticking, although it was the cause of the sound. Ben's nose was ticking.

Outside, in the hall, someone heard it. But a sound so much more ominous had recently preceded this new ticking—the sound of a dead body falling plop on to a floor—that for several moments only the echo of that horrible plop filled the listener's ears.

Then, as the front-door was reached, the ticking claimed attention, and the listener paused, hand on door-knob.

Was it the clock? Surely not! The clock had stopped again.

'Click! Click!' Pause. 'Click! Click!' Pause. 'Click-click!'

Click, not tick. Clocks went tick. What went click?

The figure by the door, revolving this theory, delayed departure. The clicking went on. It was the only sound in the silent, gloomy house. It came, obviously, from the staircase. It might be a rat or something. A board creaking. A window-frame rattling. Not that it really sounded like any of these things . . . but what else *could* it be?

Suddenly the clicking changed in character. It became more violent. It wheezed. It whistled. It choked.

With a gulp, the figure darted from the door. Across the hall, and up the stairs. The figure was almost sobbing. As it reached the turn at the half-landing it stopped, clutching the bannisters.

'Kerchaw-wahgug! Click-click!' said the clock.

In a trice the case was open, and Ben was falling out of it into Molly's arms.

'Ben!' she murmured. 'Ben! Ben!'

There was nothing else to say. She lowered the spluttering form, easing it to the ground with a strength that seemed impossible from one so frail and frightened. The form became still, and she bent over it in agony.

'Ben!' she whispered, close to his face. 'Ben!'

''Sall right,' came the very faint response. 'Don't worry. I'm dead.'

She shook him gently.

'Oi!' protested the form, feebly. ''Eaven's rockin'!'

Heaven ceased to rock. It now began to pat. This seemed to be more welcome to its temporary inmate. But he still rebelled.

'Git away, Noah!' he gasped. 'I got somethink helse ter do yet! I'm goin' ter jump!'

There was a terrible convulsion on the floor. Molly jumped, too, as the form rose galvanically to a sitting posture.

''Old me,' said Ben, and lay down again.

A minute went by. Then Ben spoke again. His eyes were tightly closed.

'Is that you, Molly?' he asked.

'Yes, Ben,' she answered.

'Let's feel a bit of yer!'

She touched his face with her hand.

'Lummy, that's nice, that is,' murmured Ben. 'Keep it there. Funny, ain't it?'

She kept it there. Another minute went by. Then Ben sat up a second time. Now his eyes were open.

''E must 'ave give me a crack,' he said. 'Oi! Where are yer?'

'Here,' she replied, touching him again. 'Take it easy. There's plenty of time.'

She didn't think there was, but for the moment she had to pretend it.

'Ain't there a light?' murmured Ben. 'This dark's fair gettin' on me nerves!'

'Mr Lovelace switched them off before he went out,' she told him.

The name whipped his sluggish mind.

'Lovelice! That's right. That's wot the Spaniard ses. Oi!'

'What?'

''As Lovelice come back yet?'

'No.'

'Wot abart the other chap? Don Diablo?'

'He's gone out.'

'Wot for?'

'I don't know. Perhaps—'

'Wot?'

'Perhaps he's gone to wait for Mr Lovelace at the gate, or in the lane.'

'Wot! Leavin' us two 'ere?'

'But he thinks you're safe in—in the clock,' she pointed out.

'One day I'll mike 'im sife in the clock!' growled Ben. 'Yer know, I'm torkin', but I feel sick.'

'Perhaps you'd better not talk?'

'No, I gotter tork. Me marth keeps me mind orf me stummick, like. Besides, miss—Molly—I gotter know wot's 'appened. Wot abart you? *I* was in the clock, but *you* wasn't. You—'

'I was locked in the room upstairs, so he thought I was just as helpless. If he couldn't get in, I couldn't get out.'

'Oi! Is that a shadder dahn there?'

'Where?'

'Now it's movin'! Oi!'

'Nothing's there, Ben!'

'No more it ain't. It was you. Yer seem ter keep bobbin' abart, like. Fust a mile orf and then a hinch. Yer know, bein' a penjulump tikes some gettin' uster. Where was we? Oh, yer couldn't git aht of the room hupstairs. Well, 'ow *did* yer git aht?'

'That doesn't matter—'

'I wanter 'ear!'

'All right. But—we ought to be going.'

'So we ought.'

He jumped to his feet like a rocket and fell down again. 'That's funny,' he reflected. 'Me joints 'ave gorn orl jelly.'

He felt Molly's arm under his neck. He had never been happier and more wretched in the whole of his existence. Queer, how life mixed it. In his ear Molly's voice whispered.

'Lie still! Don't try to move any more. Wait till you know you can.'

''Fraid I gotter wait,' he muttered. 'But—look 'ere! You better pop orf!'

'You say some funny things sometimes, Ben,' answered Molly, 'but that's about the funniest I've heard! Me pop off? And leave you here? Off your nut, Ben, aren't you?' She changed the conversation quickly and determinedly, reverting to her interrupted story. 'I got out down the chimney, Ben. I broke a chair up till I got a long, narrow bit and—shoved.' She shuddered. 'Then I went over the whole house trying to find you.'

'Go on!'

'I'd just given you up—I thought Pasquali must have

217

taken you out with him or something—when I heard you in the clock.'

'Go on!'

'And thank God I did! Just think, Ben! If I hadn't—'

'I vote we *don't* think,' he suggested. 'Wot I wanter know is 'ow you knew Don Diablo 'ad gorn?'

'I heard him close the front-door, though he did it ever so softly.'

'Not like the bang 'e give that hother time?'

'No, Ben. He meant us to hear the other time—and that's how I got caught.'

'Wotcher mean?'

'Why, he never left at all that other time. It was just a trick. I don't know whether he let you get away on purpose or not, but when I began to get out of the window—you remember, I gave you five minutes start—he was standing at the bottom!'

'Lummy!'

'Yes, it was lummy! He meant to nab me as I got to the ground. But I just spotted him in time, and nipped back as he got hold of the rope and tugged.'

''E might 'ave killed yer!' gasped Ben, indignantly.

'He might,' Molly nodded, 'but life's full of might's. He didn't kill me. He got the rope, though—and so, just now, there was only the chimney left. Ugh! That was the nastiest job *I've* ever tackled.'

'Yer know,' said Ben, 'wot I'm livin' for is ter put '*im* up the chimney.'

'And what *I'm* living for is to get miles away from it!' retorted Molly. 'How do you feel?'

'Like a bit o' skin rahnd a jig-saw.'

'Do you think you can move?'

'Yus, with a bit of 'elp. Funny, it was you larst time, wasn't it? We're takin' turns.' He had been lying flat. Now he sat up shakily. "'Allo—I've jest thort o' somethink. I fahnd a match in the trine comin' back. A 'ole one. It's in me pocket. Let's 'ave a light.'

He fished for the match, and discovered it. He struck it. The light flickered on Molly, and he stared at her.

'Trouble's good fer you, ain't it?' he said. 'Yer've filled out in front, like!'

Molly glanced down at her increased figure, and the matchlight played upon her smile.

'That's not me, Ben,' she answered. 'That's your cap.'

'Blimy, I'd fergot orl abart that!' exclaimed Ben.

'I haven't, Ben,' replied Molly, the smile now vanished. 'I've found out what they're after.'

'Go on!'

'Yes, Ben. In the lining. A letter. I expect that man White put it there before he passed the cap on to you—'

'Fer me ter pass on ter Lovelice!' blinked Ben. 'Well—of orl the sorce—'

He felt Molly's warm breath suddenly on his fingers. She had blown out the match.

'Quick!' she whispered, seizing his arm. 'Someone's coming!'

27

Blade Against Bullet

The words were barely out of Molly's mouth before there was a definite sound at the front-door. A second later the staircase was empty, and the two late occupants were in the darkness of the upper landing.

The front-door opened. They heard it open, but they did not hear it close. Someone entered. They knew the hall towards the staircase, and they prepared for further flight. But all at once the steps ceased, and were followed by a low exclamation.

Somebody else was entering.

And now the front-door did close, and the first person turned swiftly. They heard the quick swing round, though they could see nothing.

'Don't move!' said the second person. It was Don Pasquali's voice. 'I have a knife.'

The first person answered, with admirable control:

'You carry two, then?'

The second person's voice was Mr Lovelace's.

Don Pasquali smiled. The smile was in his words as he responded:

'Life is risky business. And more big risk if you know too much!'

'Obliged to you for the warning,' retorted Mr Lovelace, dryly. 'But how you expect to use your knife in the dark happens to be one of the things I *don't* know! Any more than I know why you suggest using it.'

'Shall we have some light, then?'

'I'll supply my light after you've supplied yours! What's your game, eh?'

'I ask, too, what is your game?'

'As this happens to be my house, I think I'm entitled to the first questions,' the old man rapped out. 'Trespassing may be permitted in Spain, but it doesn't happen to be permitted in England.'

'And you?' inquired Don Pasquali. His voice still smiled. 'You always do what you are permitted?'

'That's my business!'

'Also, mine.'

'I see. Blackmail!'

'Blackmail?' Now Don Pasquali did more than smile. He laughed. 'A good joke, that! Dios! You English can be funny.'

'I'm glad you think so,' observed Mr Lovelace. 'You'll probably need your own sense of humour pretty badly before long. You know, of course, that you are in the news?'

'In the news?' repeated the Spaniard. 'What is that?'

'You're wanted. The police are after you. You know what the word "police" means, I take it?'

'Oh, yes. But what do the police want me for?'

'Gawd, 'e's a cool 'un!' whispered Ben, and felt a small hand over his mouth.

'Have you ever heard of a man called Mr White?' inquired the old man.

'Ah! Mr White?'

'Yes. Somebody killed him yesterday in Southampton.'

'Poor man!'

'In a taxi. With a knife. It must have been a very quick job, because the murderer doesn't seem to have had time to pull the knife out again.'

'So?'

'I'm telling you, Mr Spaniard. Now, it would be interesting if the knife you say you're holding at this moment is a brother of the knife that was found sticking in Mr White's chest, wouldn't it? The police have got that knife, you know. They think it came from Spain.'

'They think, also, that a sailor come from Spain,' answered Don Pasquali, after a moment's pause. 'They think he bring the knife from there, perhaps.'

'Oh, they're after the sailor, as well,' admitted Mr Lovelace. 'I expect they'll hang the pair of you. Unless—'

There was a silence. The little hand again pressed over Ben's mouth; but, this time, unnecessarily.

'Unless?' queried Don Pasquali.

'Well,' said Mr Lovelace, slowly, 'if I were given complete particulars—and if events took a certain course—I might help to arrange things so that only the sailor swung.'

'Oh, but you will have to do that, of course,' said the Spaniard.

'Have to?'

'Or, perhaps, *you* swing, too?'

222

'And what should I swing for?' asked Mr Lovelace.

His voice was still steady, but the listeners above noted a new tone in it.

'A dead man in a clock?' suggested Don Pasquali.

Now there was a longer silence. Ben found that his companion had crept a little closer to him.

'But why all this in the dark?' came the Spaniard's voice. 'It is time *now* for the light, eh?'

'I agree,' said Mr Lovelace, shortly. 'I'll turn on the main switch.'

They heard him move from the foot of the stairs and go to the back of the hall. They heard something click. Then they heard him return to his place by the stairs.

'Now turn on the light,' said the old man. 'The switch is by the door, just where you're standing.'

They heard another click, but no illumination followed.

'There is nothing!' frowned the Spaniard.

'Oh, yes, there is,' answered the old man. 'There is a revolver. Now we're fifty-fifty. Or, shall we say, fifty-one—forty-nine?' And, as the Spaniard gave an angry exclamation, he added, 'I can just make you out against the glass of the door, Mr Spaniard, and I've got you nicely covered. I shall see you if you move—so perhaps you *won't* move, eh? One to Great Britain.'

'I, also, see you!' exclaimed Don Pasquali.

'Forgive me,' retorted Mr Lovelace, 'but I know my house too well to believe you. My head is below the casement window, and you can only guess where I am by my voice. Then I have six bullets, and you only have one knife. I think we'll continue in the dark, as we are, for just a few moments more. Do you mind?'

Don Pasquali did mind, but he was not going to spoil

his chance by giving way to his anger. He had waited before, and he could wait again.

'You are clever,' he conceded. He had managed to force back his smile. 'So I do not mind. To work with a fool—that is the pity. *You* know that, eh?'

'What do you mean?' demanded the old man.

'Your Mr White,' answered the Spaniard. 'He was a fool. Or he would be here now, not me.'

'Yes, you're going to tell me about Mr White,' rapped out the old man. 'You're going to tell me all you know about him, and then I'll judge whether he was a fool or not.'

'Oh, yes, he was a fool,' insisted Don Pasquali, softly. 'The fool that expect too much.'

'Well, well, go on!' snapped Mr Lovelace, for Don Pasquali had paused.

'I go on—yes, I go on,' replied the Spaniard. 'I tell you a story. You send Mr White to Spain, do you not?'

'Maybe. And maybe not!'

'We will say that you do. It will save time. We will say that you try for a long while to find out something about one certain person. I say his name, eh? It is Mr Joseph Medway. You will see it on the placards. Oh, a great man! He become more great—but only if all go smooth with him now, at this moment. And so if you find out the thing you have heard of Mr Medway, it will bring a big sum of money to you, because Mr Medway will not want you to tell to others what you find out. It will ruin him. Only—you must be sure. It is no good if you are not sure. So you send Mr White to Spain, to make sure.'

'This is certainly an interesting story of yours, Mr Spaniard,' commented the old man. 'I must undoubtedly hear the end of it. If I like the end of it, maybe I'll decide not to shoot you.'

'Ah, you will not shoot me,' answered Don Pasquali, confidently.

'What makes you so certain of that?'

'The end of the story. It has, you see, a surprise.'

'And, maybe, I also have a surprise. Meanwhile, suppose we proceed? Mr White, apparently on my instructions—'

'—goes to Puerbello, where you have found there is a lady. A lady who is quietly there, earning no money, but receiving it. Now, who is it send the money to her for so many years? A lawyer. Yes. A lawyer! A lawyer—so you find—of our big friend on the big poster—Mr Medway.'

'And when Mr White reached Puerbello?' inquired Mr Lovelace.

'Oh, then it is very sad,' sighed the Spaniard, mockingly. 'For the lady is just dead. In a house that is mine from my father two years ago. The rent is not all paid. The poor lady, she owes me money. I am, you see, her—what is your word—landlord? And so, of course, as there is no one else to do it, I look through her things, and I find a letter.'

'Ah!' murmured Mr Lovelace.

'It is a letter written many years ago. It is sign by our friend Mr Medway. She should have burn it, I think, but she keep it. Just one little letter, to hold to her heart, eh? And *I* find that letter, Mr Lovelace, and so I say it is my letter, and not for you or for your Mr White. Is that not so?'

'Certainly,' agreed the old man, 'and I expect Mr White thought so, too, and offered to buy it from you?'

'Oh, yes. Twenty-five pesetas. Not enough! Fifty, then?

No. A hundred? And always more eager. So I ask myself why—'

'And he tells you why?'

'Just a little,' smiled Don Pasquali. 'As you say, enough.'

'You were right, Don Pasquali, to call him a fool,' said Mr Lovelace.

'Ah! You know my name?'

'Mr White telephoned it to me a few minutes before you killed him.'

'Then you know, also, the rest of my story, eh? You know that he attack me, when I want my share, and leave me for dead? And steal the letter—eh? *Steal* it—'

'I have agreed he was a fool,' interposed Mr Lovelace, testily.

'More than a fool!' flashed the Spaniard, holding out a scarred hand. 'See, this is his work! Don Pasquali does not forget!' He dropped his hand to his side, and shrugged his shoulders. 'So! You know. I follow him. To England I follow him. Perhaps he find this out. Who shall not know—if you do not? Perhaps you find out by some—what is your word?—agent, and perhaps you send to Mr White a wireless on board his ship that I am here in Southampton first? And so Mr White he get what you call the wind up. And so he must think what to do. And so he knock off the cap of a fool of a sailor. And so he buy him a new one, hiding first the letter in the lining. And so I kill Mr White. But the sailor with the cap—he escape.'

Above, the sailor was wondering how to escape. He turned his head to whisper to the girl at his side—and found there was no girl at his side . . .

'Yes, the sailor escaped,' Mr Lovelace, below, was saying. 'Mr White, then, was not the only fool.'

'The sailor escape from you, also,' replied Don Pasquali. 'Where is he? And where is the cap? As you say, Mr White was not the only fool!'

'You think I have the cap?' queried Mr Lovelace, suddenly.

'I know you have not the cap,' answered Don Pasquali. 'I go outside to watch. I see you return. You do not see me, so you do not act! And so I know by your look, by your way, by your walk, that you have not the cap.'

'Really?' exclaimed Mr Lovelace. 'After all, Don Pasquali, you seem to be quite clever!'

'Not so bad,' agreed Don Pasquali.

'And where does your cleverness lead?'

'To the surprise at the end of the story.'

'The surprise being?'

'Oh, no! We must arrange a price for it, Signor Lovelace. The price Mr White would not arrange.'

'Well, let's hear the price.'

'We share. As you say just now, fifty-fifty. In Spain we hear the British are just. Is it so? Or is it not so?'

While Mr Lovelace considered his reply, Ben felt a sudden touch at his shoulder. His companion had returned . . .

'Very well, I agree,' said Mr Lovelace. 'Now, what is your surprise?'

'It is in the clock,' answered the Spaniard. 'Someone is there who will tell us where the cap is.'

Mr Lovelace snorted with annoyance.

'Are you fooling?' he exclaimed. 'I left a dead man in the clock!'

'And I leave a live one there,' retorted the Spaniard, with triumph. 'The sailor. Go and look!'

'Bah! We'll have some light on this!' cried the old man, and suddenly darted towards the back of the house.

The Spaniard waited by the front-door. Above, Ben whispered, 'Ain't we goin' ter do nothink?'

'In a second!' came the reply, so faintly that Ben was not sure whether he had merely guessed it.

'Switch on!' called Mr Lovelace's voice.

Click! The hall was bathed in light. On the half-landing the door of the illuminated grandfather clock stood open, revealing its emptiness.

'Dios!' cried Don Pasquali.

'Well, what did you expect?' barked Mr Lovelace, as he returned to the hall. 'When I came in, a second before you, a match was glowing on the stairs. Our sailor's up on the next floor somewhere—and now, by God, we're going to catch him!'

28

Cornered

Molly could be quick, but either she had underestimated the speed of her enemies or the situation beat her. She had barely begun the whispered instructions for which Ben was tensely waiting before Mr Lovelace and Don Pasquali were on the staircase, and an instant later Molly herself was scampering up the next flight.

Normally Ben would have scampered with her. He did not do so because of the beginning of the instruction he had received. 'Stop—hide—and when I've drawn them off—' Molly had whispered, and then the top of Mr Lovelace's head had flashed into view, and she had gone. There had been no time to work out what the order meant, or whether one agreed with it.

What the order meant, however, soon became clear. As Molly's feet pattered, with significant noise, up the second flight of stairs the pursuers reached the top of the first flight, and they continued on their way upwards without pause. To his amazement Ben found the main staircase clear . . . And Molly had meant that he should use it, cross the hall, and make his escape!

Escape? Lummy! Did she imagine that he could think of his own safety while she was being pursued by a couple of murderers? What had he done to deserve this low opinion? Almost indignantly Ben swung round towards the upper staircase and shouted:

'Oi!'

As he lurched towards the stairs, a figure turned and came flying down towards him. A hand—it was scarred, though he could not see it—seized his collar, and he felt himself being propelled back to a wall. Then Mr Lovelace's voice called down the stairs, 'Have you got him?' and Ben's captor responded with a triumphant, 'Like a flea!'

A few moments later, a light was switched on. It illuminated a queer scene. Molly was seated on the lower stair of the second staircase, with Mr Lovelace standing over her, while Ben himself was squatting in a corner squinting up at the Spaniard's knife.

'Good! A double capture,' commented Mr Lovelace, sarcastically. 'An unexpected pleasure!'

'Do we want them both?' grinned Don Pasquali, making a pass at Ben with his knife. 'Or shall I get rid of this one?'

'No, not yet,' replied Mr Lovelace. 'He can live a little longer. But watch out for tricks.'

'That's right,' muttered Ben. 'See I don't shoot hup suddin like a Jack-in-the-box and 'it yer!'

'He might even do that,' said Mr Lovelace. 'He did it to me not long ago at Waterloo. But I'm more interested at the moment in another of his tricks. Tell me, Ben, how do you manage to drink dope without being affected by it?'

'Nah, then, not so much o' the Ben!'

'And not so much of *your* sauce, my man! Speak up! I asked you a question!'

'Wot was it?'

'Why didn't my tea put you nicely to sleep?'

'Pah! Does it matter?' interposed Don Pasquali, impatiently.

'If I think it matters, then you can be sure that it matters!' retorted Mr Lovelace, tartly. 'Kindly leave me to manage this in my own way. I believe in learning other people's tricks, and I am still waiting to learn this one.'

'Which 'un.'

'If he refuses to answer, Don Pasquali, you can prick the top of his head—'

'Beast!' cried Molly. 'If you touch him, I'll—'

'Yes? What?' inquired Mr Lovelace, blandly. 'Stay still, young lady, or it will be the worse for both of you. I'll deal with you in a minute!'

'That's orl right—doncher worry, miss,' said Ben. 'E's like that blinkin' monkey they 'ad at the Zoo—yer mustn't hirritate 'im or 'e spits. The reason 'is cup o' tea didn't send me ter sleep was 'cos I didn't drink it. Now 'e knows. We ain't *orl* mugs!'

'Apparently not,' nodded the old man. 'And did you afterwards let your lady friend out of her room?'

''Ow could I?' answered Ben. 'Door was locked, weren't it?'

'I seem to remember a chimney?'

'Yes, yes, he go up the chimney,' interposed the Spaniard, 'but he have to go out of the window, because—' He grinned. 'I block the chimney up.'

'I see,' murmured Mr Lovelace, contemplatively, and his eyes rested for a moment on Don Pasquali, and on

231

his knife. 'Up the chimney, and out of the window—and so to Waterloo! Eh?'

'Wotcher arskin' for? You know!'

'And then back from Waterloo?'

'Well, I'm 'ere, ain't I?'

'With—a cap?'

'Eh?'

'You still have that distressing habit of prevarication, I note. I said—with a cap.'

Ben gulped. Now what? He had sworn to Don Pasquali that he hadn't got the cap, but Mr Lovelace knew he had got the cap, only now he hadn't; Molly had, and he wasn't going to let nobody know *that*, blimy he wasn't, not if the Spaniard dagger came down into his head and made a hole a yard deep . . .

'That's right, he did come back with the cap,' said Molly, 'and much good it'll do you!'

And, pulling it out of her frock, she held it out to the old man. On the point of exclaiming, Ben desisted. He had caught Molly's eye.

Mr Lovelace seized the cap swiftly, but did not examine it at once. Molly's tone, even more than her words, caused him to pause. When he turned the cap over and looked at the lining, his face grew dark.

'Sorry to disappoint you,' observed Molly, coolly, 'but my gentleman friend really *isn't* such a mug as you've taken him for!'

The gentleman friend strove to conceal the fact that his brain was spinning. What the blazes was happening? Mr Lovelace had the blinkin' cap at last, and didn't seem in the least glad about it.

'The lining's been slit!' he rasped.

Now Don Pasquali's face darkened, and his fingers tightened on his dagger.

'Of course, the lining's slit,' retorted Molly. 'Do you suppose he was going to bring the contents back to this place? Not likely!'

'But—the cap!' cried Don Pasquali. 'He bring that—'

'Certainly! It's a nasty night, and a cap's a covering,' answered Molly. 'I tell you, Don Pasquali, you may have beaten my gentleman friend with your spoof message, but my gentleman friend beat you to a frazzle in the end! He smelt a rat, and he deposited the contents of the cap in a safe place before he came here. If I'd known that myself I wouldn't have troubled to make him throw the cap up to me just before you opened the door to him.'

While Ben digested this amazing ingenuity—it was the first he had heard of it!—she ran on.

'Do you want to hear the rest of the story? Here it is, Pasquali. After you put my gentleman friend in the clock— don't worry, you'll pay for it all one day—I managed to poke my way down the chimney, and I got him out. He was as nearly dead as anyone I've met, but I'm beginning to think you can't kill Ben, and perhaps when *you* know it you'll stop trying! God, you've killed one man each, haven't you? and that ought to be enough for twenty-four hours!' She turned on Mr Lovelace fiercely. 'Yes, and *you'll* pay for what I saw you do, too, before we've finished with you! Who is that poor fellow you killed—and why did you kill him?'

During the first part of this outburst the Spaniard had looked dark, but by the time it swung from him to Mr Lovelace he had suddenly overcome his first anger and was regarding the excited speaker with admiration.

'See, she has the fire!' he exclaimed, with a laugh. 'Like that animal my friend here mention, she can spit!'

Mr Lovelace, on the other hand, was far from laughter. He was scowling heavily.

'Do you think you are wise, young lady?' he demanded.

'Wise? Ask me that in twenty-four hours,' retorted Molly, 'then we'll see who's wise!'

'Aha!' cried Don Pasquali, his white teeth gleaming. 'She is what you call—the one? In twenty-four hour! Yes, we see! She will think different, too!'

'What do you mean?' snapped Molly, angrily.

Mr Lovelace also turned towards Don Pasquali, as though for an explanation of something concealed in his tone.

'*She* know what I mean,' smiled the Spaniard. 'When it is all over, and she is more calm. Oh, but I like to see her spit. Her eyes, then, are more pretty than the precious stones she can wear. *She* know!'

'Stop that rot!' ordered the old man, in a rage. 'D'ye think this is a love parlour? Any more of that sort of talk, you idiot, and I'll soon change the tune!'

Don Pasquali began to get into a rage himself.

'You think I stand that?' he shouted. His moods changed more swiftly than the old man's.

'You'll stand what I tell you to stand,' replied Mr Lovelace. 'You'll stand my ordering you to keep your voice lower, to begin with!'

'So! And now *you* stand something!' But it was noticeable that Don Pasquali's voice had dropped. 'You answer what the lady ask! You tell us who is the man you kill, and for why!'

Ben glanced covertly at Molly. During this altercation

he had been wondering whether it could be turned to account, and he had been studying positions. He had watched the point of the Spaniard's knife, and the angle of the old man's revolver, and in particular he had watched Molly, ready to spring to her side or essay a header over the balustrade at the slightest sign from her. But, to his disappointment, and rather to his surprise, she did not give any sign. Was she just trying to work them up, like? Or was she playing a deeper game still?

He knew that Molly's brain would not remain dormant during a scene of this kind. It would be working, working, working. Her brain went on long after his stopped. So he continued to watch her, and to try and read her, and to be ready for her . . .

'Possibly, in turn, we all have fits of idiocy,' said Mr Lovelace, now in complete control of himself again. 'I hope this will be your last, Don Pasquali, and to ensure that it is—just for that reason, and not for any other—I'll answer the lady's question and tell you who the man is I killed, and why. But don't take your attention off the lady's gentleman friend, or you may find *your*self killed before I can tell you—he looks a little restive.'

'Oh, I watch him,' muttered the Spaniard, waggling his knife.

'When you go to 'Ell,' said Ben, 'I 'ope yer drops right dahn onter one o' them things!'

'The man was killed,' proceeded Mr Lovelace, appearing to derive a cynical pleasure from his confession and from the contempt of his audience it implied, 'because he disobeyed me, and because he tried to run away. Even in small matters those who are working for me must obey me. One of this man's duties—to make my point clear—was to post certain letters, periodically, to a certain individual—'

'Ah! Medway!' interposed Don Pasquali, with sudden increased interest.

'Joseph Medway, M.P.,' replied Mr Lovelace.

'Letters to warn him, eh? To tell him what will happen if he is not good?'

'Why, Pasquali, you seem to know quite a lot about the game,' commented Mr Lovelace, 'but please don't interrupt any more. The letters were, as you say, to warn Mr Medway. To prepare the ground, so to speak. Of course, they were not signed, and I gave orders that the man who posted them—he also wrote them, at my dictation—I am quite careful, you see—should select a different postal district each time, and that none should be anywhere near Wimbledon Common. I now have reason to believe,' the old man went on, 'that—to save trouble, perhaps, or time for the cinema— every communication was posted at the pillar-box at the corner. In other words, that every communication bore a local postmark.'

'And for that you kill him?' exclaimed the Spaniard.

'For that I might have killed him,' answered Mr Lovelace. 'Actually, I killed him because, when he heard of what had happened in Southampton, he got in a panic, and tried to escape. Of course, I could not let him escape, could I? He knew too much.' He shrugged his shoulders. 'So he had to be dealt with. That is how I deal with anybody who knows too much and who tries to escape. Perhaps you will make a note of it?'

Now he turned to Molly, as though dismissing Don Pasquali from his mind.

'You, young lady, will certainly have to make a note of

it. Both you and your gentleman friend. Through your
folly you undoubtedly know too much, and you have only
one way of postponing the inevitable results of your folly.
That is by telling me the *truth*, this time, about the contents
of the cap. You say your friend has hidden it? That may
or may not be so. But it strikes me as far more likely that
you have hidden it. And where more likely than on your
person—'

'Aha! Let *me* search her,' cried Don Pasquali.

There was brutal appreciation of the job in his tone. Mr
Lovelace noticed it. He also noticed Molly's instinctive
shudder, and the growl from Ben's corner.

'Well, now,' he murmured, 'of course—that *would* be an
idea?'

29

The Mind of Mr Lovelace

Molly Smith had told thousands of lies in her life, and if veracity is an essential qualification for Heaven she had lost her chance during her first year of speech. Her parents had lied before her, and she had been brought up to accept the process of lying as naturally as the process of eating or doing her hair. But there were moments when, despite her history and her family traditions, she could speak the truth as well as anyone and could leave no doubt about it in her hearer's mind; and now occurred such a moment. She looked at Mr Lovelace straight in the face, and said,

'If that dirty Spaniard searches me, I'll be dead when he does it.'

''Ear, 'ear!' added Ben, fervently. 'And so'll I!'

Ben's remark made no impression. Molly's, on the other hand, did. Mr Lovelace regarded her intently for a moment, and then nodded thoughtfully.

'I believe you mean that,' he answered.

'Then, you've got a grain of sense in your head, after

all,' replied Molly. 'I mean it to the last ounce of life in me.'

'But sometimes we mean more than we can achieve,' the old man pointed out.

'That's true,' agreed Molly, 'but this doesn't happen to be one of the times. If you think it is, you don't know me.'

'Very well. We will suppose this isn't one of the times,' said Mr Lovelace. 'We will suppose that, when you are searched by Don Pasquali, you are dead. Will that matter to me so very much? However much it may matter,' he added, cynically, 'to Don Pasquali?'

'Of course it'll matter to you!' Molly flashed back. 'You'll have a third murder to explain away. I suppose there's a limit to the number you can hide? Yes, and this murder would do you even less good than the others, because you wouldn't get anything for it, Keep your eyes on me while I repeat something I've already told you once. I haven't got what you want. It's not on me.'

Mr Lovelace kept his eyes on her. They seemed to go right through her. Then he withdrew them, and turned them on the Spaniard.

'Again, Don Pasquali, I am inclined to believe her,' he said, 'so what are we going to do about it?'

'If you believe her, I do not!' retorted Don Pasquali, shortly.

'Then you still suggest searching her?' queried the old man.

Don Pasquali looked at her, hesitating.

'I could, of course, weaken her first with a bullet,' the old man went on. 'That might prevent the greater tragedy. Well?'

Don Pasquali compromised.

'Shall we search this one first?' he proposed.

'The best way ter search me is ter git a fishin' rod,' said Ben, 'and ter drop the 'ook dahn me 'oles.'

'I know a better way,' rasped Don Pasquali.

And he began a less sporting method.

'Yer'd do it quicker with both 'ands,' grunted Ben. 'Shall I 'old yer knife for yer?'

'Silence!' exclaimed the Spaniard.

'No, let him go on,' interposed Mr Lovelace. 'I like to hear him.'

'Well, would you like to *search* him?' retorted Don Pasquali. 'He wriggle more than a fish!'

''Oo wouldn't?' retorted Ben. 'A stacher'd wriggle if it 'ad 'ands like your'n messin' abart its ribs. Oi! Why doncher git a spide? Then yer could git right hinside me skelington!'

The search proceeded and concluded. It produced nothing. As ever before it may be noted that it omitted Ben's left boot.

'There y'are,' muttered Ben, as he re-arranged himself. 'Orl work and no profit! 'Corse, don't mind turnin' me hinside hout afore a lidy!'

'*Will* you be quiet?' exclaimed Don Pasquali, angry and disappointed.

'Yus, *you* be quiet arter you've 'ad yer trahsers pulled rahnd back ter front!' retorted Ben. 'Jest becos' I wasn't born in Bond Street d'yer think I ain't got no delercate feelin's?'

Don Pasquali wiped his brow with a red handkerchief, and turned towards Mr Lovelace.

'Watch him!' said Mr Lovelace, sharply.

Don Pasquali swung round again. An instant later Ben would have been on his back.

'But, come, don't kill him,' said Mr Lovelace. 'You really are a fool, Don Pasquali.'

'He is best dead!' cried the Spaniard, hotly. His knife was touching Ben's neck.

'And, with him, our chance of learning where the letter is?' replied Mr Lovelace. 'Fool is too kind a term for you!'

'Now 'e'll say "Deeoss",' murmured Ben. 'It's orl 'e knows.'

But the Spaniard said nothing. For the moment the psychology beat him. He worked best in big spaces and among simple, heavy minds. Confined in an upper landing and surrounded by British mentality, he was not at his best.

Mr Lovelace, on the other hand, retained his coolness, and arrived now at a decision. Far better than Don Pasquali, he understood the psychology he was up against and the peculiar nature of the human riddles he had to solve. He understood the impossibility of dealing with Ben and Molly as he might have dealt with an ordinary couple. Deliberately and callously he had considered the idea of torture, and he had decided against the process because the chances of success were outweighed by the chances of failure. He had had to kill one dog already because, on the death of its master, it had made too much noise. Ben, he felt convinced, was capable of even greater noise.

'Listen,' he said. 'We are going to get this situation clear. If the letter I am looking for, and am going to find, is not on the girl—and I do not think it is—then it must

be elsewhere in this house or outside it. That's to say, it
was either taken out of the cap while you and I were
talking in the hall, Don Pasquali, or it is in that secret
place not a hundred miles from Southfields station where,
according to this girl, our friend Ben has hidden it. By
the way, what's *your* version of that story, Ben? *Did* you
hide it, as she says, or has the young lady a strong
imagination?'

'Corse I 'id it,' answered Ben. 'Think I'd bring it back
'ere?'

'Then will you save a lot of time and trouble by telling
me where you hid it?'

'Likely, ain't it?'

'Perhaps you don't know where?'

'Wotcher mean?'

'I mean, perhaps there isn't a secret place at all?'

Ben strove hard to keep his end up, but this cross-
examination distressed him. He wished Molly could have
done the answering for him. She could deal with nasty old
men with searching eyes . . .

'I see, you know quite well what I mean,' observed Mr
Lovelace.

'Well, this is wot *I* mean,' retorted Ben, 'and doncher
git up on wrong tracks jest becos' my mind ain't like a
hexpress trine! Corse there's a secret plice! And corse I
ain't tellin' yer where it is. And yer can search the 'ole
o' Sarthfields—search till yer blind—and yer won't find
nothink. 'Cos why? When I 'ides a thing—well, I *'ides* it!
This ain't children's 'Unt the Thimble.'

Mr Lovelace smiled and murmured,

'I very much doubt whether I *would* find anything.'

'Yes, but I *make* him tell!' exclaimed Don Pasquali

242

suddenly. He flourished his knife, but the old man brought him up with a curt order.

'None of that, Pasquali!' he ordered, sharply. 'If you're not careful, you'll ruin everything. The position is quite clear. I must search the inside of the house—with the lady here—while you and Ben go to Southfields.'

'Eh?' jerked Ben.

The proposal did not seem to appeal to the Spaniard, either.

'We must leave no stone unturned, Pasquali,' continued Mr Lovelace, speaking authoritatively. 'And this is the only way. You will take Ben to Southfields, and you will use what persuasion—outside this house—you may think fit. What is the time now?' He glanced at his watch. 'Eight o'clock. So late! Well, I will give you two hours. That is, till ten o'clock. By ten o'clock you will have returned here with or without the letter—but, of course, with Ben. Meanwhile, by ten o'clock, my own search this end will either have proved profitable—or not.'

'And if I have not the letter, and you have not the letter?' inquired Don Pasquali.

'Why, then there will be only one more place to look,' replied Mr Lovelace, 'and that will be on the lady herself. We are giving her, as you will see, two hours' grace.'

Don Pasquali stared at the old man, then broke into a smile. 'It is good!' he cried. 'I find the letter at Southfield, or I search the girl here at ten!' The smile vanished. 'Unless *you* find the letter while I am at Southfield!'

'We must each trust each other,' agreed Mr Lovelace. 'Am I not trusting you, if you are lucky at your end?'

'How so?' frowned the Spaniard, obviously temporising.

'Why, if you find the letter at Southfields, you will be as free to proceed without me—'

'As you will be, if you find the letter here in the house?' interposed the Spaniard.

'Precisely.'

'Then why not search here together, and go to Southfields after, if we do not find the letter?'

'How long after?' answered Mr Lovelace. 'You forget, Pasquali, that time happens to be a factor in this case. Here is your cap, Ben. It is no longer interesting.'

Rather surprisingly, Don Pasquali gave way as Ben caught the cap that was tossed to him.

'Yes, yes, it is good!' he nodded. 'I see, you are right. As before. It is good!'

And, without more ado, he prodded Ben with his knife.

'Oi! Wot's that for?' exclaimed Ben, jumping.

'For you,' replied the Spaniard. 'Down the stairs, now. Quick. You hear him say Time is important!'

Again Ben felt a prick. Again he jumped. Before he knew it, he was on the staircase, with the Spaniard behind him.

'Don't move!' murmured Mr Lovelace to Molly.

He had caught the indignation in her eye, and he noted the quick stiffening of her body,

'Don't move,' he repeated, softly, and now his revolver touched her almost caressingly. 'And—don't speak. I know when you are serious. Now *I* am serious,'

There was no doubting it. Molly, as well as Mr Lovelace, could read signs. Silent and motionless she waited, while Ben descended the staircase, urged by the Spaniard's knife—crossed the hall—unwillingly opened the front-door—and went out into the night . . .

The front-door closed. Mr Lovelace and Molly were alone. Mr Lovelace laughed quietly.

'No—not for a minute, even yet,' he said. 'We will give them time. Time, the factor, eh? Time to get well on the road to Southfields!'

'You think that Spaniard won't double-cross you?' muttered Molly.

'If he gets the chance, he will certainly double-cross me,' replied Mr Lovelace. 'That is why I had to pretend your silly story might be true. To make *him* believe it. But he will not get the chance—or the letter. The letter is here. All he will get at Southfields will be a policeman. Now, where can I put you, my dear, while I telephone to the police-station?'

As Molly stared at him she fought against an odd, traditional instinct of admiration for even crooked cleverness.

'The policeman will come here, too,' she said, feeling stifled.

'Even if the police-station receives only an *anonymous* call?' responded Mr Lovelace. 'Well, if the policeman does come here—and eventually, I admit, he is bound to—what will he find? Just evidence of fresh deeds committed by a Spaniard and a sailor—burglary—murder—worse?'

He shrugged his shoulders, while the cynical smile that was rarely absent played round his lips.

'And I fear the policeman will also find,' he added, 'that these desperadoes have frightened an old man away. Yes, the policeman may even think that they have killed the old man, and hidden his body. There will be a coin or two on the floor, to support the theory—and maybe an over-turned chair, eh? But it will not really matter by then what the policeman thinks. The old man, by that time, will be very far away.'

Suddenly the revolver pressed into her so hard that it hurt. 'Now!' ordered Mr Lovelace. 'Get up!'

30

The Mind of Don Pasquali

As the front-door closed behind them, Don Pasquali gave a little chuckle. Freed from the dominance of the old man, his own dominance reasserted itself, and his personality grew and expanded on the dark door-step.

'Signor Ben, I have no brain,' he murmured, his teeth gleaming whiter than ever as the heavy, sensual lips parted in a malicious grin. 'You hear what he say? "You really are a fool, Don Pasquali! No, fool is a word too kind!" So! Well, watch the fool—watch from the earth where the insects lie!' The Spaniard's foot shot out and sent Ben sprawling. 'Now turn and see what the fool do! But do not get up, or the worm is cut in half!'

Ben hardly heard the sneering words behind him. His descending eye had caught something white on the earth. It gleamed for an instant, then vanished as Ben's body flattened over it.

'Turn and watch, do you not hear?' ordered Don Pasquali.

Ben rolled round slowly. His mind, also, was rolling. That white thing.

'What is the matter?' demanded the Spaniard.

'Me cap fell orf, that's orl!' muttered Ben, sitting up stupidly.

The Spaniard looked at the cap. It lay on the earth beside Ben, and Ben's hand was over it. The Spaniard had no idea that something far whiter than Ben's hand was under it.

'The cap that is no longer interesting,' said Don Pasquali, with a frown. 'Well, we talk of that in a minute. But, first see how I use my knife!'

Ben put up his hands quickly; the knife, however, did not come in his direction. It flashed towards the porch, sawed something, then flashed away again.

'Do you know what I cut just now?' asked Pasquali.

'Yer 'and, I 'ope,' replied Ben.

'I cut the telephone wire,' observed Don Pasquali, boastfully. 'Now Mr Lovelace cannot tell the police that you and I go to Southfield! Not so bad, eh? For a fool?'

He was parading himself before Ben, driven partly by vanity and partly by the necessity of re-creating himself as a factor to be reckoned with. He had not made much of a show inside the house while the old man had been ordering him about. He needed to wipe out the memory.

Ben also had a need. If Don Pasquali was not the fool Mr Lovelace took him for, Ben must not be the fool Don Pasquali was taking him for. 'On'y the trouble with me,' thought Ben miserably, 'is that I *am* a fool!'

Still, one spends one's life trying not to be, so even now, while grovelling on the ground like the lowliest worm, Ben did not give up trying. P'r'aps, if he swallowed his natural feelings, like, *he* could be subtle, too!

'Go on!' he murmured, for a beginning.

Don Pasquali did not quite catch the implication, so Ben explained.

'Yer don't mean 'e was goin' ter ring hup the pleece?' he said, incredulously.

'Oh, yes!' smiled Don Pasquali. 'And then, he get all!'

'Wot! Double-cross yer?'

'Perhaps! But, now, he cannot! I see to that. Get up!'

''Arf a mo'—'

'Get up! Quick! Or I kick you up!'

Ben leapt to his feet, and the Spaniard's boot missed him by half-an-inch. In his hurry he left his cap on the ground. It seemed, with the Spaniard's eyes on him, a million miles off.

'Now we walk a little away, and then we talk,' said Don Pasquali.

'Wot abart?' asked Ben, trying not to look as though his sole thought was the cap.

'You hear when I tell you.'

'Eh?'

'What do you wait for?'

'Oh, nothink! But me 'ead's cold, see? Larst time I 'ad a 'air cut, chap said I was goin' bald.'

He stooped half-heartedly towards the cap, and the Spaniard laughed.

'It is no use now!' he exclaimed. 'It is no longer interesting!'

He drew back his foot to kick the cap before Ben could grab it.

'Gawd! The front-door's hopenin'!' cried Ben.

The Spaniard spun round. Ben leapt upon his cap. As the Spaniard turned back to him he clapped the cap on his head, and the white paper he had grabbed up with it

crackled thunderously as it was pressed down on his hair.
The Spaniard's brow darkened.

'A trick, eh?' he exclaimed.

'Yus,' admitted Ben, while his heart thumped. 'Wot's
wrong with me 'avin' me cap? It ain't worth nothink ter
you now. See that old devil in there givin' it back ter me
if it 'ad bin! But, o' corse, if you think we got time ter
waste torkin' abart it—'

'No, we have not!' snapped Don Pasquali. 'But if there
are more tricks, Dios, you pay for them!'

'Carn't yer think of nothink but Deeoss?' muttered Ben.
'*We* got lots more!'

The Spaniard seized Ben by the shoulder, and trundled
him away from the house. The trick appeared momentarily
to have unnerved him again, for he did not say another
word until they had nearly reached the gate. Then he
stopped, and gave Ben a shake.

'*Now* we talk,' he said.

'After we git ter Sarthfields?' replied Ben.

'We see about Southfield!' replied Don Pasquali. 'Perhaps
we do not go to Southfield!'

'Eh?'

'Perhaps there is nothing at Southfield? Then I go back
very quick!'

'Wot—back ter the 'ouse?'

'Why not?'

Back to the house? Ben didn't want that. He thought
hard. He must keep Don Pasquali out of the house . . .
Don Pasquali, also thinking hard, watched Ben closely.

'Yes, why not?' repeated Don Pasquali. 'You tell me,
Signor Ben! Why not?'

'It'd be silly,' muttered Ben. 'Jest silly!'

'So? Well, perhaps *I* do not think it silly! Mr Lovelace would he send me to Southfield if he thought the letter was there—?'

'Corse 'e wouldn't!' agreed Ben, his mind beginning to wake up. ''E thinks it's still in the 'ouse!' He chuckled realistically. 'Fer a clever man, 'e's the biggest mug I ever come acrost!'

'Why?' demanded Don Pasquali.

'Lummy, ain't it pline?' retorted Ben. 'Ain't it pline as a pike-staff? 'E's so clever, that bloke, 'e's *too* clever, if yer git wot I mean. You 'it it yerself when yer torked abart orl this fool business. 'E ain't a fool 'cept in thinkin' heverybody helse is a fool—you and me.'

'You, too, eh?'

'Yus! Me! D'yer think they tike *hennybody* in the Merchant Service? Mr Lovelice thinks you sich a fool that yer won't git on ter 'is gime, and sime way 'e thinks me sich a fool that I'll play *inter* 'is gime! See you not cuttin' them telerphone wires! And see *me* not 'idin' the letter afore I come back 'ere—'

'It is true, then!' interposed the Spaniard, excitedly. 'It is true that you hide the letter somewhere outside the house?'

Ben summoned a look of utter incredulity to his face.

'Yer don't mean you didn't git onter it?' he exclaimed. 'Lummy, I thort *you* was a bit cleverer, like. Corse I 'id it. It's "somewhere in Sarthfields," as they sed in the war. But Mr Lovelice don't believe it—'e thinks it's still in the 'ouse, the idjit, and 'e tries ter double-cross yer—and now if yer want yer charnce ter do a bit o' double-crossin' yerself— well, it's your'n fer the arskin'!'

Don Pasquali's eyes grew more and more searching.

'And you?' he said, suspiciously. 'You, also, do your bit of double-crossing?'

'That's right,' nodded Ben. 'And I hexpeck yer ter give me a drink fer it! Any'ow, I'm cornered, ain't I, so wot's the good o' kickin'?'

'As you say, it is no good for you to kick,' agreed Don Pasquali.

He turned his head and glanced towards the house. His hand, still holding his knife, was within a few inches of Ben. A quick jerk, and the knife might be wrested away!

'Yus, but I'll bet 'e's watchin' me aht of a corner,' thought Ben. 'This is one of '*is* tricks—ter see if I reely mean ter be good!'

So he resisted temptation, and a moment later Don Pasquali turned back to him.

'Come,' he said. 'We go.'

They passed out through the gate. The lane looked like a black tunnel, for the tall trees that lined it almost met overhead.

'Which is the way to Southfield?' asked Don Pasquali.

'This way,' replied Ben, pointing the wrong way.

'And how do we go?'

'I sold my Rolls-Royce larst week, so we'll 'ave ter walk.'

'How far do we walk?'

'As fur as Sarthfields.'

'Idiot! How far is Southfield?'

'Oh. Couple o' mile.'

'Then we do it in half-an-hour?'

'That's right.'

'And when we get to Southfield?'

'Eh? Oh! When we git ter Sarthfield we git the letter.'

'But where *is* the letter?'

'I'm goin' ter show yer, ain't I?'

'Oh, no! Oh, no! You *tell* me!' smiled Don Pasquali. 'You tell me *now!*'

'Yus,' said Ben, 'and then you nips orf and—orl right, orl right, put yer knife away. You're in a 'urry, ain't yer? It's in a shop.'

'A shop, yes! Go on!' exclaimed Don Pasquali, impatiently.

'Well, I am goin' on. In a shop. A terbackernist. Chap I knows is lookin' arter it for me.'

'Diablo—!'

'Doncher worry, 'e's orl right. I sived 'is live once, divin' orf Brighton Pier in a ragin' sea, so 'e'd do anythink fer me. "'Ere, 'ide this, will yer?" I ses ter 'im. "And don't let nobody 'ave it but me." "Orl right, Ben," 'e ses, "I ain't fergot wot you done fer me, divin' orf Brighton Pier, and with the wives fifty foot 'igh—"'

'Yes, yes, that is enough!' interrupted the Spaniard, casting his eyes heavenwards. 'Dios, the next time you dive you have a big stone round your neck! What is the name of the shop?'

''Oo?'

'The name of the shop! Of your friend—'

'Oh. 'Iggins. 'Arry 'Iggins.'

'And Signor 'Iggins, he sell tobacco?'

'That's right.'

'And where is he?'

'Eh?'

'Where is the shop of Signor 'Iggins?'

'Ain't you 'urryin'? 'Igh Street. 'Arry 'Iggins, 'Igh Street.'

'The number?'

'Height.'

'Can you write?'

'Wot for?'

'Can you?'

'Yus.'

'Then write now.' Don Pasquali produced a pencil and a piece of paper. 'Write and say to Signor 'Iggins that the letter is to be give to me!'

'No fear!'

'No?'

Ben felt a sharp jab in his back. He wrote. Don Pasquali took the piece of paper back, read it, and pocketed it.

'That is good,' he said. 'Now, if we get apart, it will not matter. Walk now! And quick. Or shall I prick you again?'

They began their journey. Southfields grew farther and farther away. Ben strove for a brain-wave.

He must get rid of the Spaniard somehow! He must get rid of him before he discovered that he was being led astray. The first job had been to put distance between Don Pasquali and Molly. The second was to see that Don Pasquali never got back to her.

A little way ahead, gleaming darkly through a thin line of trees, was a black surface. A star shone in it, proving it liquid. Ben turned his head towards it, wondering whether he could make use of that silent, unruffled surface.

The next moment he found himself sailing through the air. There followed a splash. The star shivered. Ben went down to meet it.

31

The Mind of Ben

A splash and a dancing star were the last things Ben heard
and saw for some while, but presently both hearing and
sight returned to him, and he realised that he had not been
extinguished from existence even yet. 'If them 'orrible noises
is comin' out of me,' he thought, 'I'm orl right!'

The things he saw were almost as horrible as the noises
he heard. They were waves ninety miles high, making rings
around his chin; and his chin, as far as he could determine,
was paddling. The things he saw were partly responsible
for the noises he made, and the result of both was an
impetus that seemed by some violent but unscientific
method to be propelling his chin. The chin went forward,
paused to drink one of the ninety-mile waves, went forward
again, and then paused for another drink. 'If I can keep
on makin' the noises afore the wives stop me,' thought
Ben, 'I'll git somewhere, that is, if there's anywhere ter git.
On'y,' he warned Fate, in case Fate wanted to keep him
on earth a little while longer, 'I can't drink much more,
'cos I'm full, and that's a fack!'

Fate heard the warning, and held a branch out to him. He grasped it and pulled. He pulled himself to another branch, and then to another; and when at last a wind-milling hand came down on grass, he discovered at the same moment that the water wasn't bottomless, and that his boots were touching ooze.

You can't walk on ooze unassisted, but now the kindest branch of all stretched out over the grass and said (or so Ben swore), 'Catch hold, Ben—I'm on your side!' So he caught hold, and he hoisted himself out of the ooze, and he slithered himself on to the grass. And there he lay for several minutes, in an orgy of blissful relaxation, without a single care in the world.

The world, however, doesn't believe in too much bliss, and in due course the cares returned. They returned on the wings of realisation. Ben sat up suddenly, while his reviving mind snapped back sharply to the moment before he had descended into a Surrey pond and disturbed a star.

Don Pasquali had thrown him in. Just as he was thinking of throwing Don Pasquali in! Where *was* Don Pasquali?

He looked around, moving his head gingerly to avoid noise. He saw no sinister form. He heard no sound. Don Pasquali had vanished.

Well, Ben would have to vanish, also. That was obvious. The question to be decided was, where should he vanish to?

While beginning to revolve this point he gazed at the water from which he had just dragged himself. It looked ridiculously smooth and peaceful. There were now no waves at all—they had been the creations of Ben's own splashing—and nobody would have realised the agony

that calm expanse could produce saving one who had
tasted it . . .

''Allo! Wot's that?' wondered Ben, as his eye caught a
small dark object on the water's edge.

He stretched forward and touched it. He touched it
gingerly, because it might be a wild cat or anything.
It proved to be his cap.

'Well, I'm blowed!' he muttered. 'You and me carn't lose
each hother, can we?'

He turned the cap over anxiously, and rejoiced at what
he saw. The paper he had picked up from the earth just
after leaving the house with Don Pasquali was still inside
the cap. It had half-slipped back into the torn lining.

'The 'oming instinck!' reflected Ben.

He extracted the paper and looked at it. He could make
nothing out in this light, but he knew what it was; he had
known all along; and, as he stared at it, he found himself
piecing its recent history together, and reconstructing its
adventures since he had tossed it up to Molly at the window.

She had caught it. She had taken possession of it. She
had examined it. She had ripped the lining and found the
letter in it. So much Ben had gathered from her a moment
before Mr Lovelace, followed by Don Pasquali, had
returned to the house.

But what had happened afterwards? They had waited
together in the darkness of the upper landing. She had
slipped from his side. He remembered that now. He remembered putting out his hand and missing her. And then she
had come back. What had she slipped away for?

Why, it was obvious! She knew they were about to be
caught. She knew the letter would be found if either of
them had it. Even if it remained in the house, it must be

found. So she had slipped into the only room that had an unlocked door on the upper landing—the room in which the dead dog lay—and she had dropped the letter out of the window . . .

'Lummy, if she ain't clever!' marvelled Ben. 'Clever as they mike 'em!'

And, while he continued to ponder—for it was necessary to follow Molly's mind in order to make up his own—he saw the completeness of her scheme and of her intention. 'Quick—hide—and when I've drawn them off—' her whispered instruction had begun. If there had been time to conclude the instruction she would have added '—Nip down the stairs—the coast will be clear—and out of the house. The letter will be outside somewhere, under a window. Find it, and take it—'

Where?

Well, now he had found the letter! In a roundabout way, her plan was working! But what was the conclusion of the plan? Where *did* she mean him to take it? Yes, and what of herself, in the meantime?

Sitting on the edge of the pond, Ben struggled to work the problem out. There were four possibilities, and not only the fate of the letter, but the fate of Molly, probably depended on his choosing the right one. He surveyed each in turn, and wished his brain had been in a cooler condition for the job.

'Fust, go back ter the 'ouse. Wot abart it?'

Apart from sharing Molly's danger, he could not see any advantage in this course. Mr Lovelace was in control at the house, and would remain in control. To return, with the letter in his possession, would merely be playing into his hands. And, when Don Pasquali returned, also, after his fruitless journey to Southfields, the complications would increase. For Don Pasquali would obviously return. Unless—

'Nummer two, go arter Don Pasquali ter Sarthfields, and stop 'im! Wot abart that?'

How *would* Ben stop him? How, at this instance, would he even find him? There was, of course, no 'Arry 'Iggins, of Height 'Igh Street. The second alternative seemed even more hopeless than the first.

'Nummer three—tike the letter ter the pleece.'

That might have been Molly's intention. Get bobbies on the job, and let them clear it up!

But in the clearing-up process, Ben would be cleared up, too! And Molly, perhaps, as well. Ben was quite ready by now to risk his own security, but he wasn't going to risk Molly's. In fact, Molly's security was the only thing he cared a brass farthing about, and the more he thought of the police, the less he believed they would be of any assistance in that direction.

'Fust thing they'll do is ter clap 'old o' me and tell me ter 'old me tongue,' he reflected. 'See 'em listenin' ter the story I'd 'ave ter tell 'em. "We've got yer now, and yer'll wait till yer spoke ter, see?" That's wot they'd say. And afore I can tell 'em wot they got ter do it'll be too late!'

Too late, Ben decided, was any time after ten o'clock.

Well, what about the fourth possibility? What about going to Joseph Medway, M.P., by whom the distressful letter was signed? Was *that*, after all, what Molly would have told him to do?

The more he thought of the fourth possibility, the more he warmed to it. If the police wouldn't help him, Joseph Medway might! In fact, that would be the price Ben would claim for the letter! Medway was a big pot—the sort who could pull strings! Unless he pulled them and got Molly out of her scrape, he shouldn't be got out of *his* scrape.

Yes! Now he'd got it! Now he'd got the plan he'd been searching for! Little Ben would only help Big Ben on terms!

And thus Ben turned blackmailer himself, but with the highest of human motives.

'Yus, but where does Big Ben live?' he thought suddenly, 'and 'ow am I goin' ter find 'im?'

As though in answer to the thought he became conscious of an uncomfortable pressure on the inside of his left foot. For a moment he concluded that something had worked inside the boot while he had been in the water—a bit of wood off the top or a bit of congealing mud off the bottom. Then he remembered the tiny card-case he had found by the gate of Greystones, and the lady's visiting card with the name Violet Medway upon it.

'Yus, and the haddress'll be on it, too!' he exclaimed.

He dived towards his left boot excitedly. Lummy, here was a bit of luck! Yet was it luck? There seemed to be some plan behind it all, some settled scheme that connected all these fragments of happenings together and built them into a picture that Ben had been destined, even while a ship was ploughing its way Southamptonwards, to complete.

It was through no coincidence that the young lady had visited Mr Lovelace on the same day that Ben had been propelled into his house. They had both gone there on the same business, though from different angles. Ben had gone, unconsciously, to deliver a letter. The young lady—had gone to receive it?

'S'pose she's 'is dorter,' reflected Ben, while his hand fumbled with his boot, 'and s'pose she knows abart them letters of warnin', like, and s'pose, when I fust come acrost 'er, she was wonderin' if they'd bin posted in that there pillar-box, 'avin' seen their postmarks, like, 'cos they *'ad* bin posted at that pillar-box, 'adn't they, and s'pose she's bin tryin' ter find the 'ouse, and seein' me s'pose she gits suspishus like, and follers me, and sees me go in, and arter a time goes in 'erself, pertendin' she was faint like, and then s'pose when I'm hup the chimbley and the old man's gorn fer that glass o' water she arst for not wantin' it she jumps up, well, didn't I 'ear 'er, and looks arahnd quick fer the letter, and finds somethink helse, though I'm blamed if I knows wot, but didn't I 'ear 'er gasp arter she'd hopened a drawer? . . . Blarst it, it's got hunder me 'eel . . . Yus, and then orf she goes, and drops the blinkin' card-case, and I picks it hup, and 'ere it is, comin' aht o' me boot, orl ready fer me ter go to 'er 'ouse and say I fahnd somethink she lorst. And then, when I gits fice ter fice with 'er, I ses, "Yus, but 'arf a mo', yer don't 'ave it if yer don't tike me quick as blazes to yer farther," and then, when she does that, I ses to 'er farther, or wotever 'e is to 'er, I ses the sime thing, see? I ses I got somethink I've fahnd that *'e's* lorst, and I ses to 'im, "Yus, but yer don't 'ave it if yer don't go quick as blazes ter the 'ouse where I finds it, with me, with lots o' bobbies, yer'll want a lot, and if yer don't stop Parlyment fer a bit while yer git my friend Molly away from a old man wot's doin' Gawd knows wot to 'er, yus, and a Spaniard wot's goin' ter do a lot more if we don't git there afore ten o'clock, see? And you gotter see that Molly don't go ter prison or anythink like that, but you can do wot yer like ter me, that don't matter, so long as you look arter 'er and git 'er away from wot she's goin' through nah, at this minit. Yus, arter that I'll give yer the letter, but not afore, so don't you think it!"'

From which it will be gathered that Ben's mind was working more swiftly than his fingers.

But at last the fingers reaped their reward, though not until the sodden left boot had been removed, and at last the little card-case was secured.

Of course, he couldn't read the address on the card. It was much too dark, and he hadn't a match. But he slipped the case into a pocket that had no holes above card-case size, squelshed his boot on again, and rose. All he needed now, to complete the preliminaries, was a light.

He received the light the next moment. It came to him from the road, in the form of a constable's lamp.

32

Conversion of a Constable

'Hallo!' said the policeman. 'Been havin' a swim?'

Ben looked at the policeman, but didn't see him. All he saw was the blinding light of the lamp, and for an instant it extinguished the far more feeble light in his mind.

'I asked you if you'd been havin' a swim,' repeated the policeman.

'That's right,' answered Ben. 'Practisin' fer the Channel.'

'Bit late for that, isn't it?' replied the policeman.

'Not if yer 'eart's in it,' blinked Ben. 'Goodnight.'

The policeman did not take the hint. He played his lamp up and down Ben's moist frame, and then proceeded,

'Well, let's stop being funny and have the truth. What happened? Did you fall in?'

'Fall in!' retorted Ben. 'There's a hidea! No, I stood on the top o' St Paul's and dived.'

The policeman frowned. But clearly he was not going to be budged by sarcasm. His tone became a little more ominous as he relinquished one point and started on another.

'What are you doing here?' he demanded.

'Gettin' dry,' Ben told him.

'Would you like to come along with me to a place where you'd get drier?' suggested the policeman.

'Wotcher mean?' answered Ben, uncomfortably.

'There's a nice fire at the police station.'

'I ain't doin' nothink!'

'No, you're not even answering questions when they're asked you,' agreed the policeman.

'You try, with the sun in yer eyes,' responded Ben. 'Switch orf yer light, and then p'r'aps I'll get me thinker back.'

The policeman removed the lamp from Ben's eyes, though not before he had climbed over a broken fence that divided the lane from the field, and had got within seizing distance of his victim.

'That better?' he inquired, sarcastically. 'well, now let's see whether your thinker improves a bit. What are you doing here?'

'I've toljer—'

'How did you fall in?'

'Slipped on a loose stone or somethink.'

'Let's see the stone!'

'Yer can't.'

'Why not?'

''Cos that fell in, too.'

'Well, where's the place?'

'Jest where yer lookin'.'

'I see. So you were standing there, eh?'

'Right fust time.'

'Why were you standing there?'

'I don't know wotcher mean.'

'Yes, you do! You know very well what I mean! What I

264

mean is that I want to know why you left the lane and came into this field? Were you trying to get away from anybody?'

'No!'

'Think again.'

'I 'ave. 'Oo'd I wanter git away from? I 'adn't met you then!'

'There's plenty of other people,' the policeman pointed out, and suddenly Ben found the light full on him again. 'A couple of people in a lorry, for instance. Do you know anything about them?'

'No,' replied Ben, while his heart missed a beat. 'Wot 'ave they done?'

'*They've* not done anything.' retorted the policeman. 'What've *you* done?'

'Me?'

'Yes. Is there some water still in your ears?'

'Well, I don't think I done anythink lately—not since I run orf with the Bank of Hengland.' The policeman laid a hand on his shoulder. 'Lummy, heverythink's crooked to a bobby! Do yer 'ave lessons in bein' suspishus?'

'*You're* going to have the lesson,' returned the policeman. 'Come along!'

The official hand tightened on his shoulder. Ben realised that the situation was becoming desperate. Even if he were taken to a police station and nothing were proved against him, valuable time would be lost and his plan of saving Molly would be frustrated. But probably something *would* be proved against him, despite the fact that there was nothing to prove, and meanwhile Molly would remain at the mercy of a murderous old man and a worse than murderous Spaniard . . .

'I tell yer, I ain't *done* nothink!' he exclaimed, earnestly. 'Yer can't tike a feller up fer fallin' in a like!'

'I can take a fellow up for acting suspiciously,' answered the policeman.

'Am I hactin' suspishus jest becos' I don't throw me arms rahdn yer and kiss yer—'

'And also for bearing a strong resemblance to a man the police are looking for,' continued the policeman.

''Oo's that?'

'P'r'aps it's you.'

'P'r'aps it's Kitchener!'

'Have you ever been to Southampton?'

'Never 'eard of it!'

'Have you ever been to sea?'

'Nah! Spent orl me life hinland.'

'Well, you can repeat those answers to the inspector, and maybe he'll think more of 'em than I do! Now, then, that's quite enough of that! Pick up your cap, and get a move on.'

'Oi!' protested Ben.

But he was in the grip of the law, and in a few seconds he found himself back in the road.

This was the end of all things. Perhaps, if he had gone straight to the police, he would have got a hearing, after all, but a man who was dragged to the station as a suspect would find very little sympathy. A night in a cell, and, when morning came—nothing would matter! . . . Yes, but it wasn't morning yet . . .

'Better come quietly,' advised the policeman.

'Yus, but look 'ere,' cried Ben, desperately, 'you got this orl wrong!'

'You can prove I'm wrong at the station—'

'Yus, and a nice fool you'll look! Now if yer'll give me a mo' instead o' marchin' me along as if I was a frog I'll tell yer somethink that'll mike yer look like a fool the hother way rahnd. 'Oo knows, p'r'aps it'll give yer a stripe—'

'I suppose you *can't* help talking,' said the policeman, as he kept Ben moving.

They were getting farther and farther from Greystones.

'Yus, but don't yer want me ter tell yer 'ow I *reely* got inter that there pond?'

'You can tell it to the inspector, now.'

'Well, I'm goin' ter tell it ter *you* now, see? I was chucked in.'

'Were you?'

'Yus. By a blinkin' Spaniard—'

'What's that?' exclaimed the policeman, sharply. 'A Spaniard?'

'Yus.'

'Well, then, that *fixes* you, my man—'

'Wotcher mean?'

'Why, the sailor we're after is working with a Spaniard!'

'A lot you know!' retorted Ben. ''E's tryin' ter git away from the Spaniard. Yus, and a murderin' old man, too, wot's got a gal in 'is clutchin' 'and, like, and I can tell yer where the old man is, see, but not the Spaniard, 'cos 'e chucks me in, see—'

'Ease down, ease *down*!' interrupted the constable, and his grip tightened as well as his tone. 'We'll hear all about it presently.'

'Yus, but presen'ly's no good!' exclaimed Ben. 'We gotter go there now, see?'

'We've got to go to the police station now,' retorted the constable.

'That ain't no use—'

'*Will* you be quiet? Another word, and I'll clap the bracelets on you, do you hear?'

'Orl right! And yer know wot'll 'appen?' cried Ben. 'A gal will be murdered, and the chap wot's murdered 'er and wot's murdered a man, too, yus, and a dawg, 'e'll git away, and the Spaniard wot murdered the feller in Sarthampton'll git away, and they'll go on murderin'. Lummy, it ain't sife, and it'll be your blinkin' fault jest 'cos yer 'ain't the sense ter know the truth when yer met it and wouldn't go ter the 'ouse wot I could tike yer ter, and ter blow yer whistle ter git orl the hother bobbies wot's abart on the job, too, but instead yer lug me along wot ain't no good ter nobody 'cos I ain't done nothink, ter lock me up in a cell orl night while blood's runnin'—'

He paused, panting. The policeman had also paused. At last it seemed as though something beyond the mere capture of Ben was penetrating his conscientious and cautious mind.

The lane they were in was still deserted, but somewhere ahead glimmered lights, and the noises of traffic came faintly on an evening breeze.

'If you're trying to pull my leg—' began the policeman, slowly.

'Yus! I look like it, don't I?' answered Ben.

Once more the policeman threw his light full on Ben's face. The eyes that winked in it, framed in beads of sweat, winked with earnestness.

'And you can take me to this house?' continued the policeman.

'Ain't I tellin' yer?' replied Ben.

'Where is it?' asked the constable, and Ben noticed that he was fingering his whistle.

But neither Ben nor the constable noticed that a figure had crept out of a hedge and was now standing only a yard or two away; and before Ben could answer the constable's question, or the constable could bring the whistle to his lips, the figure leapt forward and dealt the constable a savage blow.

The constable went down like a log.

'So! You would say where, eh?' muttered the assailant. 'Signor Ben—you are one dam fool!'

Don Pasquali glared into Ben's face. Ben stared back, like a hypnotised rabbit. Then Ben performed one of his amazing acts.

He curved himself and dived down to the prostrate policeman. He seized the whistle, gave it a wrench, made another dive to escape the now-descending Spaniard, and found himself free with the whistle in his hand.

He blew it. It shrilled terribly through the evening air. He heard the Spaniard emit an untranslatable oath. He blew again. The Spaniard vanished.

Now Ben was alone with the prostrate policeman. He had done his best; he had summoned aid; but who would believe that the policeman had not given the first blow on the whistle, and that it was not Ben himself who had followed this with a blow on the policeman's head? And who, after that, would believe that Ben's story, even if he were allowed to repeat it, had been anything but a ruse to divert the policeman's attention in order to fell him?

In sudden panic he turned and fled. The whistle was still in his mouth. He blew deliriously as he ran.

33

Good and Bad

The average nightmare is suffered horizontally. Most of Ben's were endured vertically; and not even in the sense of merely standing up. He endured them, more frequently, running along, while others also ran along with outstretched hands to seize him. That was why he had to keep on running along.

He ran along now, with nightmare seething around him. From every hedge, from every dark turning, from every black shadow, imaginary creatures leapt out, summoned by the police-whistle which he still unconsciously blew. It was a full minute before he realised that he was whistling to every constable in South-West London to come and arrest him.

When, in a momentary pause in the nightmare, realisation dawned, he gasped, "Strewth!" and opened his mouth so wide in amazement that the whistle fell out. He picked it up again, lest lying in the road it should form a clue and should call to the finder, 'Ben has passed by here—carry on!' and put it in his pocket; but since his pocket was even wider open than his mouth the whistle promptly fell out into the road again.

When our minds are fevered we revert to the simplicity of the savage, and everything in life becomes either good or evil. There are no subtle sums to work out, no complicated computations. Existence swings back to us from the multitudinous stars to be, once more, the Rule of Two. Half of it is with us, otherwise good; half of it is against us, otherwise bad. Our job is just to sort out which is which.

Ben's mind was fevered. Remember that, in addition to his mental and spiritual woes, he had had a physical ducking. And so the police-whistle, bounding for a second time into the road, first from the hole in his mouth and then from the hole in his pocket, now became definitely sinister. It was an enemy. A snake. Sent to trip him up, to thwart him. 'Why, you're even wasting valuable time looking at me!' it grinned up to him. Yes, grinned. You couldn't get away from it. '*I'll* do you in!'

'Will yer?' said Ben. Yes, said it. He was talking to a whistle. He was in a bad way. '*Will* yer?'

He lurched down upon it and seized it again. He expected it to struggle. To his surprise, it came quietly. But, as he thrust it into another pocket, this time keeping his hand in the pocket as a sort of extra lining, he heard the whistle's little brothers and sisters shrieking 'We're coming—we're coming' in the distance, and he started to run again. One man against a thousand police-whistles isn't fair!

Presently he blundered into a little boy and knocked him over. In his primitive condition, all little children were Good. They were so small, and it was such damn bad luck on them, because everything else was so big. He

stopped—real heroism, this, but the germs of Christianity
live even in the savage, forming his most enduring part—
and picked the little boy up again.

'Lummy, 'ave I 'urt yer?' he mumbled. 'Wunner if I've
got a penny fer a sweet?'

Where was the little boy? He wasn't there! He had never
been there! It was the little boy Ben had knocked over the
day before, or the century before, in Southampton during
a similar flight from the police. His mind was working
backwards.

He had held conversations with a police-whistle and an
imaginary child. 'Am I goin' potty?' he inquired of himself.
There was really a very good chance of it . . .

Oi!

He was off again.

His hand, gripping the sinister police-whistle, was still in
his pocket. While he had been speaking to the imaginary
boy it had begun to grope for an imaginary penny, and had
slightly changed its position. In so doing it had established
a new contact. New contacts are our protection against the
numbness of old ones. Ben's hand had been numb. But this
new thing that touched it with a new sensation in a new
part tickled him, and broke through the monotone of lulled
sensation; and, all at once, the dead hand became living
again, and imparted life also to the brain.

'*Card-case!*' he muttered.

That's what it was! The little card-case! He'd stuck it
into this pocket after taking it out of his boot, just before
the policeman's lamp had blinded his eyes. His mind rushed
back to the moment.

If the policeman hadn't been there he would have taken
the card-case to a light—not a policeman's lamp!—and

read the address on the card it contained. Yes, that was what he had been going to do, wasn't it? Well, the policeman wasn't here now. Ben could *still* do what he had been going to do. And, lummy, the need to do it had become trebled since the postponement!

Ahead gleamed a lamp-post. Heath and common were still around him, but he had the sensation that he was nearing traffic. Traffic was Bad. The lamp-post he was Good. He tottered up to it, and, releasing the police-whistle (which had probably now learned to behave itself) he brought out the tiny case.

He extracted the card from the case. For the second time he read the name 'Violet Medway' on it. For the first time he read the address: 'Mallow Court, Mallow Road, Fulham.'

Fulham! That wasn't so far, was it? Just across the river, wasn't it?

A young man came round a corner.

'That's funny,' thought the young man, a second or two later. 'I thought I saw a fellow by this lamp-post!'

The fellow was now by another lamp-post . . .

Violet Medway. Mallow Court. Mallow Road. Fulham. And what would Violet Medway, of all that, say to a dirty, perspiring, panting scarecrow when he called upon her? More important, and claiming precedence, what would the scarecrow say to her?

While his eyes darted up and down the road—for hunted humans, unlike hunted hares, cannot see both ways at once—he rehearsed a little speech.

''Ere, I got yer card-case, miss,' ran the speech. 'I fahnd it, see? Where's yer farther? If it is yer farther?'

'What do you want to see my father for?' the lady would ask.

''Cos I got a letter for 'im—'

Hallo! Had he? Ben clapped his hand to his head. The cap was not there.

Ben leaned against the lamp-post and cried. A voice recalled him from his unmanly display.

'Is this yours?' inquired the voice.

It was the young man, who had followed him from the last lamp-post.

Ben seized the cap. The young man smiled.

'Cheer up!' he said, amiably. 'The worst is yet to come!'

The words, in Ben's view, expressed an impossibility. But the amiability of the words was, for the moment, more important. In another of those primitive flashes it suddenly occurred to Ben that this young man was Good.

'Can I do anything for you?' asked the young man.

His hand went into his pocket. Ben shook his head. Not that he objected to money, on principle, but just now he wasn't thinking of it. Perhaps this young man could help him in another way.

'Lorst me bearin's, sir,' murmured Ben.

'Well, I've found your cap for you, which should remedy your upper bearings,' answered the young man. 'What other bearings need attending to?'

Ben didn't know what the young man was talking about, but he went on:

'Could yer d'reck me ter Ful'am sir?'

'Fulham,' repeated the young man, and gazed north-eastwards. 'It's sort of over there,' he said, waving in the direction of the gaze. 'Keep onnish, and bear rightish, and you'll come one day to a big wide road. It leads to Putney Bridge. On the other side lies Fulham.'

'Thank 'e, sir. 'Ow fur is it?'

'Not very fur. Say, one or two milesish—but more twoish than oneish. Hallo! Hark to the cuckoo! Or is it a police-whistle?'

Only one thing in the whole world could have detained Ben at that instant. The young man produced it.

'By the way,' he said, 'is this yours, too? It seemsish to be Spanish.'

He held out the letter. Ben seized it with a sound inherited from an ancestor of the Cainozoic Age. The young man had never heard the sound before, and did not even know it existed. The next moment, scarecrow, cap, and letter had all three disappeared,

'Poor beggar, if ever there *was* a poor beggar,' mused the young man. 'But I wonder, just the same, whether little Edward has been quite wise?'

We will leave him to his wonder. He has served Ben's purpose, and ours; and ours, now, is to follow Ben into the north-east, reflecting the young man's friendliness because we know of Ben what he merely sensed.

Soon the open country and the secluded lanes were behind the fugitive, and he joined the human current once more. He struck the wide road towards which he had been directed. Cars passed him, flashing by with yellow eyes. All the yellow eyes looked ominous to Ben. The cars were Bad.

It may seem odd that, even yet, the police did not close their net around the man they had been hunting for so many hours. It may seem unreasonable and impossible. But there are a few people, and Ben was of these few, who lacking every other qualification for Life's grim struggle, are granted gifts for running away quite unknown to the majority of folk who face the struggle with other weapons.

A stag on Exmoor may evade all the combined craft of men and hounds who are especially trained for its capture. A large pike has lived in a small pond for many years, simply through its ability to evade. Without a trap, can you catch a mouse?

And so Ben reached the bridge and crossed the Thames to Fulham because he was the world's best dodger. He was the D'Artagnan of running, not through, but away.

In Fulham, with London now buzzing all around him, he risked one more human contact. It would have been impossible to find Mallow Road without it—and precious time was flowing on. He chose an old lady, because she might not be able to see him, and she certainly would not be able to catch him. Touching his cap, he asked her,

'Beggin' yer pardon, mum, but could yer d'reck me ter Maller Court, Maller Road?'

'Eh? This is Mallow Road,' answered the old lady.

And then her grip suddenly tightened on a black bead bag she was holding, and she hurried away.

Not only was Ben in Mallow Road, but only a few feet distant was an imposing brick post with 'Mallow Court' written on it. For a moment his heart quailed. How was it possible for a man in his condition to gain a hearing in that impressive edifice, where, he noticed, beggars and hawkers were not welcomed—or Bens, apparently, either?

'Yus, but I *got* somethink!' he thought, to counteract the impotent sensation that was running up and down between his stomach and his heart. 'And if I don't git Molly aht o' that 'ouse afore ten o'clock, wot's it matter if they set a 'undred dawgs on me?'

A church clock chimed the half-hour. Half-past nine. Lummy! He shoved the gate open.

The gate he shoved open was the front gate. By all the social rules he should have shoved open the side gate. He was not in a side-gate mood, however, for people who receive you through side gates have no imagination, and his business was with their superiors. If necessary, he was going to fight his way fistically into Mallow Court, and the nearer he began to his goal, the better.

So he mounted a brilliantly illuminated white flight till he reached a marble step at the top, closed his eyes, and rang the front-door bell.

The front-door bell was Bad.

34

At Mallow Court

Violet Medway, daughter of Joseph Medway, M.P., heard the bell from her sitting-room on the first floor, but did not pay much attention to it. She was absorbed in the contemplation of a cheap grey unused envelope.

Beside the cheap grey envelope, on a little walnut table the reverse of cheap, lay a packet of similar unused envelopes. The packet had a band round it, and was complete. The single envelope had not come out of the packet.

Another envelope also claimed attention. It was of the same family, being identical in shape, size, colour, and quality, but it had this difference: unlike the others—the single envelope and the envelopes in the packet—it had been through the post. It bore stamp, postmark, and writing.

The stamp was a penny-halfpenny stamp. The postmark was Wimbledon. The writing was block writing, and ran, 'Very urgent. Joseph Medway, M.P., Mallow Court, Mallow Road, Fulham, S.W.'

The flap of this envelope was still stuck down, and it had not been opened.

In the middle of her contemplation she raised her head and called, 'Come in,' in response to a knock on her door. A maid entered, with rather a flushed face.

'What is it, Maud?' asked Miss Medway.

'If you please,' answered the maid, 'there's a man brought this.'

'Brought what?' queried Miss Medway vaguely.

But all at once her vagueness vanished, and her eyes grew bright. They were blue-grey eyes, and their brightness had dazzled many people. The brightness was due at the moment, however, to the tiny card-case extended to her by the maid.

'Where did he find it?' she cried, jumping up.

'I don't know, miss,' replied the maid. 'He wouldn't say.'

'Wouldn't say?'

'No, miss.'

'But, surely—'

'He wouldn't even give it up till Procter got it away from him, miss! There was quite a scene. He said he must give it to you personal! Talk about mad!'

And, while Miss Medway continued to stare at the card-case, the maid ran on,

'Come to the front door! Fancy that! And when Procter told him to go round to the back he said—well, what *didn't* he say! One of them bag-snatchers, I expeck. They snatch your bag, and then have the cheek to call and ask for a reward—'

'Where is he now?' exclaimed Miss Medway, interposing swiftly.

'Procter was still trying to get rid of him when I left them, miss,' responded the maid, 'but when Procter gives me the case, because that rascal, you never saw anyone so

279

dirty, really, he was trying to get it back again, well, miss, I thought I'd better bring it to you at once before he—'

But Miss Medway did not stay to hear any more. She ran quickly out into the passage and towards the main staircase.

From the hall below rose strange sounds. Such sounds had never been heard in Mallow Court before. They were the vocal accompaniments of a delirious human windmill, and as Miss Medway reached the highly-polished balustrade and stared down the human windmill was carrying all before it. The 'all' was a portly butler who, a couple of minutes earlier, had been immaculate.

'Procter!' cried Miss Medway.

Procter did not reply. He was too busy ducking. He ducked to the floor. The human windmill sprayed forward over his back. And now Proctor rose, having resolutely secured the windmill's two feet, and began conveying his unusual burden towards the front-door. His attitude resembled that of a man carrying a sack of coal. It was live coal.

'Put him down!' ordered Miss Medway.

Procter hesitated, and the hesitation proved fatal. The sack of coal escaped and bounded towards the staircase. At the curved half-landing Miss Medway met it.

The meeting, apparently desired by both, produced nothing for a few seconds. They merely stared at each other, the one in the perfection of evening toilet, the other fit for the scrap-heap. Above them and below them panted domestics, their chests heaving with spiritual and physical emotion, while from a wall the picture of a former Medway gazed down with obvious disapproval.

Then Miss Medway spoke.

'Who are you?' she asked.

'I got ter tork ter yer, miss!' gasped the gate-crasher.

'Haven't I seen you before?' demanded Miss Medway.

'That's right,' muttered the gate-crasher. 'Pillar-box. Oh, Gawd, I am feelin' ill!'

The next moment proved that Miss Medway was one of the Good things. She grabbed the visitor by the arm, held him firmly for a second while he became limp— 'Funny,' thought Ben, ''ow yer 'its people when they're narsty, but goes orl jelly when they're nice'—and then lugged him upwards towards her room despite the combined consternation of a butler, a parlourmaid, and a deceased baronet.

Ben's limpness lasted for the complete journey to the doorway of Miss Medway's sitting-room. When he spied the room itself through the doorway, he stiffened. A latent social instinct stirred, whispering that this was no place for him. Shaded lights. Elegant chairs. Dazzling cushions. A desk good enough for a Pope . . .

But she led him in, and before he knew it she had closed the door and he found himself standing bashfully in the presence of a lady whom he only had a right, strictly speaking, to meet in books.

'Yer know,' he heard himself saying, 'I feels sorter faint like.'

He discovered a chair being pushed under him. Yes, this lady was undoubtedly one of the Good things.

'Now, can you talk?' she asked, kindly.

'Yus,' murmured Ben. 'That's wot I come for.'

'You came to return my card-case.'

'Yus.'

'Where did you find it?'

'Ahtside a 'ouse called Greystones—' He saw her eyes flicker, and he added, 'Yer knows it, doncher?'

'How do *you* know I know it?' she demanded, rather sharply.

But then she went on, her voice softening, and her eyes watchful, 'Oh—of course—by the card-case.'

'No,' answered Ben. 'By the chimbley.'

'By the—'

'Chimbley. I was up it, see?'

She did not see. He tried to explain.

'That's right. It was when yer called this arternoon. and pertended ter be goin' orf inter a faint, like. Well, I was up the chimbley, and—and I know wot yer was lookin' for. *Now* d'yer see?'

Whether she did or not, he perceived that his information had gripped her interest. After all, why try and explain things? There wasn't time, even if there was ability. The only thing that mattered was to keep her interest alive, and to bring it up to the point he wanted. So he ran on, unconscious that her interest was rendering her less friendly.

'But yer didn't find wot yer was lookin' for, did yer?'

'I found something,' she retorted, and glanced towards the single, unused, cheap grey envelope. She seized it, and now Ben found that she was challenging him. 'Who are you? You haven't told me yet! Are you that man's servant? Because, if you are—'

'Eh?'

'—I'll tell *you* something!' She held up the envelope. '*This* was in that house! Yes, I found it in a drawer while you were up your chimney eavesdropping—'

'Eaveswottin'—?'

'—and it's the same kind of envelope that has contained all these anonymous threats—'

'Oi, miss—'

'Be quiet! Listen!' she cried, and her imperious voice temporarily cowed him. 'I was sorry for you at first, but now I find that you belong to the house, and have been used to spy on me, I'm going to give you in custody! You can disguise writing, but you can't disguise a postmark. It was the postmark that led me at last to the shop where these envelopes were bought—though they couldn't remember who had bought them. It was the postmark that led me, after heaven knows how much searching, to the pillar-box where I guess now they were posted. When I came upon you hanging around there—no, don't interrupt me!—I could see by your manner that something was wrong, and I followed you to your house—'

'Fer Gawd's sake, miss—' Ben managed to gasp, but she cut him short again, and the combination of her anger and his weakness was too much for him. He could fight a butler, but an indignant lady in evening-dress, all powdered and scented . . .

'I followed you to your house, and after screwing up my courage I went in! It's a wonder now that I came out alive, and perhaps I wouldn't if that vile old man had known all *I* knew—'

'Yus, and that's nothink ter wot *I* know!' burst out Ben, now jumping up and almost crying with desperation. 'Do yer know that yer vile old man's a murderer? Do yer know that 'e's killed 'is servant—not me, 'cos I wouldn't be 'is servant not fer the Crahn Jewels—and that 'e's killed a dawg, and that 'e's in with a Spaniard wot's killed another bloke, and if we ain't quick they'll start killin' a gal, yus, and now don't *you* hinterrup'! I tell yer, it's this gal wot's sived yer blinkin' letter, I'd 'ave give it up long afore this, on'y she 'olds on, like the good 'un she is, and gits the letter aht of the cap, and then chucks it aht of the winder, but they don't know that, see, they don't know I've got it, they think she's got it, and they're goin' ter search 'er at ten o'clock—the Spaniard's goin' ter, my Gawd—and 'ere we're standin' torkin' abart it and doin' nothink but you tellin' me I'm in with them jest becos' I gits hup a chimbley ter git *away* from them, and heverythink goin' rahnd and rahnd and rahnd like it is now, and bobbies arter me fer doin' things I 'aven't, and bein' chucked in a pond, d'yer think that does a chap any good on a hempty stummick, and then bein' clapped into a clock, no that was afore, and then bein' twisted by a big bully of a butler . . . 'ere, wot's 'appenin'? . . . the room's goin' rahnd agine! Oi! Where's the ceilin'? The floor's comin' hup and 'ittin' me . . .'

She caught him as he swayed. Scent floated through the storm. He found himself back in his chair. And, in the distance, he heard a voice that seemed to be telephoning: 'He's left the House, you say? . . . How long ago? . . . Any minute now? . . . Thank God . . .'

35

Voices—Present and Past

When Joseph Medway let himself into his house—it was eighteen minutes to ten—he was not in the happiest frame of mind. He had anticipated that the morrow would be the most triumphant day of his life, and that besides paving the way to a new era of British prosperity (for all idealists imagine that they merely have to get their ideals accepted to bring about the Millennium), it would also pave the way to a new era of political prosperity for himself. His bill, fathered by an approving but cautious Government that refused to be wholly responsible for it because of its anti-foreign nature, aimed frankly at alien interests. Britain for the Britons was its key-note, and let Europe look after itself.

But there has never been an idealist, political or otherwise, without enemies, and Medway's enemies had become particularly rampant on the eve of the bill's introduction. Doubts which he had not previously allowed to enter his optimistic mind oppressed him on his way home. The atmosphere of the House had been nervy, and he discovered that his political opponents had been busier than he had imagined.

He felt pretty solid with the biggest personalities. His trouble was going to be the rank and file.

This, however, was not the only matter that troubled him. If the atmosphere of the House at Westminster was nervy, so was the atmosphere of his house at Fulham. Anonymous communications, containing veiled warnings, had pestered him, and at first he had thrown them into the fire with the contempt they deserved. Even when his daughter Violet had caught him once in this act of destruction, and had insisted on knowing the cause of his passing frown, he had not seriously worried. He had left the worrying to Violet, and wished heartily that she had been as unimpressed by the absurd documents as he was.

'My darling,' he had said only that morning, when she had tried to invest him with her interest. 'Pooh!'

'Pooh to you!' she had retorted. 'Haven't you ever heard of Bolshevism and Blackmail?'

'I have also heard of Feminism and Female,' he had answered, 'and of women's proneness to panic. What you want, my dear, is a round of golf.'

The golf had not materialised; the panic had. In the evening he had received a vague message over the telephone to which he had not attended. The message had been conveyed to him with deliberate vagueness by a secretary conversant with his employer's unreceptive mood. Then, later, had come a second message. The secretary, being no longer trusted by the other end of the telephone, had been forced to bring Sir Joseph personally to the disturbing instrument. And Sir Joseph was now on his way home.

'Though the chief reason for my return,' he told himself

a dozen times during the swift journey in his car, 'is because there is really nothing to keep me any longer at the House, and in the circumstances an early night seems eminently sensible.'

It never assists the sweetness of your mood when you are attempting to deceive yourself, and this explains the mood of Sir Joseph when he let himself in with his latch-key. Procter, hovering in the hall, did nothing to help matters. Procter looked as nervy as Sir Joseph was trying not to be.

'What's the matter, Procter?' demanded Sir Joseph, irritably.

For something was obviously the matter, unless Procter had St Vitus's Dance. And even that alternative would not be soothing.

'If you please, Sir Joseph—' began Procter.

But he got no further. Sir Joseph had turned his head suddenly towards the front-door. A sound had diverted his attention. The sound of heavy, hurrying feet. A moment later the bell rang, accompanied by a sharp, imperative knock.

Sir Joseph removed his eyes from the door for an instant and glanced at Procter. Procter made a half-hearted move-ment to answer the bell, but Sir Joseph saved him the trouble. He answered it himself. An inspector and a constable stood on the doorstep.

'What's this?' inquired Sir Joseph, sharply.

'Beg your pardon, sir,' replied the inspector, 'but we're after a man we believe called here a few minutes ago.'

'I don't know anything about it,' frowned Sir Joseph, and his frown deepened as the voice of an old lady, who was gripping a black bead bag, shrilled from the street,

'I know this is the house! Mallow Court he asked for. I'm sure of it!'

Procter's voice sounded behind Sir Joseph:

'That's right, sir. A man came here—I was just about to tell you—'

'Yes, yes, but surely he isn't *still* here?' demanded Sir Joseph, rounding on the butler.

And now another voice answered him. The whole thing was ridiculous, distracting! Every time Sir Joseph asked a question a different voice responded from a different point! This was the fourth, and it came from the top of the staircase.

'Yes, he's still here, Father,' called the fourth voice. 'Will you please come up at once?'

Sir Joseph nodded to the inspector, who promptly entered with the constable, but Violet added quickly, 'No, only you—for just a minute!' as she saw them.

'I'm afraid, sir—' began the inspector, but Sir Joseph, who preferred managing things himself, waved him down brusquely.

'One moment, inspector,' he said. 'Let me deal with this, please.' Then, turning to the staircase, he exclaimed:

'What's all this about, Violet? Have you got the fellow upstairs?'

'Yes,' she answered.

'Well, if you've caught him, he's wanted—'

'I know, but he's quite safe,' interrupted Violet, 'and he's in my room, and nobody's coming into my room till you've come in first alone—nobody!'

Sir Joseph, who recognised the determination in her tone, stared at her in astonishment.

'Aren't you being absurd and foolish?' he cried.

'This man's dangerous!' added the inspector. 'He's knocked out at least one policeman, and if he's the fellow we think he is, there'll be a far more serious charge against him.'

He pushed forward, and now Violet turned her determined eyes upon him. A picture of General Gordon defending Khartum flashed grotesquely into her father's mind as she stood her ground with the same heroic disobedience.

'The man's *not* dangerous!' she called. 'He's stretched out in a chair, if you want to know, and he hasn't the strength of a winkle!'

'Most muscular winkle *I* ever came across!' thought the butler.

Sir Joseph looked at the hesitating inspector, and shrugged his shoulders.

'Will you accept my guarantee that the man sha'n't escape?' he asked. 'If so, perhaps it would be as well for you to remain down here for a minute or two. You'll have no difficulty,' he added, as a sergeant and two more constables came running up the front steps, 'in manning all the doors!'

'Is that your wish, Sir Joseph?' inquired the inspector.

'I would like to satisfy my daughter's whim, if you, on your side, can make it conform with your duty?'

The inspector, sure of his man, did not think it would be a bad move to conform with Sir Joseph Medway. After a short pause, he nodded.

'But only a minute or two, sir,' he said. 'It's a bit irregular— but, perhaps—in the circumstances?'

Then he turned to his men, while Sir Joseph ran up the stairs.

'Now, then, why all this?' he demanded, on reaching the top.

'It's for your sake, Father, more than anybody else's,' his daughter answered, in a low voice. 'You'll know all about it in a moment.'

'Yes, but we can't keep the inspector waiting—'

'That's why you've got to be quick.'

She led him to her sitting-room. They entered, and she closed the door. The cause of the trouble, as she had implied, lay stretched out in an arm-chair, his eyes closed.

'Who is he?' asked Sir Joseph.

'I don't know,' replied Violet, 'but he seems to have been working for you—though if you ask me why, I don't know that, either.'

'Well, well, what *do* you know—?'

'This. That he came here a few moments ago, and insisted on seeing me. He brought back a card-case I'd lost, but that wasn't his chief reason. His chief reason was that, in some extraordinary way, he got hold of something else—something for you, this time—not for me.'

'What is it?'

'He said he'd only give it to you on condition—'

'Oho! Is this our blackmailer—'

'No!' she cut in sharply. 'He's got it *from* the blackmailer! And the condition is that we go straight to the blackmailer's house and rescue a girl who's in danger there. She seems to have been working for you, too—so the request's fair, isn't it?'

'I don't understand—' muttered Sir Joseph.

'Nor do I,' she interrupted again, 'and there isn't time to try. But perhaps this will help?'

She held out an envelope. The cheap grey envelope that had gone through the post and had not yet been opened.

'Tonight?' asked Sir Joseph, snatching it.

'By the last post,' she nodded. 'That's why I telephoned the second time. But you ought to have come the first,' she added, reprovingly. 'You see, I was right, Father—it's serious!'

Sir Joseph tore the envelope open and read the contents. His face darkened. The note ran:

'Final Warning. When you read this, the writer will possess a letter worth ten thousand pounds. There are others—political enemies—who would pay the writer more than this for the letter, since its publication would so discredit Joseph Medway that his career would be ruined. But the writer, being lenient, will accept the sum named. Further particulars, as to ways and means, will follow immediately. Meanwhile, as proof of the seriousness of the matter, three words will suffice: Madrid—Puerbello—Carlotta.'

He stared at the words. He appeared, for the moment, to have forgotten that an impatient inspector was waiting in the hall below. He appeared, also, to have forgotten his daughter, and the outstretched form on the armchair, and the room he was in . . .

'Well?' said Violet.

He came back.

'And—the "something else"?' he inquired, quietly. 'Where is it?'

His daughter turned towards the motionless figure and pointed towards a cap in his lap.

'Would that be it?' she asked.

The cap lay in Ben's lap, lining upwards. From the slit in the lining peeped a corner of the letter. Sir Joseph dived towards it, but found Violet's hand on his arm.

'If we take it from him, while he's in this condition,' she said, 'we take it on trust, don't we? We fulfil the condition?'

Without replying, Sir Joseph slid the letter out of the lining. He glanced at it, and a faint, strange smile came into his eyes. His daughter had never seen him smile like that before. He turned the letter over, and looked at the signature: 'Joseph Medway.'

And, once more, he appeared to forget the room he was standing in, and all it contained, saving the time-yellowed sheet of paper in his hand.

'Is that—*it*?' murmured Violet, recalling him.

'Yes, this is it,' he answered, slipping the letter into his pocket, and turned towards the recumbent figure in the arm-chair. 'We will fulfil the condition.'

36

Meanwhile, at Wimbledon—

'With the exception of the gentleman called Ben,' said Mr Lovelace, lighting a cigarette, 'we are all of us cleverer than we have been given credit for.'

'Why not except yourself, as well as the gentleman called Ben?' replied Molly.

She could speak, but that was all she could do. Her wrists and her feet were bound. The mark of her sharp little teeth on one of Mr Lovelace's wrists implied the necessity.

'Would you like to hear why?' smiled the old man. 'Very well, I'll tell you.'

He walked to the window and peered out. All was still and silent in the dark garden. Then he turned, and, placing a chair which commanded a view of both the window and his prisoner, sat down.

'*You* are cleverer than I gave you credit for,' he began, 'because the letter is *not* in the house, after all.'

'Yes, you've looked pretty thoroughly, haven't you?' she exclaimed, fiercely.

'Yes, very thoroughly,' he agreed. 'I'm sorry I wasn't able to wait for Don Pasquali before making the strictly personal search.' He regarded his hand. 'But you shouldn't have bitten me. Admit, you began the roughness.'

'If only I'd been a little quicker—'

'You would have more than bitten me? I'm sure of it! That was why I had to demonstrate my knowledge of Ju-Jitsu. There is, you see, a limit to your cleverness—as also to Don Pasquali's. Now, Don Pasquali was cleverer than I gave *him* credit for by reading my mind and cutting the telephone wires. As he had obviously spotted their location before it's rather surprising he didn't cut them earlier. But then there are distinct limits to Don Pasquali's cleverness. That will be proved before long—when he comes back.'

'If he hadn't cut the telephone wires,' she retorted, 'he would never have come back!'

'You mean, the police, acting on my advice, would have caught him at Southfields?' answered Mr Lovelace, and his voice was momentarily dolorous. 'Yes—that *was* a mistake of mine. I was too certain—as I've admitted—that the letter was here. But the letter isn't here. And the police haven't met Don Pasquali at Southfields. So my error corrects itself automatically. And I don't repeat errors.'

'That's got to be proved, hasn't it?'

'It will be, very shortly.'

'I say, you do love talking big, don't you?' she chided him. 'When you get down to rock bottom, it's about all you can do.'

'H'm! *You* say that?' he inquired grimly, regarding her cords.

'My dear Father Christmas, the most brainless bully God ever created could knock a girl on the head and tie her up.'

'Not if the girl was you,' Mr Lovelace denied. 'However, I'm quite ready to convince you that I am not the most brainless bully God ever created, if you'd care to hear any more?'

'It'll take some doing,' she scoffed, playing on his vanity.

He gave a sudden grin. He knew she was playing on his vanity. He didn't mind. He had something to be vain about.

'Listen,' he said, after another glance at the window. For a moment he thought he had heard footsteps. 'Let us work this position out through sheer logic. The Einstein Theory, eh? If the letter isn't inside, it must be outside. Do you agree?'

'I'm not saying anything.'

'So it's fortunate for me that what you might say is quite unimportant. Now if the letter is outside, it would either be on Ben, or in the garden—you might have thrown it out of a window, for instance—'

'You've searched the garden, haven't you?'

'Yes. But if it was there, I searched too late. Or it would be in Southfields—or somewhere else. But wherever it was, my opinion of Don Pasquali has so increased that I am pretty sure he will find it. You see, when I am not by to restrain him, a man of his Southern temperament wouldn't stop at torture.'

'Yes, you really *are* a beast—!'

'A beast at bay, shall we say? It may explain what is to follow. A beast at bay has to adopt drastic methods!' He spoke bitingly. Was he defending himself before God, or just before his Vanity? Louis XI prayed to the little saints around his hat to forgive him for the sins he was about to commit. 'But, for the moment, we are talking of Don Pasquali, who will get the letter from Ben—'

'And then, obviously, walk straight back into the Spider's Parlour!' interrupted Molly, scornfully. 'And you think yourself clever!'

'I am afraid I do think myself clever,' the old man confessed, enjoying the instant. 'The reason Don Pasquali will return is because he will hope to walk back into a *lady's* parlour—though I admit some people think that is the same thing.'

'You're worse than a beast, Mr Lovelace,' said Molly, with a little gulp. 'You're a devil.'

'But always, please, a clever devil. Yes, Don Pasquali will return, because *you* are here—'

'And I'll tell him you've searched me already!'

'My child, is your own cleverness evaporating now?' asked the old man, affecting a pained voice. 'If he has the letter, why will he want to search you for it?'

'But suppose he hasn't—?'

'I refuse to suppose anything so depressing! The torture, in such a case, would have to be visited on you. So we will suppose that he *has* the letter. And we will also suppose that he refuses to give it up, or pretends he hasn't got it—I am quite ready for his twisting. In that event I shall bargain with him. I am certain, when we get to genuine market prices, he will prefer you to a musty old letter written twenty years ago.' Molly was looking beyond him towards the window, as though expecting to see the

Spaniard's face materialise there at any moment. 'But you need not fear a long bout of unwelcome attentions from him, I shall make sure that I get the letter first—and, afterwards, Don Pasquali will not live long. I shall, of course, have to kill him.'

He waited again for her, for some comment. She again disappointed him, as before, by stubborn silence.

'The police will think, naturally, that *you* have killed him,' he went on.

Now she wrenched her eyes from the window at that, and he smiled at his victory.

'Ah—that wakes you up, eh?' he chuckled. 'Now, you must admit, I am clever? Don Pasquali, having himself killed—let us count them—a man in Southampton, his accomplice, a sailor—'

'What?' she gasped, her will-power nearly snapping.

'Well, we may assume the sailor,' said Mr Lovelace. 'It's hardly likely that he has allowed your gentleman friend to wander around loose? Please do not interrupt the inventory! . . . No. 3 is a dog. A mere detail. The dog, the police will assume, was guarding the house. No. 4, a man-servant. He, also, was guarding the house. No. 5— perhaps—myself. But that, after all, will be a police theory only. The police will search for my body, and then give up. Another sad, unsolved mystery! Four victims will be enough, however, and my body, of course, will be on the Continent. Yes, and with the letter upon it. It is rather a pity that I shall have to complete the business with Medway from abroad—'

'But do you think *I* won't say anything?' cried Molly.

'I'm afraid you will not be able to say anything,'

answered Mr Lovelace. 'Don Pasquali will have wounded you fatally with his knife, I regret to say, before you shot him with my pistol. You will be unbound when you are discovered, of course, and your finger-prints will be on the revolver.'

Mr Lovelace rose from his chair, and walked to the door. Molly noticed that he had now taken the revolver from his pocket, and was holding it close to his side.

'And when I am abroad,' he murmured, softly, 'I will send Mr Joseph Medway, M.P., a copy of the letter that has given us all so much trouble. He wrote it twenty years ago, none too wisely, to a charming lady whom he met while he was attached to the British Embassy in Madrid. As he was already married, it was unfortunate that he became the father of this attractive lady's child. The lady moved to a small village called Puerbello, and he paid her for her silence. Now the lady is dead—and he shall pay me for mine.'

Even in her own extremity she was able to detach her mind and think of others. After all, if Ben were really dead . . .

'I've met some pretty low things in my life,' she said, surprised that she was still able to find her voice, 'but I've never even *thought* of anybody as low as you. Pickpocketing's a virtue. Do you really and truly suppose that, even if you can work this devilish business from abroad, you'll get your money?'

'From one source or another,' he answered, as he opened the door a crack. 'If Medway doesn't pay me for the letter, there are others who will, and who'll ask no questions. You see, young lady, I don't *start* these devilish businesses.

My mind is much too pure.' He peered through the crack.
'The seeds are sown by others—personal enemies, perhaps,
or business enemies, or political enemies, or international
enemies. People whose names are too respectable to do
more than sow the seeds. I am merely a middleman. I
carry out orders. Unwritten ones. But sometimes the
middleman scores the most. He has, you see, alternative
markets . . . But these matters are beyond you . . . Your
brain cannot soar above pickpocketing. Otherwise you
might have gone farther. Tell me, do you hear anything?'

All she heard through the door-crack was the ticking of
the grandfather clock—the ticking that sounded only when
the clock was empty and the pendulum was free to swing.
But the old man evidently heard more, for an instant later
he slipped from the room and closed the door softly behind
him.

Then Molly heard what Mr Lovelace had heard.
Somebody was outside the window; close to it. And she
noticed, for the first time, that the window was open a
crack, as the door had been. Just a tiny crack at the bottom,
through which fingers . . .

The fingers were long and brown. She recognised them.
She recognised, too, the scar on a hand when the hand
came through, turned, and pushed the frame upwards.

The lower part of the window was now open wide. A
dark face filled the gap. The old man's deduction had been
right. Don Pasquali had returned.

The face peered in cautiously. The unpleasant eyes noted
the room's emptiness saving for the girl. When they
noted the girl, they became more unpleasant. Beneath a
perspiring brow, the eyes smiled.

'So!' whispered Don Pasquali.

He slipped through the window like a great cat. He came forward. She stared at him helplessly.

'Where is he?' asked the Spaniard, in a low voice.

She felt numbness gripping her. She had fought against similar numbness many times during the past hours, but this time the numbness seemed to be winning. A minute ago, she had conceived nothing lower than the old man. Now there seemed nothing lower than the Spaniard, with his hot, hateful breath, and his shameless, devouring eyes.

Should she tell him where the old man was? Should she say that he was just outside the door, listening? It might save Don Pasquali! But did she want him saved? If one of them had to die . . .

'Where is he?' repeated the Spaniard.

Her eyes rested on his knife. He had not entered the room unprepared.

'Cut me free,' she gulped, 'and I'll tell you.'

'Oh, no! You tell me first!'

'I'll tell you nothing! Where's Ben? That's what *you've* got to tell! Where's Ben? Oh, my God! Have you—killed him?'

The Spaniard grinned suddenly. This was a good idea.

'Oh, yes—I kill Ben,' he answered.

Molly closed her eyes, then opened them in terror as she felt Don Pasquali draw closer.

'He have to be killed,' continued Don Pasquali, 'for the trick he play! Southfield? Pah! As if I believe that!' He stretched forward his hand and touched her shoulder. '*You* have the letter! I know all along! But I have to deal with

Signor Ben first. And now I am back. And, see, I keep well the appointment!'

He held up the hand that had touched her shoulder, while from the hall sounded the preliminary wheeze of the grandfather clock.

'Now it strike!'

The clock struck ten.

'So! And now I search you, as it is arrange! Very clever, to hide the letter on the pretty little body, and think it is safe there! Not from Don Pasquali! It is where I like to find it!'

The hand was on her shoulder again, and she re-lived the nightmare of his visit to her bedroom in Southampton. But this was a worse nightmare. Then she had not been bound, and could put up a fight.

'Wait!' she gasped. 'Don Pasquali!'

'Wait?' he laughed. 'There is no time to wait. The police will be here if he wait!'

'But I haven't the letter—I haven't—I haven't!'

'*You* say so. But *I* say you have!'

'I swear I haven't.'

'No good! I am sure! All the time, the letter is here, and you try to fool me!'

'But Mr Lovelace has already searched me—'

'Oho!'

'There's a bruise on my shoulder—that's how I got it—'

'Sst!' came the hiss. But he paused. 'Mr Lovelace—I forget him—yes, when I look at you!' he murmured. 'And you will not say where he is! Perhaps you do not know? Perhaps, as you say, he search you—and find nothing—and run away?' He frowned, while considering the possibility.

Then he shrugged his shoulders. 'Well, well, I search you, just the same. But first I make sure of Mr Lovelace. The door shall be locked, eh?'

He turned and walked towards the door. As he did so, it opened. The next moment he fell to the ground, shot through the heart.

37

'I'm Goin'!'

Twelve minutes before Don Pasquali died, Ben suddenly opened his eyes in Violet Medway's arm-chair to find her father looking down at him.

'Wot's 'appenin'?' he asked.

'We're just off to save your friend,' answered Sir Joseph.

'Eh?'

The next moment he was on his feet. Big Ben pushed him down again. Little Ben got up again.

'He's like that,' Violet whispered to her father, and her father nodded, imagining he could handle him. He had yet to learn that Ben was harder to manage even than Parliament.

'Don't worry,' said Big Ben, soothingly. 'We know where the house is—we'll see your friend comes to no harm.'

'Wotcher mean?' replied Ben.

'We mean that you're to stay here—you're not well—and that we'll bring your friend back to you.'

'Wot—me stay 'ere?' said Ben.

Sir Joseph frowned slightly, beset by a momentary doubt.

'You've recovered pretty smartly, my man,' he observed. 'I thought you were nearly dead?'

'Bein' nearly dead's nothink ter me,' retorted Ben. 'When I'm dead, I'll larf! Oi! I'm goin' hover!'

He swayed. Big Ben caught him.

'I'm goin' with yer,' breathed Little Ben, in Big Ben's chest, 'and nobody's goin' ter stop me, see?'

Big Ben looked perplexed. His daughter, substituting instinct for logic, decided for him.

'Let him come, Father,' she said. 'I think it'll be best.'

And so, instead of remaining stationary, the sitting-room and the landing rolled backwards through Ben's worn-out brain, and the staircase went back, too, albeit not quite so smoothly, and a small army of constables was encountered at the bottom. Here Ben became an immediate centre of attention, and a momentary view of an inspector's grey moustache was not reassuring. But he repeated to the grey moustache, 'I'm goin' with yer, see?' and then the grey moustache vanished, and reappeared beneath features that were now a little less forbidding.

'I'm not quite sure about it,' said the inspector.

'I'm quite sure about it,' said Violet Medway.

'I think she's right,' said Big Ben.

'I'm goin'!' said Little Ben.

Then they all vanished again, and while hurried preparations were being made another face loomed above Ben's. It was the face of Procter.

'I'm goin'!' said Ben.

Procter did not reply. When the world is turning upside down it's no good butting in.

Another face flitted by. It was the face of Maud, the maid. It made a large circle round Ben, as though he were a museum exhibit. Its object was to obtain a closeup for the sake of subsequent descriptions, by an eyewitness, in the kitchen.

And then some of the other faces reappeared, and the imposing hall, through which a ragged man had windmilled his way to the staircase, now went backwards into history with the staircase and the upper passage and the elegant sitting-room; and Ben was on the front-steps again, descending to the street with assistance.

A knot of people stood in the street. Also, two cars. Ben might have been a bride leaving a church from the interest he attracted. One of the people pointed to him excitedly as he neared the bottom of the steps. She was an old lady clutching a black bead bag.

'I'm goin'!' Ben told her.

In another sense he appeared already to have gone, for during this last lap of his strange journey he was oblivious to nearly all that was happening around him. Only the knowledge of Molly's danger kept him functioning. Only that knowledge had brought him safely to Mallow Court, had conquered within the space of twenty minutes, a butler, a society belle, an M.P., and a police inspector. Only that knowledge had startled him out of a dead trance, causing him to resemble a deflated balloon that had suddenly filled itself with air, and had given him the slogan, 'I'm goin'!' to hang on to.

The entire dictionary had been reduced to those two words. He almost forgot, while he repeated them like a Litany, what they meant. All he knew was that, when any immediate difficulty presented itself, when anything disturbed a kind of black stream that was carrying him onwards, he had to say them. Then everything was all right.

The black stream was rather peaceful, though it was

disturbed by a vague procession that flashed by him in a contrary direction and vanished behind. Lamp-posts. Streets. Yellow eyes from other cars, and from illuminated buildings. A bridge. Water, with reflections. More lamp-posts, more streets, more yellow eyes, more illuminated buildings. Then fewer lights. Fewer eyes. Darkness rushing through darkness . . . rushing both ways . . .

And vague, distant voices through the darkness.

'You should have got in touch with us before, sir.'

'I don't believe in paying compliments to anonymous letters!'

'But these contained threats, you say?'

'Which only my daughter believed in.'

'Well, the lady was right, wasn't she—'

Meaningless voices. Droning on quietly, a thousand miles away. Far from the shores of the black tide that was carrying Ben on.

Between him and the voices grew other things. They passed like a succession of vast shadows, flitting into the haven of history. A rolling ship, with a cap flying from a deck, and a figure flying after the cap. Ben's figure. A cow, soft-eyed and troubled. He'd known that cow at some time or other. Where was it now? Gone—and in its place a taxi-cab, with a dead man in the corner, and a knife sticking in the dead man's chest. The phantom taxi passed. The black stream suddenly tilted to one side and raced dizzily downwards. It seemed for the moment to be trying to pour Ben out of it. He felt himself rushing downwards towards a bush that hung on the edge of a vast, yawning precipice . . . But he hung on . . .

'I see, miss. But, when you left the place, why didn't you communicate with us at once?'

'I telephoned to my father at the House.'

'And I'm afraid I didn't pay much attention to the message, inspector.'

'Well, *then* was the time for her to have got in touch with us.'

'Come, inspector! Would she get in touch with you concerning a matter of blackmail—involving her father's honour? The letter, as we have since discovered—the letter found in the cap—is written in Spanish to a woman who—'

'Father!'

'—bore the writer an illegitimate child.'

'You needn't give me the details, sir. They don't concern us at the moment—'

'No? But the writer, who was already married, behaved abominably! He was attached to the Spanish Embassy, and he made an excuse for leaving Madrid on account of the unfortunate incident. His cousin went out to fill his post. The baby died.'

'It really isn't necessary for you to tell me this, sir.'

'But I'd rather, inspector. It may be the surest way in the end of preserving the details inside this car—though, of course, it places you under no official obligation. As a matter of fact, I'm telling my daughter, also. She did not know that I was sending money through my solicitor to Carlotta D'Albert . . .'

Train-smoke. Fog. They came belching down the dark river of Ben's mind, full of swiftly-moving figures. He escaped from them all. Two of the figures that had been behind him were now ahead of him. The dark river was bearing him close to them, closer and closer, while voices from another world droned on:

'Poor little baby!'

'Yes, and poor mother of the poor little baby! Both dead! And poor, foolish father of the poor little baby—dead, also.'

The voices stopped droning for a few moments. Then one continued:

'He died a few weeks after his cousin went to fill his position at Madrid. It was this cousin who told Carlotta the news of his death—and who, taking pity on the lady, continued the payments that had been arranged. Both cousins were christened Joseph—and the second Joseph might have fallen for such an attractive lady as Carlotta D'Albert—but for the example of the first.'

Another lull. Was the river slowing?

'Then—father—the letter—?'

'Cannot hurt me, my dear, even if it *is* made public,' said Sir Joseph. 'Just somebody else's memory, that's all. Perhaps, inspector, you'll help us to keep that memory intact?'

The inspector did not reply. His hand had made a sudden grab, and had caught thin air, while the thing he had grabbed at slid out into the lane.

'Where's he gone?'

'Hoy!'

'Catch him!'

But in these last few yards of the race there was no chance of catching Ben. The black river had slowed and stopped, and had then suddenly become a black tumult, and as he tumbled out into the road he tumbled up again in a single bump. He did not know what he was doing. All he knew was that he was doing it, and that, somewhere in the blackness, a face was beginning to appear—a face he had not dared to materialise in his mind before lest it should turn him into sobbing impotence.

But now the face was close at hand! It was staring at him—anxiously, fearfully, beseechingly. He sobbed, yes, but not with impotence. Each sob brought activity to his limbs, and added an explosion to the twisted engine within. Before the occupants of the rescuers' cars realised that Ben was out of the leading one, he was through the gate of Greystones and speeding along the drive.

Even in his delirium he stuck to the grass. When he came round the final curve and was forced upon gravel, he ran lightly, on tip-toe to the front-door. The front-door was open.

He ought to have been surprised. It was all too easy. But he was not surprised. All this was nothing to do with him. God was taking a hand, and when God takes a hand it's all right, see?

Another door stood open. Again he wasn't surprised. He passed through the second doorway. A Spaniard lay on the ground, dead. Beyond the Spaniard was a girl, bound. But Ben's eyes did not rest on either of these. They rested on the figure of an old man with a revolver in his hand. . . .

Two arms and two legs, spraying out from a whirling blotch of body in the middle, swooped on top of Mr Lovelace. He raised his revolver, to find it wrested from him. And now he was on the ground, struggling to retain consciousness of a world that had suddenly gone mad, and that was, therefore, hardly worth the compliment of remembering. So he gave up trying, and ceased temporarily to remember it.

Five seconds later, the inspector, followed by his constables, leapt into the house. The sight that met him astonished even his hardened eyes. A tightly bound girl was in the throes of violent hysterics, two men lay on the floor—one dead, the other unconscious—while a third swayed round dizzily and gulped, in a voice of choking triumph:

'And now, inspector, yer can '*ave* me!'

The arms of the law went round Ben as he swooned—but they went round very gently.

THE END

Also available

Murderer's Trail
J. Jefferson Farjeon

Ben the tramp is back at sea, a stowaway bound for Spain in the company of a wanted man—the Hammersmith murderer.

Ben, wandering hungry through the foggy back alleys of Limehouse, is spooked by news of an old man murdered in Hammersmith—and runs! He crosses a plank, slips through an iron door, and goes to sea with the coal. But so does the man who did the murder, and a very pretty lady who did not. Along the way, the Atlanta loses a stowaway, a pickpocket, a murderer, a crook, a wealthy passenger, the third officer and a lifeboat. And that is how Ben gets to Spain . . .

'Ben has never perhaps been quite so entertaining, both in thrills and in laughter, as in this story.' DAILY MIRROR

'The grimness of the story is relieved by many delightful touches of humour.' THE WEST AUSTRALIAN

Also available

Little God Ben
J. Jefferson Farjeon

Ben the tramp, a self-confessed coward and ex-sailor, is back in the Merchant Service and shipwrecked in the Pacific in this quintessentially 1930s comedy thriller.

Tired of being homeless and down on his luck, the incorrigible Ben has taken a job as a stoker on a cruise ship. But his luck doesn't last long when they are all shipwrecked in the Pacific. Seen through Ben's eyes, the uncharted island is a hive of cannibals, mumbo-jumbo, and gals who are more scantily clad than any he has ever seen. And every time he tries to bluff his way out of a situation, he just bluffs himself further in, somehow convincing the natives that he has god-like powers . . .

'His dialogue is invariably amusing.' DAILY MAIL

'Ben is not merely a character but a parable. He is a mixture of Trimalchio and the Old Kent Road, a notable coward, a notable hero, above all a supreme humourist.' TIME AND TIDE

Also available

Detective Ben
J. Jefferson Farjeon

Ben the tramp, the awkward Cockney with no home and no surname, turns detective again—and runs straight into trouble.

Ben encounters a dead man on a London bridge and is promptly rescued from the same fate by a posh lady in a limousine. But like most posh ladies of Ben's acquaintance, this one isn't what she seems. Seeking escape from a gang of international conspirators, Ben is whisked off to the mountains of Scotland to thwart the schemes of a poisonous organisation and finds himself in very unfamiliar territory.

'Jefferson Farjeon is a master of the particular art of blending horrors with humour.' SUNDAY TIMES

'Ben is a sheer joy.' GLASGOW HERALD

Also available

Ben on the Job
J. Jefferson Farjeon

Ben the tramp, with his usual genius for trouble, runs into danger when he finds a dead body and decides to help out.

Ben knew that whenever his thumbs were itching, something 'orrible' was about to happen. Sure enough, on one foggy afternoon of itchy thumbs, the hapless Ben is implicated in criminal activity by the police—the kind of mistake it isn't easy to explain. Doing a runner, Ben hides in the basement of a deserted house, where he discovers the body of a well-dressed man, shot through the head . . . and much more trouble than he bargained for.

'Jefferson Farjeon is quite unsurpassed for creepy skill in mysterious adventures.' DOROTHY L. SAYERS

'Continues the adventures of Mr Farjeon's already popular creation, Ben, the Cockney tramp.' MORNING POST